D0445101

UNPUNISHED

UNPUNISHED

a mystery

CHARLOTTE PERKINS
GILMAN

Edited and with an Afterword by Catherine J. Golden and Denise D. Knight

THE FEMINIST PRESS
AT THE CITY UNIVERSITY OF NEW YORK

NEW YORK

Published in 1997 by The Feminist Press
at The City University of New York
311 East 94th Street, New York,
New York 10128-5684

First edition.
02 01 00 99 98 97 5 4 3 2 1

The Feminist Press would like to thank
Nina Baym, Joanne Markell and Genevieve Vaughan
for their generosity in supporting this publication.

Library of Congress Cataloging-in-Publication Data

Gilman, Charlotte Perkins, 1860–1935
    Unpunished : a novel / Charlotte Perkins Gilman; edited
    and with an afterword by Catherine J. Golden and Denise
    D. Knight. — 1st ed.
    p. cm.
Includes bibliographical references.
ISBN 1-55861-170-3 (cloth: alk. paper)
ISBN 1-55861-185-1 (pbk: alk. paper)
I. Golden, Catherine J. II. Knight, Denise D., 1954–. III. Title.
PS1744.G57U56   1997
813'.4—dc21   96-53526
                          CIP

Text design and typesetting by Timothy Shaner.
Printed on acid-free paper by McNaughton & Gunn, Inc.
Manufactured in the United States of America.

CONTENTS

Editors' Acknowledgments

After spending much of our professional lives engaged in research on the work of feminist writer, activist, and theorist Charlotte Perkins Gilman, we are delighted to have the opportunity to present the first published edition of her final full-length fictional work, *Unpunished*. While this edition developed out of our own interests in Gilman, the support of other individuals and our home institutions helped us to bring it to fruition. We wish to express deep thanks to the following people for their assistance during various stages of this project: Terri Wise and Connie Brooks of Skidmore College, who worked tirelessly as student assistants; Alan Wheelock of the English Department at Skidmore College; Skidmore College for providing a Faculty Research Grant in support of Catherine's work on the text; Tim Prchal at the University of Wisconsin—Milwaukee, for pointing us to some excellent resources on detective fiction; Anne Cranny-Francis of Macquarie University, Sydney, Australia, for her helpful insights into the genre of contemporary detective fiction; the reference assistants at Lucy Scribner Library, Marilyn Sheffer and Esther Gillie, for helping us obtain Gilman resources that were not readily available; Dawn Van Hall of the Sperry Center at the State University of New York College at Cortland for preparing the photograph of Gilman used on the jacket. We are indebted to Mary Maples Dunn, Director of the Arthur and Elizabeth Schlesinger Library at Radcliffe College, and Eva S. Moseley, Curator of Manuscripts, for their cooperation in allowing access to the manuscript of *Unpunished* and for granting permission to publish. We also extend our gratitude to Florence Howe, Jean Casella, Sara Clough, Elizabeth Chilton, and Sara Cahill at the Feminist Press for their guidance, advice, and expertise. Finally, we thank our husbands, Michael S. Marx and Michael K. Barylski, for their support, encouragement, and good humor.

Catherine J. Golden
Denise D. Knight
February 1997

A Note on the Text

The text of *Unpunished* has been taken directly from Gilman's revised and unpublished typescript in the collection of Charlotte Perkins Gilman Papers at the Arthur and Elizabeth Schlesinger Library at Radcliffe College, box XIX, folder 232. (Another copy with penciled corrections is located in folder 231; those changes have been incorporated into the version in folder 232.) To the greatest extent possible, we have attempted to preserve, rather than to correct or "improve," Gilman's original text and style. In cases of obvious typographical errors, missing punctuation (e.g., quotation marks to introduce dialogue), or absence of new paragraphing (e.g., when a new speaker is introduced), we have silently emended the text to enhance readability. For example, *behing* has been corrected to *behind*, *bood* to *book*, and so on. Some spellings have been regularized; for example, the name *Flannigan* appears in a variant form as *Flanagan*; likewise, *aunty* appears also as *auntie* and has been made consistent throughout. In addition, numerous comma splices have been silently corrected with semicolons and periods, and occasional fragments have been silently emended by changing semicolons to commas. Some dashes, particularly when used in conjunction with other punctuation, have been eliminated. Any insertions of missing words are indicated by brackets. Ellipses in the text are Gilman's.

A set of texual notes is included in the back of this edition. Allusions to words, events, people, biblical verse, or objects that might be unfamiliar to the contemporary reader, or that might benefit from clarification, have been elucidated in these explanatory notes. The existence of a texual note is indicated by an asterisk in the text.

C. J. G.

D. D. K.

UNPUNISHED

This story has murder enough to satisfy the most demanding, applied in a manner decidedly unusual. It has crime enough for our present day taste, but the criminals are all out of order. There is a pair of most amiable detectives, and another one far from amiable. The mystery involved is not merely in the usual question of who did it, but in the unusual one of who did it first. Some of the tale is amusing.

Charlotte Perkins Gilman

"Extra! Extra!"

"**E**xtra! Extra!" chanted the tenor, along one side of the echoing canyon of an uptown block.

"Uxtra! Uxtra!" boomed the bass against the high-shouldering apartment houses on the other side.

But Bessie Hunt had spent an instructive year in newspaper work, and was not impressed. She went to the window it is true, and leaned far out, but it was not to watch the flat-dwellers "bite"; it was the far more feminine interest of looking for her husband. If she leaned as far as she could she could see him away up the long block.

Her business experience, though varied and interesting, had not dulled, but rather sharpened the delight of "doing her own work"—at least in doing it for Jim. There were times when things went badly with Jim and she promptly leaped into the breach as it were and took a job again, so that intermittent housework still seemed rather in the nature of a prolonged and pleasant picnic for two.

"I like it, Jimmins," she insisted, when he protested that she was far too able a woman to be cooking for two; "I like it, same as you like to go camping and cook your own fish. It's poor economy but it's lots of fun."

He had phoned her that he would be home early, and hungry, and she had one of his pet dinners ready. No husband being visible up the street she returned to the diminutive kitchen and contemplated the preparations with satisfaction. There was the funny little round chunk of a roast, that looked like a fillet, but was by no means so tender, the only kind she could buy small enough for two. Yes, it was done, but covered tight, sizzling away—she turned the gas down a bit more. Fried sweet potatoes, all hot and ready. Tomato, lettuce, everything was all right; table as neatly set as geometrical design. Jim did hate a mussy table, with the dishes "thrown on any old way."

"Almost six—he ought to be here. He said he'd be home before six. I believe he's got a case—he sounded as if there was something doing." With which meditations she returned to the window and risked her life again.

Yes, there he was, the most inconspicuous of average men, with his nose buried in a newspaper too, but she knew him unerringly. Then the upward look, the waved hand, the swift ascent of the four flights, and Bessie's skittering rush down the long narrow hall to open the door, with quite honeymoonish greetings, in spite of four years of marriage.

"Anybody'd think," said Jim, as they managed to walk together in the yard-wide space, "that you were fond of me!"

"Let 'em!" Bess cheerfully proclaimed. "I am, and I don't care who knows it. But say—you've got something, haven't you?"

"I have that," he replied emphatically. "But not a word do you get out of me till I've got something else, namely my dinner."

He helped her put on the dishes, remarking for the hundredth time, "I'm so glad you don't set a tenement-house table, Bess," at which she smiled and solemnly producing a foot-rule measured from the edge of the table to each end of the platter. They ate in contented quiet for a time, and presently Bessie asked, "Is it a murder, Jim? A real mysterious detective kind of murder?"

But he only grinned sweetly and remarked, "You certainly can fry potatoes to beat the band. Each slice seems to have had personal attention."

"It has," she proudly explained, "as you well know. Every last one of 'em has a dust of salt, a shadow of sugar and a bit of butter—couldn't do it with mass production! And now where are they?" she protested tragically. "Gone! All gone! And nothing to show for it!"

"Nothing but a happy husband," said Jim peacefully. "That's an awful good pie, Bess. If you *could* improve on the last one I should say you had. And now if you'll leave the dishes awhile I'll help you with 'em later. I know you are bursting with curiosity."

"All right. You go smoke while I put the eatables away. The dishes can sit in the sink and soak—do 'em good."

She hurried things off the table, and came to sit by her husband before the small glowing electric heater which supplemented the efforts of a moody radiator. A card table was drawn up beside her with plenty of paper and sharp pencils, for him to use if desired, and she sat at attention with her stenographic pad taking occasional notes.

"I'm mighty glad I've got you Bess, instead of a sheep like my dear Watson. Being a stenog comes in mighty useful, doesn't it?"

"The more trades the better is my motto. Now go ahead. Won't you just tell me first what it's all about?"

"Not a word, Bess. I want you to get it straight, in sequence, just as I did. I want your impressions on each step of it too, and please ask questions as to details; I may leave out something. It's big, I'll tell you that much."

He drew himself up and leaned forward, elbows on knees, eyes studying the pattern of the rug. "Now then—

"You know I had to rush over to Brooklyn early, to catch Ross Akers before he went out on his calls, and ask him some questions about the Williams affair. He'll tell me anything unless it's against that 'hippocritic' oath of theirs. They were just finishing breakfast, asked me to sit down. Funny family."

"Describe," said Bessie, scribbling away.

"Well, you know Ross, big, handsome, distinguished, cordial and yet with an air of bitterness about him, sort of incongruous. But he's all brains, competence, good natured too, except for that odd strain. And this morning he seemed, somehow, excited, but trying not to show it. Well his father's dead, and he's saddled with three foolish females. A stepmother about forty, Ross is somewhere the same age I should think, and two young stepsisters, sixteen and fourteen, say, the kind that do up their faces in the street cars. Frail little things all of them, dead weights on Ross."

"It's a shame," said Bessie. "And he such a hard working man. Anything to prevent stepmama from earning her own living?"

"Nothing but total incapacity, I should say. Well, while we were talking the 'phone rang and Ross went to it—here's his end of the call. 'Yes. Yes of course. You don't say so! Yes, I'll come at once. Very well, I'll bring someone; we'll be right over.'"

Jim paused a moment. "This may be pure imagination, Bess, but you know my professional attitude—"

"I ought to by this time," laughed his wife. "It's universal suspicion, ruthless continual suspicion. You'd suspect your mother of being a German spy. I don't doubt you suspect me of a number of Black Pasts, and of leading a Double Life, even now!"

"I don't believe even you could get up a double dinner like that," he assured her with a kiss. "But seriously Bess, Ross' manner was—queer."

"Queer how?"

"As if—as if—you know how doctors are, kind of smooth and reassuring—"

"Bedside manner?" she interpolated.

"Yes. Well he sounded almost—frightened. That's too strong, nervous is the better word. Of course I didn't know the other end of the talk, but he was evidently excited. He's a mighty good doctor, and a good friend, but—"

"But your spear knows no brother. Do go on."

"He came back to the table, drank off his coffee without sitting down, said he had to hurry off, and asked me to go with him. He got his little bag and we set off at once. And he began to talk right away. Said this patient of his was worried and asked him to bring someone—an officer perhaps—her brother-in-law hadn't come down and they couldn't get into his room."

"Aha!" cried Bessie. "We are on the trail!"

"He said it was only a few miles, but you know how Brooklyn is, we got caught in traffic, early as it was, held up over and over again, and he kept on talking. Seemed as if he was glad to.

"'This Mrs. Warner is a patient of mine,' he said. 'So is her brother-in-law, Wade Vaughn—the criminal lawyer—you know him?' I told him I did." He looked at Bessie, who raised her head to return the look, nodding soberly.

"Yes, we know him," she agreed.

"'She says he hasn't come down to breakfast, that he won't answer when called, bedroom door locked, office door locked, she's worried.'

"'Why don't they break in?' I asked him.

"'They're all too much afraid of him. It's a queer family.'"

Jim broke off and turned to her again. "You see, Bess, he spoke as if he wanted to talk more, and at the same time seemed afraid he might say too much. 'What kind of a man is Mr. Vaughn?' I asked, to kind of help him out, and he replied grimly, 'One of the most unpleasant men I ever knew.'

"'And what kind of a family?' I wanted to have him relieve his mind you see."

"I see, Reynard,* I see. Relieve his mind and furnish yours. Go on, do."

Jim smiled at her and went on. "'You old investigator!' said he, wiggling his car out of a jam. 'The fact is, Jim, I've brought you along on the chance that there may be something to investigate. He had enemies enough!'"

"'Had?' said I. 'Then you think—'

"'I don't really think anything yet,' he answered cautiously. Then we were stuck again and he got fidgety. Do you remember anything about old J. J. Smith, Bess?—that was found paralysed on his own doorstep, about eight years ago?"

"Seems to me I do," she agreed. "I was a kid stenog and I heard the girls talking about it. Some tragedy, wasn't there?"

"Yes. He told me all about it. Smith was a widower, had two daughters, worshipped them but ruled them with a rod of iron, had them educated at home. Awful domineering old chap. This man Vaughn was his lawyer and close friend. He wanted to marry the younger girl, Iris. Old man highly approved, daughter didn't. Then the girls ran away. Iris married a minister, Sydney Booth. Other one married an actor named Warner, was on the stage with him. Father furious, swore he'd disinherit them, never see them again and so on. Willed all his money to Vaughn."

"Was he very rich?"

"Not for New York, a million or two I guess. Well Mrs. Warner had a son, Mrs. Booth had a daughter; the families [were] together in an auto accident. Hard lines Bess: both husbands were killed, Mrs. Booth shell-shocked so to speak, Mrs. Warner more or less crippled and disfigured. And while she was still unconscious—concussion of the brain and all that—Vaughn takes the whole lot to his house—father would not see 'em you know—and persuades the half crazy Mrs. Booth to marry him, right off."

Bessie sat up straight. "What!"

"Yes ma'am. What, indeed. That's what he did. Well that complicated matters for Smith and he made a new will—Akers has seen it—left a skimpy trust fund for the support and education of the children. All they get on majority is a paltry thousand apiece. If the girl marries, with Vaughn's consent, under twenty-one, her husband gets fifty thousand. And all conditioned on their absolute obedience. If they are 'rebellious like my daughters' the will said, they were to have nothing."

"Grand old man!" remarked his wife. "Leave anything to the rebellious daughters?"

"Income of three hundred dollars a year. Well, the half crazy one died, killed herself—"

"Oh yes!" cried Bessie. "That's when it was all in the papers."

"—and he's kept Mrs. Warner as his housekeeper, and taken care of the children."

"She *stayed* with him! Oh how could she!"

"What else could she do? Remember she was crippled, lives in a wheel chair mostly, and her face disfigured—and all the chance the youngsters had of getting what belonged to them dependent on this obedience—see?"

"I see," she remarked slowly. "I see a lot. Look here, would they inherit it at his death?"

"Smart girl! No they wouldn't, as far as I can see. They are no relation to him. Well, that's what Akers told me. 'All this is public knowledge,' he said. 'The will's on record.'"

"How old are the children now?"

"Girl eighteen, boy nineteen, I believe. The accident was in 19—1920 I think. [Smith] never spoke after they got him into the house. That was left to Vaughn like everything else, and after his wife died he moved into the old house, with the whole family."

"Isn't it about time you got there?" she suggested. "I want my crime!"

"How do you know there is a crime, you bloodthirsty little thing?"

"What else is all this fuss about, Mr. Detective! Get on, do."

"Very well. We reached the house about eight-fifty. Young Warner opened the door. Nice looking chap, well-built, slim, tall, rather dark, evidently worried and trying to maintain a noble calm. They call him Hal. I've seen him before somewhere, and his cousin too. We enter the front hall, doors right left and back, stairs facing us at left. We are shown into room at right and I am introduced to Mrs. Warner, in her wheel chair, and to Miss Iris Booth. Akers very popular, especially with Mrs. Warner."

"Observing man. What made you think so?"

"Just the way she looked at him, the way he held her hand a second longer than was necessary, sense of—relief in the atmosphere."

"And he?"

"He had an air of assuming responsibility, but that's natural in a family physician. He explained to Mrs. Warner that I was an old friend of his, and that in case there was any ground for her fears I should be a thoroughly trustworthy person to rely on; put it on thick. 'Now we must set your mind at rest. Where's Joe?' he asked."

"'Joe's gone,' she said. 'Didn't I tell you? They've all gone, all three of them.'"

"Oho!" remarked Bessie. "The plot thickens!"

"I'll say it thickens! I tell you Bess, this is some story. Well, she began at the beginning, speaking quickly, told how the young people went down early and found there wasn't any breakfast and not a servant in the house. They went up to their rooms and looked, beds made, everything neat, not a box, bag or piece of clothing, gone clean as a whistle. Hal told his mother and she said for them to get something to eat and they did, and brought up her breakfast. Mr. Vaughn, it appears, does not wish to be wakened in the morning, but always comes down between eight and half past. You see they were all afraid of him, evidently. But she got worried, the servants disappearing so, and they knocked at his door. He didn't answer, not to loud knocking or calling.

Door locked, and the door to his study or office or whatever he called it locked also. That was the one at the left as we entered. So she got more worried and sent for Akers. 'It did seem as if you would never get here!' she breathed intensely, sort of squeezing her hands together."

"Describe," Bessie urged, pencil waiting.

"Woman near forty I should say. Dark soft hair. Dark eyes, shade over one eye. Puckered scar on cheek—pulls her mouth up on one side. She must have been badly cut up in that accident and it was pretty poorly patched I should say. Expression pathetic and brave, trying to put up with a bad job and look pleasant. Then this fright—of course she was nervous, holding it in. Sort of wrapper on, long, covered her feet."

"How much of a cripple?"

"She can walk a little, but it hurts her. Gets about in the chair, and the boy carries her up and downstairs."

"And the girl?"

"Blonde, slender little thing, big appealing sort of eyes, blue, long lashes. Gentle mouth, quivered easily, quite pretty. (Boy looked as though he'd say very pretty!) Awfully upset of course. But Bess, they had one marked characteristic in common, those two young things and the woman—astonishing self control. You know how people act in a case like that—well they didn't, none of them. I got an impression of unusual excitement and at the same time this unusual control."

"Impression noted—do go on with story; I'm thrilled."

"Ross took command at once. 'You and Iris stay here. We'll try the bedroom first. He may have had a seizure of some sort.' So he and I and the boy went upstairs. Vaughn's room was over the parlor, right side of the front as you go in. There was no key in the lock, but after trying them from all over the house we found one to fit and got in. Bed hadn't been slept in. Room all orderly and quite unoccupied. We went down and told the others. They were more frightened than before, naturally. So now we tackled the office door, the northeast corner room. This time the key was in, but Hal said he'd get his tools, that he had some pliers he thought would turn it.

"While he was gone his mother said to me, 'Mr. Hunt, in case there has been any—foul play—I wish to engage you to investigate it.' I tried to reassure her, said we mustn't anticipate trouble, but she smiled a funny crooked smile and suggested that it was sometimes wiser to do just that.

"The boy came back with his tools, and while he was fussing with a pair of long-nosed slender pincers, the bell rang. Nobody was pleased. It certainly was no time for callers. But this one rang again, loud and long.

"'Let me go,' says Ross, and opens the door, just a little. But the man pushed right in—and who do you think it was, Bess?"

"Give it up," she replied promptly.

"Think of the last, the worst, the most undesirable person to have bursting on such a position as we were in! Gus Crasher."

Mrs. Hunt dropped her pad and stared. "Whe-e-w!" she whistled. "How opportune! Evidently you are not going to have this case all to yourself!"

"By no manner of means," he agreed. "But listen, my dear. This Crasher person was all dolled up, new suit, new hat, terrible neck-tie, white flower in his buttonhole. He looks around, glares around you might say, evidently not at all glad to see me. Then he marches over to Miss Iris and tries to take her hand, but she gets behind her aunt's chair. Also her cousin comes between them. Ever see Crasher mad, Bess?"

"No, nor do I want to. When I think of that man being a detective I'm almost ashamed that you're one."

"Gus is a good sleuth all right, but rather shady, I'll admit. Anyhow there he was, glaring at the boy, visibly resenting all of us. Then he pulled himself together. 'I came ahead of time for fear of some slip-up. I think you have an engagement with me this morning, Miss Iris,' he remarked pleasantly. Such an expression on his face—like a self-conscious rat-trap!

"The child drew herself up, cold steady little voice, 'You are mistaken Mr. Crasher.' Ice was warm to it.

"'You'll find I'm not mistaken,' he says with a large smile. 'Hasn't your steppapa explained it clear enough yet?' Then he looks around at the rest of us and especially at young Warner with absolute triumph and back at her. 'You and I are going to get married this morning.'

"'We are not!' she shot at him. 'Not this morning nor ever!' She turned to the boy with a kind of sob—'Make him go away!' she cried. He was more than willing.

"'You'd better clear out Mr. Crasher,' he said as stiff as you please. 'Evidently you are not wanted here.'

"Crasher stood there like a particularly unpleasant bull with a few matadors bothering about. 'We'll see about that. Where's Vaughn?' Nobody answered for a minute and then Ross said, 'You had better come back later if you wish to see Mr. Vaughn.'

"Crasher looked at him, whirled round and looked at me. 'What's up here anyhow?' he demanded. 'What are you doing here, Hunt? Where's Vaughn? I'll find out!' He goes to the door and finds it locked.

"Crasher knocked and pounded, shook the door handle,

shouted to Vaughn with no more success than we had, and turned upon us fiercely. 'You open that door young man or I'll call the police and have it broken open.'

"'Precisely what I was about to do when you intruded, Mr. Crasher,' said young Warner. 'If you'll get out of my way—'

"So Crasher stepped aside, and after a little more fumbling the boy turned the key. The door opened inward; he rather stood back from it and pushed it wide open so we could all see into the room."

"Yes? Yes? For goodness sake don't stop to be dramatic, Jim."

"You'd think it was dramatic all right if you'd been there, Bess. We were all in a huddle outside the door. In the middle of the room was a big flat-topped desk, chair on the far side, facing the door. Mr. Vaughn was sitting there, a little slumped down against the back, staring straight at us, dead."

Sufficient Murder

Mrs. Hunt refused to be shocked. "Quite as I expected," she said drily. "Do go on dear. Suicide or murder?"

But Jim suddenly got up from his chair and marched around the little room, his hands in his pockets. "I'm no chicken, Bess. I've seen both often enough—some pretty gory ones too. But this—" he came back and took a chair opposite her, leaning forward, tensely, "—Bess! That man had been killed four times over. Or four ways at once. Possibly five."

She stared, paling a little. "What can you mean, Jim?"

"Listen now, get it down straight. I was looking at each one of them. Mrs. Warner sat there in her wheel chair, and he in his desk chair staring right at her. She was just *set*, holding tight to the arms of her chair, *tight*. Harry stood by her, his hand on her shoulder, tense as a bow-string. The girl was holding on to his arm, close; both of them trembling a little, no wonder. But

Bess—they didn't any of them look surprised.

"Crasher marched in at once, and I after him. Ross Akers too. We drew back the curtains, pulled up the shades, let in a glare of light, then went closer to examine the body, not touching anything of course . . . There was a bullet hole in his right temple. There was a long bruise on his head from front to back; he was bald enough to show it. There was a knife sunk in his neck, inside the collar bone, sunk to the hilt. And, if you'll believe it there was a cord around his neck too . . . "

Bessie sat staring at him, her eyes large with horror. "What's your possible five?" she breathed.

"That I'm not sure of. But there was a decanter on the table partly filled with whiskey, and a glass by his left hand with a few drops in it. Crasher looked at it, smelt it, wet a finger tip and tasted it. 'Thorough job!' he said. 'Poison!' Then Iris laughed."

"Laughed? *Laughed*!"

"Yes. Laughed herself into hysterics, sobbed, cried. Dr. Akers took her upstairs, and Hal carried his mother up too.

"Crasher watched them go. He seemed more excited than was natural for a dick of his experience—stood looking at that dead man, not with any sort of pity or horror for his end, but with a sort of balked rage that was dreadful, his big fists opening and closing.

"'And what are *you* doing here?' he demanded suddenly.

"'Just what you are,' I told him. 'Interesting case. Hadn't we better call the police?'

"'You go and call 'em,' he grunted, but I preferred to watch him. We went and looked at the windows, all unfastened, one open—on the Field Street side. There was another door, locked, key gone. We came back to the desk and stood examining it with the utmost care. Suddenly he gave a start and looked at the side window as if he'd heard something, and I was fool enough to look too—that trick almost always works, unless one is watching for it—and in that instant I *think* he took something off the desk. If he did it was very small—I'm not sure anyhow."

"Never mind," his wife encouraged him. "What kind of a room? Find any 'clues'?"

"Not a clue. We didn't look for fingerprints. A bookcase— law stuff, a safe behind the door, a table by the front windows, a long flat divan with cushions and a rug. No signs of disturbance. There wasn't any more to discover, apparently, so to anticipate him I rang up headquarters and gave them the news. About then Akers and young Warner came down, both of them looking pretty determined and the boy as if he could bite nails.

"'Mr. Crasher, my mother has engaged Mr. Hunt to take this case,' said Hal, stiffly, 'and requests you to leave the house.'

"Crasher eyed him surlily. 'Leave the house, eh? And suppose I won't? I intend to wait here till the proper authorities arrive.'

"'There are three of us, Mr. Crasher,' put in Akers. 'If you will not leave at the request of the lady of the house we will put you out.'

"Hal Warner is a big husky boy and looked as if he would enjoy a scrap. Akers and I size up pretty well. I opened the door for him and he went. He didn't look pleased though.

"Akers went poking about the room. 'I suppose you haven't found anything?' he said. 'And if you didn't I'm sure I can't.' He was methodical, looked at each window, and when he came to the fireplace he studied it a bit. There was one of those fitted iron things closed over it. 'Does that come off?' he asked. Crasher and I had paid no attention to it, having so little time for careful search, but now I squatted and worked at the thing. It came out easy enough. In the grate was a pile of burned papers, quite a lot I should say, and on top of the pile was a list of names roughly printed instead of written, and a brief note on a piece of an envelope—'Vaughn's private business is closed out.'

"Ross stood up and drew a long breath. And you never saw a man look so relieved. He grew inches—lifted his shoulders as if a ton had dropped off. Hal started to grip him by the hand, but thought better of it and suppressed his interest.

"'Let's show that to mother,' Hal said, and we went upstairs.

"'Thank God!' was her comment, and she looked at Ross with her eyes shining. Then she turned to the boy, 'Hal dear, I think I hear that taxi, please pay him and send him away. And take Iris. If she can get a brisk walk before the police come and start an inquisition, I think she can stand it better. But first put this back and shut up the grate. Let the police find it. Oh, and Hal—if they are here when you come in just remember to tell exactly what has happened this morning—except about Crasher. Surely, Mr. Hunt'—she looked at me appealingly—'we need not tell them about Crasher, need we?'

"I thought about it a minute, and concluded that she needn't.

"'He's nothing to do with the murder apparently,' I told her. 'I guess you don't have to mention it—unless they ask you. And then if they find he was here and blame you, you can say you only answered questions.'

"'I hate to drag in all that about Iris,' she said, and I didn't blame her. So the kids went out and then she turned to me, steady as you please.

"'Mr. Hunt, it is a great comfort to have someone to consult at once. Dr. Akers tells me we must have a lawyer and has recommended a friend of his.'

"'Philip Anderson,' Ross put in, 'You know him—'

"So I added my good opinion to his and she seemed pleased, but went on—'Just now I feel the need of a detective more than a lawyer. The police will fasten on the servants of course and look for them. No doubt they will suspect us all. But what I am afraid of is that man Crasher. It is true that Mr. Vaughn had arranged to have him marry Iris—he is ferociously in love with her . . . I know something of his methods and his abilities. So I wish to engage you not only to find out who are the murderers, but to combat and disprove false charges such as I have good reason will be made.'

"I won't swear that's verbatim, but it's pretty close. And knowing Gus [like] I do I wouldn't put it past him to do something of the sort if he had reason. He looked mad enough this morning to make a lot of mischief. She said I might need money for expenses, and handed over fifty dollars."

"Sensible woman!" approved Mrs. Hunt.

"Then she went on and told us a tremendous story. I judge it to be the truth and nothing but the truth, but a long way from being the whole truth. It appears that that suspicious old father of hers had rigged up a contraption in his room, connected somehow with the telephone, by which he could sit there and listen to talk in the kitchen and in his study below—Vaughn's room. This good lady has her father's room and got on to the trick by accident, and made the most of her opportunities.

"'My brother-in-law was a blackmailer,' she plumped at us, hurrying to get it across before the police came. 'He took advantage of his professional position, clients' confidences and so on, and used that man Crasher to gather evidence for him. It was blackmail on a large scale. People came as "clients" to consult him "professionally," but most of his "profession," in this house at least, was receiving tribute from his victims. He lent money too, mortgages and so on.' Then she looked at Akers with that little crooked smile of hers, and said, 'There's one comfort in all this trouble—nobody can collect on ashes.'"

"So that's why he was looking so relieved, downstairs," proclaimed Bessie.

"Very likely," Jim agreed. "Looks as if he'd had a grip on Ross. And I suppose the rest of the stuff was other people's notes and beautiful bunches of evidence for his pretty business."

"And who burned 'em, do you think?" inquired his listener.

"I don't think yet, not anything. I'm just giving you the case as I got it."

"Why do you suppose she wanted to cover that grate again and let the police find the ashes for themselves?"

"Hold on, friend wife, I haven't got to guessing yet. It's too thick. She ran on, telling us about those absconding servants. They were among his victims it appears, and worse off than the rich people who only had to pay cash. He had some sort of evidence of crime held over them, true or false she didn't know, but it was enough to keep them in a sort of slavery. She thought the man, Joe White, might have killed him long ago, but, that Crasher had the women's 'dossier' too, and he knew it . . . Bess—"

"Yes, what is it?"

"That woman was under a tremendous strain!"

She giggled. "That must be masculine intuition, Jim. Of course she was. I should think a five-fold murder would be enough to strain anyone. And she's quite smart enough, I judge, to know that everyone in the house will be under suspicion. Then the relief at getting rid of him—seems to have been a most unpopular gentleman. And she's dead right about Crasher. If there's any way he can fix it on one of them I don't doubt he'd be willing. What about that marriage?"

"There's your 'True Woman,'" Jim jeered, retaliatively. "'What about the marriage,' of course. And at that you're dead right my dear, as you usually are. If you've got a shadow of sympathy for [the] corpse, give it up. You remember about that 'obedience' clause in the will?"

"Yes. Well?"

"She told us what she had overheard on Monday afternoon. He had put the screws on that pretty child that she must marry Crasher Wednesday morning or he'd pack them all out of doors—and he'd called to get her, an hour ahead of time. It appears she was to inherit some of her grandfather's money, if she married with her guardian's consent—and those two Christian gentlemen made a bargain, though Crasher kicked some, by which Vaughn was to force the girl to marry Gus, and he was immediately to hand back the money that went with her."

"She should have refused! You can't drive a girl like that, nowadays."

"Maybe you can't, but that's what he did. Said he'd ruin Dr. Akers too. You see it would have spoiled the boy's college prospects, cost them the little money they had to look forward to, and no girl of her age and nature—she's a sweet little thing, Bess—could stand up against all that, the aunt being crippled and all. It was an awful jam. Nevertheless, her aunt got on to it, wouldn't hear of it, of course, and they were about to leave, this morning, when this happened."

"So that's why she would have none of him when he turned up. And Gus Crasher is robbed of his bride on his wedding day, and turned out of the house! If those people do stand to gain anything by Vaughn's death—"

"If they do," said Jim slowly, "they certainly are up against it. Motives to burn, opportunity *ad lib*, and Crasher after them! . . . Well, about then the police came bounding in, Moore and Flannigan and Clargis—he's a plain-clothed man—and Tom Davis to look at the body. They were quite impressed, for policemen. I can tell you, Bess, there was a sense of accumulated—shall we say ill-feeling about that murder, rather beyond the ordinary.

"Tom took a good look at the body, Akers agreeing with him as to the approximate time of death, early the previous evening, and he went off. Autopsy later. The others began to question us at once. Akers had to leave for his professional calls so Clargis began on him. He answered up like a little man, told a straight story from my call at his house up to the minute, except about Crasher and opening the grate. I had given them the same stuff while the docs were busy, told them I was engaged on the job, and they let me stay. Clargis is a good fellow anyway; we often help each other.

"Then he summoned Miss Iris. The child was pretty calm; that little walk with Hal had done her good. She told all about the morning's doings, minus Crasher, even to her little walk. Hal came next.

"'Where were you yesterday evening?'

"'At the movies, first turn, *The Neighbors* just round the corner. Iris was with me. The ticket man knows us, if you want to make sure.'

"I thought they looked as if they found him a little too frank.

"'Did you hear anything in your uncle's room either before or after going out?'

"'There was some loud talking when we left; he often had callers in the evening.'

"'Men or women?'

"'Both. Oh, you mean last evening? That was a man.'

"'Did you recognize the voice?'

"'No, I don't think so. We often hear talk in there.'

"'Was there anything like a quarrel?'

"'The man sounded pretty mad, but Uncle Wade only chuckled. Aggravating little chuckle he had!'

"'You say you found the door of Mr. Vaughn's bedroom locked this morning. Was that his custom?'

"'I can't say; I never had occasion to try it.'

"'Was there another door to the room?'

"'Yes, into the bathroom, and that connected with the next room. That was locked and the key in it, inside.'

"'Who used the next room?'

"'No one. It was the guest room.'

"'And the door of the office was also locked, with the key in it?'

"'Yes. But the keyhole's so big I could turn the key with pliers.' They looked at it and agreed with him."

"Jim, my dear, you've got a memory like a dictograph," admired Bess.

"Oh, I won't swear to every word of this, but it's pretty straight. When it came to Mrs. Warner we went up to her room. She was perfectly collected, told the same story about that morning as the youngsters, to a dot, including her belief that her brother-in-law was a blackmailer. Clargis concentrated on the servants, asked how long they had been there, what references and so on. She told how her brother-in-law had installed them without consulting her, first the two women, later the man. He asked for personal descriptions and she gave them. But he was most interested in her being able to hear them talk in the kitchen.

"'Did you hear anything like a threat or plan against him?'

"She said no, but that she had heard them talking as if of a plan of escape. He pricked up his ears and demanded particulars; and she heard them Monday night, talking apparently of a getaway— 'But there's no crime in that!' she insisted.

"'There may have been considerable crime before it, madam,' Clargis answered, 'so anything you can tell us on that line will be valuable.'

"'I can't give you this exactly,' she went on slowly, 'they were all there together, Monday evening, late, talking. I was interested for I did not want to lose them. But I only gathered bits of it. Joe said, 'Bugs'll do it; he'll do anything for me.' Then something from Nellie that I didn't get, and Joe answered, 'Fast? That little sled of his will beat any police boat in the harbor.' Then the cook said, 'SSH!' But I was interested and waited. After a while Joe was audible again, and clearer, trying to reassure them. 'Not a bit of danger! Just a fishing trip you know—and connect outside the limit.' And 'Finest harbor in the world!' And 'Italian goes there all right, plenty of them there, and plenty of room for three more men, my dears!' And they laughed. They laughed a good deal.'

"'Nothing else?' they demanded, but she said that was

absolutely all. Clargis made no remark, but he was pleased and showed it.

"'Wasn't it the *Chimborazo* that sailed this morning for Rio? That would fit all right. We'll get hold of Bugs if we can, but we can reach the boat anyway. Those "three men" will be surprised when they land—thanks to you Ma'am.'"

Jim evidently did not share in the pleasure of Mr. Clargis. "They'll wireless that steamer, Bess. I'm afraid it's all up with that bunch."

"Maybe," admitted the lady. "Looks too easy to me. Wonder what they laughed about—if they did."

"You're not believing the lady?"

"I'm not believing anybody when I'm considering a case, and neither are you, Jim Hunt. Well, what happened next?"

Search and Inquiry

"Then we went over the house. I'll say this for that machine-gun murderer, or syndicate—he or she or they didn't leave the ghost of a clue. Not a cuff link, not a cigarette stub, nothing—unless Crasher did pick up something off the desk. They found a notebook on him with the combination, opened the safe, empty. As for fingerprints—not one; that horn-handled knife didn't show anything, and the glass and decanter were *clean*; they'd been wiped off!"

"Careful job!" she commented. "And thorough. Looks to me like experience."

"Yes—or a high order of intelligence. Both perhaps. As to the rest of the house—I'll make a plan of it." On the biggest piece of paper before them he hastily indicated the crossed streets, the large long southwest corner lot, the big old house, the board fence on the side and back. "Picket fence in front," he explained as he drew, "sort of narrow balcony across the front windows—you can step on it from the top of the front steps, easy. These windows are French, like doors, open on the balcony.

"There's a side door on Field Street, a gate there. Cement drive to the garage at the end of the lot—it's about a hundred and fifty by sixty or seventy, I should say. Bricked path down the middle, gate at the back, opens into an alley running from Park to Garden Street. Flower beds, grass, shrubbery everywhere, big, old, overgrown. Path from back door to side door cemented.

"Ground floor has a hall straight through from front to back, with a door in the middle. Stairs, both front and back, go up on the east side of the hall, common landing above. Vaughn's room here on the corner, northeast, then a little hall for that side door, coat closet at the end of it. Then the dining room, back of that the kitchen. Sort of pantry between that coat-closet and the center hall, opens from dining room. On the west side two big connecting parlors. Upstairs Mrs. Warner's room over Vaughn's, bathroom over the side hall, then Iris' room and one over the kitchen—the women servants had that; the man slept in the attic. West side, Vaughn's bedroom in front, bath, guest room, and Hal's at the back.

"We went over every inch, attic and cellar. All as neat as a pin. Clargis said it looked phony to him; he never heard of any servants keeping things up like that. I confess it didn't seem natural, the dead man upstairs, the whole staff cleared out, and the place on dress parade so to speak. Of course the boy's room was mussed some, and they hadn't had time to make the beds yet, or wash the breakfast things, but everything else was in apple-pie order.

"Then Flannigan, Clargis and I took the garden, went over it carefully, and at last, down by the back gate, we did find a footprint or two, at one side, in the soft earth. There was a box there by the fence, and someone had apparently stepped up on it to look over and came back. Outside the gate things were clearer. There was a trampled spot as if someone had stood about there, and plenty of cigarette stubs, pretty cheap stuff, too. Then there was a flattened place in the grass right there. The footprints came to that place, and left it again, marked deeper."

"Aha!" observed Bessie, sagaciously. "As one carrying something heavy."

"Don't interrupt and spoil my impressive story! We followed these deep prints along the side of the alley, a muddy place it was, to the second lot west, where a big bunch of lilac bushes hung over the fence; rather broken and mussed they looked. Clargis grabbed a bit of old board and slanted it against the fence; we took turns and peeked over."

"Spot where the body lay!" crowed Bessie.

"Right again. We climbed over and took a look. 'Hello!' said Clargis, 'it's Carlo! Now what would that Wop* be doin' in the alley? And who bumped him off and spilled him over here so casual like?'

"'The missing man-servant of course,' Clargis told him. 'You see there's no attempt at real concealment; he just dumped him here till he could make his own getaway. But what was the guy doing waiting by that gate so long?'

"Well, that was the sum of our discoveries. They called up the office. Remains of friend Carlo taken to the morgue, man set at each end of the alley to restrain inquirers, Moore left in the house, Flannigan took himself off, said he must get after those servants, Clargis too, and I was left to myself."

"Who's your Carlo person?" Bessie inquired.

"Oh, he's a hanger on, a stool, anybody's man for a dollar or two. Somebody hired him to watch in the alley and somebody else caught him at it. Carlo's no loss and doesn't seem to add to the excitement particularly. What's a little one-blow murder more or less beside that complication in the house?"

"All very well, Mr. Hunt, but you may find it more important than you think. No more corpses in your story?"

"No, not one, sorry to disappoint you, amiable lady."

She was looking over her notes. "You said the windows in his room were all unlocked?"

"Yes, and one open, east side, near the side door."

"Looks to me like a piece of foresight on the part of whoever did it. About what time was it when you were done with Carlo?"

"About lunch time! I was for leaving, but Mrs. Warner begged me to stay. Hal and the girl had got something together; she said she wanted to talk to me further—and I stayed. It was a funny meal . . . "

"The eats?"

"No, the folks. There they were, and two of them mere children, with a peculiarly dreadful murder in the house and policemen on watch at the doors. And they sat there as calm as cucumbers, not eating much, to be sure, except the boy; he did pretty well, but talking like—like people in a book."

"What did they talk about?"

"About my business and didn't I find it interesting. About detective stories, and did I like them, and were they true to life. About other stories, had I read so and so, what did I think of 'the trend of modern fiction'? That was Miss Iris. And it wasn't put on for the occasion; it was evidently what they were used to.

"Then Mrs. Warner caught a look of mine, and began to explain. 'I don't wonder you are a little astonished, Mr. Hunt. What surprises you is the result of living with Mr. Vaughn. That we are not grieving for him, but on the contrary relieved at his loss, is due to just that—living with him. There has been much strain and misery in this family, on our part, that is, but no matter what we felt we were required to keep up light and pleasant table talk. It has become a habit.'

"'It's going to stop being one,' protested Hal. 'I'm going to eat with my head in my plate and no more talk than a farmer!'

"'We had to do it when we were miserable, and now we are doing it to cover unseemly relief,' she added. 'But we can stop it now and talk of what we are really thinking about. Will you advise us, Mr. Hunt—tell us what we ought to do? I can see of course that in the eyes of the police we are all open to suspicion. These young folks were in at nine or near it—they might have done it. I might have swarmed downstairs like a seal and done it. Joe White is the most likely suspect, perhaps aided by the women, and there are those people coming to the office—but we are still on the list. Now none of us have ever been associated with a murder before. Except—' her face grew hard.

"'Except what?' I urged.

"'Except my sister's,' she said bitterly. 'Oh I know he wasn't in the house—but he drove her to it. He did it as much as if he'd shot her!'

"'You asked for advice,' I remarked. 'The first advice I will offer is that you, all of you, repress this—animosity. I can see that it is well deserved. I don't blame you one bit for feeling so. But it is true that you are all under suspicion, must be, and nothing can be worse for you than showing hatred.'

"'I'm afraid we've showed it already,' said Hal ruefully.

"'Yes, you all did to some extent, but that was better than pretending to affection that wouldn't have stood fire for a moment. Frankness was far wiser. But—soft pedal please!'

"They all agreed with this. After lunch we had some more talk, Mrs. Warner and I. She told me a lot. My heavens, Bessie, if any of them did kill him I shouldn't blame 'em one bit.

"She told me about Crasher. He was thick with Vaughn in this blackmailing business, collected evidence for him, all that sort of thing. But he hadn't Vaughn's facilities for covering payments.

"'I should think he would have been a rather dangerous partner,' I suggested.

"'He would indeed, but Vaughn was stronger than he was. He not only had his position and legal knowledge, but he had "the goods" on Crasher. And that is what I specially want you to do, Mr. Hunt, find out what that was; as long as that man is at large I shall not feel safe about Iris—or Hal. Why, those two men between them thought nothing of "framing" anyone who stood in their way. And I think, I can't be sure of this, that they hired still lower wretches to do still worse things for them.'

"I told her about finding Carlo, and she nodded her head in agreement.

"'Hired to watch our gate! And probably Joe found him.' She has a good head, Bessie."

"Too good!" said that lady in a darkly suspicious manner.

"Well, she freed her mind to a considerable extent, and finally I excused myself, said I'd have to be getting busy, that I wanted to take another look around before leaving. So I walked over the house again, not carefully, just to see if any general impression struck me, and then outside again. Found nothing of importance in the garden, but one thing of considerable importance out of it, and that's a witness."

"A witness! You don't mean a witness of the murder, surely."

"No, not so good as that. But a witness who has been witnessing what went on around that old house for some ten years or more."

Bessie turned over a fresh page and took another pencil.

"I was snooping around in the garden and along the paths. It occurred to me to see what the approach to those side windows was, and what windows overlooked that corner. Opposite on Field Street is an unoccupied house, blinds all shut tight. But diagonally across the house is occupied, very much so. On the second floor is a bay window built out corner-wise, looks all ways—except northeast! In that bay window I caught a moving flash of reflected light. So I went inside and upstairs, found a convenient curtain and gazed across. There sat an old lady with an opera glass, enjoying herself. Then I went to Mrs. Warner and asked her to tell me all she could about her neighbors.

"'I haven't but one,' she said, 'that's the old lady on the opposite corner, Mrs. Todd.' She lived there in the old days, it appears, when the Smith girls were young, knew their mother, was always nice to them. Later on she became quite an invalid, confined to her room. They've kept up a telephone acquaintance. She gave me a note of introduction, and I promptly presented it.

"Most engaging old lady! Quick as a bird, cheerful and sharp as they make 'em.

"'Dead, is he?' she chirped. 'I'm thankful to hear of it! Tell me all about it, young man.'

"So I told her, at considerable length. She fairly ate it up.

"'Four times over!' she gloated. 'It would have been fifty if he'd had his desserts! Marrying that little saint when she was out of her head and then tormenting her to death! *I* know!'

"She sat there in her gay little wrapper, looking as pleased as Punch to hear about Vaughn's death, and looked me over with the brightest pair of old eyes I ever saw.

"'Jack Warner says I can trust you, and I guess she's right. What do you want to know Mr. Detective?'

"I told her I wanted to know what she knew about the Smith House.

"'That, young man, would take some time,' she answered. 'You'd better give me a date to start on.'

"I told her to begin at the beginning—and she did. Gosh! I've been there most of the afternoon. She gave me a lot about old Smith, evidently didn't love him. Said she knew him when he was a young man, 'And a very opinionated young man he was, wanted to manage everything. The way he tyrannized over that poor pretty young wife was a crime,' she insisted. 'A plain crime. And the same with the girls.' I'm giving this the way she said it, as near as I can remember. 'Iris was a darling,' she went on. 'Pretty and sweet like her daughter, even more beautiful. But Jacqueline, Jack, they called her, had the character. She was handsome too, but stronger. And her devotion to her sister was simply lovely. Educated at home. Sort of housekeeper-chaperon to keep watch over 'em. But even that dragon got so fond of Iris that when the young minister began calling I think she didn't report it.

"'The big trouble began when that brute Vaughn got hold of the old man. J. J. Smith was not wicked, only domineering and unreasonable; he admired him for his ability and success as a lawyer, and they were like twins in loving to tyrannize. Vaughn made love to Iris, but she loathed him.'

"I told her that I knew about the running away and the marriage and the will. 'All right, all right,' piped the cheerful old thing. "'I skip forty years, said the bellman with tears. And proceed without further remark To the time when you took me aboard of your ship To aid you in hunting the Snark,"* That's what you are after I presume, to find out who did it. Why bother? Let the police do it, if they can.'

"'Mrs. Warner has employed me,' I told her gravely, 'not only to find who did it, but to be prepared to avert any false charges which may possibly be made. May I use your telephone a moment—to speak to her?' I asked if I might tell Mrs. Todd about her special reason for wishing me to ascertain all I could as to the murder, and Crasher, and she said 'Give Mrs. Todd the receiver, please.'

"I sat and watched the old lady's face—it was a picture. When she finally hung up she turned to me with a sort of piquant ferocity, like an enraged hen.

"'Young man!' she sputtered, 'I'll tell you everything I know. I'd be willing to tell you things I don't know, to get around that unspeakable scoundrel! Iris! Little Iris!—'"

Bessie had been swiftly taking notes as he talked, her bright face changing like an April sky. She laid down her pencil and clapped her hands at this. "Me for the old lady! Hurrah for Mrs. Todd! Go on dear—this is great!"

"I'll have to condense a good deal; she talked forever. But here's the meat of it. You see with that corner bay window she could watch up and down four ways. She had a swivel chair, and the opera glass.

"'It's a good glass—take a look,' she said. I did. I could see into Vaughn's room, over the sash curtains, see the desk and chair by it.

"'Of course he pulled the blinds down, evenings. Sometimes he forgot it till people came. And they came! Stacks of people, two, three of an evening sometimes.' (It appears he'd been doing a flourishing back-door business, Bess.) 'They'd knock on that side door, mostly, but not loud, and he'd let 'em in himself—I've seen him start to do it.

"'There's that big light on the corner, young man. I could recognize folks if they didn't take pains to hide their faces. But they did, every man-jack of them, and women more so. You can't see much of a woman's face nowadays, with those tight cowls they wear from nose to nape! But these used to duck and muffle even more; nobody could have identified one of them. But they did vary in size—there was quite a variety. Some came to the front door, some up from the alley. One man had a key to the side door, used to let himself in, quiet and quick.'

"I asked for a description of this one, and she gave it to perfection. 'Heavy shoulders, very wide. Thick nose. Thick neck. Thick legs. Soft hat pulled well down. Scrubby thick moustache—sometimes.'

"'You are a good observer, Mrs. Todd,' I complimented her.

"'I am,' she triumphantly agreed. 'I have nothing else to do. I've sat here by the hour, day-time or night-time. I've had lots of fun watching that house. This man, coming in so slinking, I particularly noticed. He used to come by daylight too, to the front door, sometimes. His clothes were different, very different, but the shape of him was not, and once he had a moustache in the evening when that very afternoon he'd been there without one. So sudden.' Bess, you'd love that old lady!"

"I should. I do now. That's Crasher, I suppose?"

"Undoubtedly. I complimented her some more, and brought her down to the present era. 'How about Monday and Tuesday this week?'

"She had seen Crasher call Monday, front door, seen him talking with Vaughn—the blinds were up—Crasher evidently excited, Vaughn calm and superior. Saw Iris come in afterward, Crasher leave, and Vaughn sit there, slowly tipping back and forth in his chair, laying down the law—

"'And that poor pretty young thing just pleading with him! I wish I'd had a gun—a rifle! There'd have been five [murderers]! And I'd have been the first, young man!' Quite a bloodthirsty old lady, Bess."

"Me too!" proclaimed that scribbling person. "I'd have been six, with pleasure! Do go on, Jim."

"All right Ma'am. Monday evening she said there were no callers. Tuesday morning Hal went out early, Iris a bit later, both home to lunch. Nothing doing in the afternoon—except that Hal was out again. Before seven a man came in a big car, to the front door. When he left he stood on the top step a little, turned and looked the house over, especially at the balcony before Vaughn's windows; then went off fast. A little later a man suddenly appeared at the side door—she said he must have come through the yard, for she was watching both streets. He went the same way, slipped out the side door and around the corner of the house 'like an eel.' The woman left her car down Field Street a bit, and walked up, quickly, her head sunk in her fur collar. She was in for some time, 'Twenty-two minutes to be exact; I've a good clock in sight, Mr. Detective, and I love to keep tabs on people.' (I tell you, my dear, Mrs. Todd's testimony is going to be invaluable.)

"'And when that woman came out she acted pretty desperate. She 'raised her arms to Heaven' as the books say—though how anybody knows which way Heaven is from a round whirling globe *I* never could see! But she raised 'em up wildly, and then clasped her hands in front and kind of shook 'em, and rushed off to her car—that woman was in quite a way, Mr. Hunt.'

"Well—I guess that's the gist of it. She talked a blue streak, some of it may be needed later, but this is what I wanted, bearing on our immediate interests. Oh, hold on, I've left out something, may be important. She saw the young folks go out Tuesday evening, and judged they were going to the movies, as they often did. But Iris came back pretty soon, ran back to be exact, and let herself in by the side door. 'Forgot her handkerchief, I bet a cooky,' said Mrs. Todd. She didn't even stop to light a light, and whisked out in a minute and went back the way she came. 'I'd know that child anywhere, with her little shiny hat and twinkling legs.'"

Jim suddenly stopped short in his account, sat up and pounded his knee with his fist. "I *thought* I'd seen those young folks before! Look here Bess, did I happen to tell you that I saw Crasher Tuesday morning?"

"Not a word. What doing?"

"He was in a taxi drawn up by the curb, downtown, and sat well back as if he didn't want to be seen. I was crossing over, and had just dodged back to save my neck and saw him plain. He was watching a girl who went into a drugstore. A girl who had just got out of a Hill Street car, and she had a little shiny hat and twinkling legs if ever I saw any."

Bessie looked at him, considering.

"Hill Street?"

"Yes, it's next to Grove you know. I stepped to the rear of his cab and waited a bit. Presently she came out. He dismissed his cab and followed her, and I followed him, just for instance!"

"Just to keep an eye on that rascal; glad you did."

"Presently she pops into another drugstore. He loafed and waited till she came out again. I was in a store on the other side of the street. That girl went into four drugstores in succession, we two on her trail. Presently she met a young man—it was her cousin I know now, and they took a Hill Street car home. Crasher followed them and I went about my business."

"And never told me a word! Nice partner you are!" protested his wife.

"Now Bess—you know I didn't get home till late and we had to hurry to get to the show—I forgot it. I'm sorry dear."

But she was thinking hard. "Four drugstores. Tuesday morning. And she runs back from the picture for a moment Tuesday evening. Jim, it looks bad, very bad. And Crasher after her. Look here Jim, we've got to see Tom Davis. Will you call him up? No, I will . . . Is that you Tom? How busy are you? Could you run up here right now for a bit of talk—it isn't nine yet. Yes, it's very important, really, and I just need you. What's that? Oh no, I'm not divorced! Jim's here, he wants to see you too."

"I do not," Jim protested. "Flirting with your old flames right before my ears!"

"Now Jim, behave yourself! He's no more an old flame than Crasher was. Of course I liked him better; anybody'd be better than Crasher! But there's only one Jim, and you know it. This is a piece of practical psychology, as you'll soon see. And now help me get those dishes cleaned up, while we wait."

A Council of War*

The dishes did not take long; neither did Tom Davis. Inside of half an hour he was there, shaking hands cordially with his "hated rival," and demanding of Bessie what graft she was working on him now.

"I'll tell you, Tom. Now look here, if Jim is your hated rival, what's Gus Crasher?"

"He's a plain skunk!" he answered with emphasis. "No, not a plain skunk, one of those they have out west—a hydrophobia skunk!"

"Good for you. Now I'll tell you what we are up against. I suppose you have examined the body?"

"Body? Which one? I've had several today."

"Vaughn murder," Jim contributed.

"Oh yes. Say—that's a murder as is a murder! And you're in on it?" Jim nodded. "We've not had the autopsy yet, but if ever a man was well and thoroughly killed, he was. He was shot, he was stabbed, he was strangled, he was knocked on the head—you saw it Jim. The reporters are crazy!"

"How about poison?" suggested Jim.

"Poison! Well you are hard to suit. Who said there was poison?"

"Crasher did."

"Not to the police, not that I heard of."

"No, he's keeping it up his sleeve. But he let it out at first, to me."

"You see he was there, and we had a look in before you boys arrived. And what do you make of this, Mr. Surgeon—a knife in the neck, a bullet in the head, and no blood. None to speak of."

Davis leaned back and whistled softly. Jim continued—"It was his habit I learned, to sit there after dinner, and drink, and snooze, and see visitors. The whiskey glass was empty. Gus smelled it, tasted it, and said, 'Poison!' Then the girl laughed. You should have seen him look at her!"

Then they told him about the case of gentle little Iris, and how her stepfather had arranged to sell her to Crasher. "And he's lost her, lost her on his wedding morning, and the man who was forcing the sale is dead . . . You know Crasher . . . "

"What do you want of me?" asked Davis slowly.

"Thought you might be able to balk him somehow. Want you to examine that *corpus delicti* with a fine-toothed microscope. Be dead sure of the order of exercises, as it were. And if he comes round after information give him some—selected. You see he'll frame them if he can, one or more of them. That's his specialty."

Then Jim told him of his happening to find Crasher trailing Iris on Tuesday morning, and that she had been into four drugstores, with him at her heels. "Now I'll find out what she bought there, and let you know. And you find out if there's any of it in him."

Davis considered. Bessie urged him a little. "We're not asking you to take sides. If Baby-faced poisoned her papa, she won't be the first one to try to get out of a hole that way. Or the heroic young cousin. Or the invalid lady herself, turning out not to be a cripple, as usual. Or all of 'em. Truth is mighty, and gets out sometimes. What we are so keen about is that an able and experienced detective, without a principle to his name, and past master of the art of 'framing,' is chomping his teeth to get even with them . . . When is the inquest?"

"Saturday I think, or possibly Monday. They can't have the funeral till I'm through, anyhow. Tell me a bit more about the family, will you? I haven't had time to read all the guff in the papers tonight."

They told him a good deal of the background of the two sisters, their escape and happiness, the terrible finality of the accident that widowed them both; of Vaughn's marrying the shattered Iris and of his literally trying to sell that child to Crasher; then holding Jacqueline in helpless dependence; of his continuous grinding tyranny over them all and the servants as well.

"Those servants haven't a Chinaman's chance, if they catch 'em," Davis opined.

"I hope they don't! If any people had a right to kill a man, they had," said Bessie hotly, to which Jim quietly rejoined.

"But there are authorities who hold that no one has such a right, without due process of law."

"Law!" repeated the lady, in no respectful tone. "Law! Huh!"

Davis was sitting with his long legs stretched out toward the radiator and his eyes on the ceiling. "Suppose we reconstruct the crime," he suggested, "and see if we can get a line on what the charming Augustus is likely to do—then we'll do it first as it were." He reached for the plan Jim had made and studied it closely. "And here's our lamented friend, Vaughn, sitting in his office like an ant-lion."

"What on earth's an ant-lion?" demanded Mrs. Hunt. "I've heard of ant-eaters; is it one of them?"

"Not at all, my attractive but ignorant young lady. It's a kind of spider. He digs a funnel-shaped hole in the sand and squats in the bottom of it, well covered up, waiting for the ants to fall in—which they do."

"I may be ignorant," she remarked with some acerbity, "but at least I know enough not to call a spider 'he,' not a working spider."

"Score one," said Tom, "I'll admit it's only the female that's dangerous. Well, however, there's Vaughn sitting in his den Tuesday evening. Alive and chuckling at six-fifty. Three known visitors, two of whom registered rage and despair so to speak. Three servants in the house with inclination and opportunity. Three members of the family who seem to be in the same position. Whew! Nine immediately possible murderers! As for motive, every one who knew him seems to have had that! . . . And little Bright-eyes over the way sees the people who go in and out. Look here, Jim, could the old lady see if anybody came up through the yard, from the alley?"

"Not possible; the house runs back too far."

"All right, then nine, more or less, might have got in and out again that way any time. That night's visitors gone by eight o'clock, you say?"

"Eight-fifteen. Admirable witness, Mrs. Todd. She'll be a scream if they call her."

Davis pursued his theme. "Then by eight-fifteen the good old man is alone to count his hard-earned wealth. As near as I could judge he had been dead, when found, about twelve hours, ten or twelve. So these little accidents must have happened before, say, ten o'clock."

"One of them must," put in Bessie smartly. "A man can die but once! You've got to center on the first death I suppose, not the later one."

"Right you are, my dear, and I will now surprise you by solemnly announcing which came first."

"Beat you to it," cried Jim. "Poison of course—never heard of a dead man taking poison."

"Nor of anyone forcibly giving it to a dead man," Bessie added drily, "poison it is."

"All agreed," pursued Tom, "if he is poisoned, that's first. In common politeness we'll attribute that to a woman, leaving harsher methods to the men. We have four women in the house with grievances to justify prussic acid, and one raging on the doorstep. Plenty of leeway. Very well. Victim takes his little drink of doctored whiskey and passes out quietly. Then—here's where we *are* up against! Four more people, or a particularly lavish homicidal maniac, come in and do it all over again—not observing that he is dead!"

"Sit where you are, Tom," cried his host, starting to his feet. "You be the corpse and I'll do the killing."

"I won't trust you for a minute, Jim Hunt. No sir! You know you are jealous of me, always were. Come on Bess, you be the victim; we won't either of us hurt you!"

"Pleasant sort of a game you are making it!" she protested, but took the chair indicated.

"He was in the habit of napping in that chair," Jim suggested.

"Only known to members of the household though," retorted Tom, "looks bad for them."

"Three of 'em are as good as convicted anyhow—"

"Yes, when you catch 'em. I've a notion those are not going to be easily turned up. And if you are right about the amiable Augustus, the other three are in serious difficulties. Now then, Mr. Hunt—you kill him first, which weapon do you favor?"

Jim favored the pistol, and advanced stealthily.

"He comes up from behind, like this, thinks he's asleep, gets right behind him and fires close to the head—and takes himself off, feeling better."

"But nobody'd garrote a dead man," Tom insisted. "And he must have been dead when garroted because he didn't struggle any."

"But they did garrote a dead man," urged Bessie. "Poison *must* have come first."

"Nobody'd knife a man after he was strangled, anyhow, Tom."

"Not if they knew it, surely. Now which would have shown the least." The two men were remembering the body as they had seen it.

"The cord first," decided Jim. "If that knife handle had been sticking up it would have been in the way. But it was a small cord and sunk in, didn't show hardly at all, and an angry person, stealing up behind"—he stole up, accordingly, with a sharp-pointed paper cutter in his hand, and Bessie bounced out of the chair.

"Your professional enthusiasm may be too much for you," she explained, and set a big cushion in her place, adding, "and that pistol wound clearly visible! *I* say poison, cord, knife and then pistol."

"Where does the blackjack* come in," sweetly asked Tom, and they fell to another discussion, finally concluding that black-jack was four and pistol five.

Suddenly Bessie asked a question. "Is there a penalty for killing a dead man?"

They looked at one another and laughed.

"Not that I ever heard of," Jim admitted.

"Might call it mutilating a corpse," suggested Tom, "but he wasn't mutilated at all, hardly mussed."

"They might [try] to prove intent to kill," Jim mused, "but after all there's only one murder. What a come-down!"

"Then we've got to look out for Crasher, and the poison, and the girl," urged Mrs. Hunt. "Tom—you concentrate on the poison, and see if you can't throw a monkey-wrench into his works."

"I will, my dear Bess. I've the ghost of a hunch already. Jim—can you find out what little sister bought in those drugstores? And let me know, first thing tomorrow morning."

"I'll be there as soon as they open, and phone you."

"It's a peach of a case," he congratulated them, with thanks for a very pleasant evening, and took himself off.

The two sat awhile in silence, and presently Bessie announced in a calm and cheerful voice, "Jim, I'm going to leave you."

He refused to be alarmed—"When? For what place? For how long?"

"And that's all he thinks of me! When is tomorrow morning early; where is the old Smith house. For how long is indetermi-nate. Do you realize that that distracted household has no ser-vant? And is likely to have difficulty in getting them? *And* that ingenious Mr. Crasher might have some up his sleeve to plant on 'em? That's where little sister gets in ahead of him! Please call up Dr. Akers right now, ask him to 'phone Mrs. Warner about the 'treasure' he has found for her. I guess he'll give me a good character. He can tell her I'll be there at seven tomorrow morning. I want to get an inside view of those people."

Jim gazed upon his wife in profound admiration. He did more than gaze; he solemnly bowed from the hips and kissed her hand.

"Bess—you certainly are the elephant's howdah! I say nothing of your ruthlessly sacrificing a loving and dependent husband, but admire you unreservedly."

Nectar for Newspapers

Not since the Lizzie Borden case had that great moral engine, the press, so thoroughly enjoyed itself. It is true there was no s.a.*—as yet, but with two men and four women in the house there was ample room for the journalistic imagination.

The headliners in particular rejoiced, and large letters assailed the eye with "The Multi-Murder!" "Wasted Death!" "Killing a Dead Man!" and similar pleasing captions.

The evening papers played merrily about with the four obvious methods of attack; the morning papers were even more profuse. Articles or interviews appeared from popular authors of murder and mystery stories, while space writers* promptly competed with them, offering theories of their own.

The absent servants were easy prey; some credited them with all the various assaults, while others hinted darkly at other motives activating other people. The journalistic morgue was opened, and all that had been known of Mr. J. J. Smith, his early life, his young wife's death, his two daughters brought up under such archaic ideas, their widely described escape and further career. All this was but nine years old; it had been produced in full at the time of the dreadful accident and the astonishing instant remarriage of one of the young widows.

Vague and ghastly hints were made of the disfigurement of the other widow, and of her being supported, in close seclusion, by Mr. Vaughn, who nobly maintained her son also, and his wife's daughter by her previous marriage, even after that lady's death. That ghastly suicide was of course enlarged upon with impressive details, and the sad life of this benevolent widower thereafter. Then was reviewed the sudden and mysterious return of the aged father falling on his own doorstep, unable to speak, stricken down with paralysis, and dying without ever explaining where he had been or as to his unexpected return. This led to a description of the will, with its harsh and unusual features, and the peculiar insistence of obedience. Some suggested that this peculiarity, and the practical exclusion of the daughters from a fair share in the property, warranted a question as to the old gentleman's being wholly in his right mind.

The more amiably inclined writers urged that Mr. Vaughn's evident benevolence, as shown by his tender care of the crippled sister-in-law, and also the full provision for the grandchildren, justified the old gentleman. Some even suggested that if more parents insisted on obedience it might be better for the rising generation.

Others again hinted darkly that one sister being dead, the other practically helpless, and the children very young, the will had been a most convenient one for the deceased.

Of him there was much vivid description, of his coming to
the city some twenty years ago, and immediate spectacular success in a noted criminal case; his further work in similar lines and
marked ability to clear his clients in the face of heavy charges.
He was favorably compared to Abe Hummel,* as equally skill-
ful, but with a far better reputation.

The worst point anyone brought against him was his incred-
ibly hasty marriage of the young widow, but an interview with
one who seemed to know him told of her distraught condition,
and that he married her as the best way to take care of her and
her sister, as well as the helpless children.

Much space was given also to the opinions of psychiatrists,
who found a basis in all this for the gravest suspicions. Here was
a young girl of eighteen. She was of course a victim of the
Oedipus complex, and upon losing her father must have trans-
ferred it to her stepfather. This obscure devotion, if for any reason inverted, might lead to terrible consequences.*

Even more suspicious was the position of Hal Warner, whose
undoubted passion for his mother might find small comfort in
her unfortunate position, and instead of gratitude to his stepun-
cle, he might transfer to him the hatred naturally attributable to
the father he had lost.

It was not so easy for these wizards to unravel the mental
attitude of the unhappy Mrs. Warner, but her known devotion to
her sister was certainly open to the most sinister interpretation,
and in her present position might lead to almost anything. It
became painfully apparent that one verse of the Scriptures was to
be relied on, and that truly "A man's foes shall be those of his
own household."*

One paper had received an untraceable anonymous letter,

poorly written and worse spelled, from someone who claimed to have personal knowledge of the deceased. "I known vorn wel yeers, he ort to bin croked befour," said this adverse critic, and there was a little speculation as to whether "befour" had any reference to the number of attacks.

The number, variety, and possible order of these gave scope to fascinating speculation, as also the unavoidable question as to whether any beyond the first was murder. "Can You Kill A Dead Man?" was demanded, and searching inquiry was made as to whether "assault with intent to kill" lost any of its guilt if the proposed victim had been killed already, involving much language of a smoothly noncommittal character, with first class legal opinion appended.

This furnished grounds for consulting moral authorities, and more than one popular minister was interviewed as to his opinions on the relative responsibility of a man who used four methods of thoroughly slaying his victim as compared with him who struck but once; and again, if more than one person had made the attack, was the first more culpable than the last. The clerical opinions were more freely given.

The sudden and complete disappearance of the three servants gave the most obvious ground for suspicion, and their success in leaving no faintest indication of where they went seemed almost proof of criminality. Still it was difficult to suppose that even an infuriated butler would choose more than one lethal weapon.

"We are confronted," said one editorial, "either with the picture of unnatural and futile spite, consciously killing a dead man over and over as it were, or with the alternative of a number of persons all happening to commit murder on this man at the same time, or nearly so. What mad coincidence could have induced four persons to select that one night for their attack?"

More practical were suggestions as to the amount of money involved, both in the probably increased fortune left by Mr. J. J. Smith, and that of Mr. Vaughn. It was easy to see that if this property was left to the family by will, or inheritable by them, a "motive" was furnished beyond question. Indeed motive and opportunity seemed uncommonly available, to all the inhabitants of the house, that is if robbery had been accomplished by the servants.

The inquest was announced for the following Saturday.

Before taking up the subsequent activities of Mr. Augustus Crasher, it is worthwhile to survey something of his previous methods. Far too conversant with human nature at its worst to place an idle confidence in anyone, his long association with Vaughn was based on harsh necessity. He had served him well, under compulsion, but cherished a secret ambition to get some hold on his employer which would warrant resisting him.

To that end he had long made use of the empty house across Field Street. First getting in one dark night like any ingenious house-breaker, he thereafter provided himself with both keys and a suitable excuse if discovered. Here he passed many a quiet evening, watching the clients who called at the side door, and sometimes slipping out and following them home.

He had a good list of these patrons or victims, and also knew much of their reasons for coming, but how he was ever to prove that they came to pay blackmail instead of to consult their lawyer was not clear. Still he popped in and out of that inconspicuous back door when not otherwise engaged, and collected evidence —against a rainy day as it were. Mr. Crasher's attitude toward evidence was like that of Mr. Wommick Jr. toward "portable property." "Git all the evidence you can," was his motto, "you never know when it will be useful."*

Quite familiar with the will of J. J. Smith, he had for some time played with the idea of marrying Iris, hoping to be so indispensable that Vaughn would not refuse him, but he had not in the least expected to find himself violently in love with her, a condition of which her guardian had taken full advantage. After Monday's interview he found himself with the girl within reach and the money out of it.

It was vain to repeat to himself the argument that he could not touch the money without Vaughn's consent to the marriage, and that consent was to be had only at the price of giving back the money; the feeling remained that he was being robbed and imposed upon, even while he triumphed in the near prospect of possessing the girl.

Dogged, acute, experienced, he turned it over in his mind.

"I've got his consent, that's the requirement. When I marry her he's obliged to turn over the money, securities likely. And then I'm obliged to return it. If I could hand him back something else—but he'd be onto that quick enough. I might take the girl, take the securities, turn 'em into cash and quit the country before he could stop me—there's places where that much would be a fortune. No—n-o—some of what he's got on me comes under extradition.

"Now if I get the girl, and get the money, and then something happens before I give it back"—he lost himself in speculations on this point. But the dominant thought remained, a warming gratifying thought, that in two days time that soft pretty little thing would be in his arms.

"Hates me, does she?" grinned Mr. Crasher. "I'll learn her!"

Meanwhile he determined that as there was notoriously many a slip 'twixt the cup and the lip, he would keep watch on his treasure during the intervening time.

"Might try to run away," he considered. "No knowing what a skirt will do!" So he supplied himself with food and drink and took up his position in the house opposite, while a temporary assistant was stationed by the alley gate with instructions, "If any girl sneaks out, scare her back."

Nothing happened to reward his vigilance Monday night, but Tuesday morning after Vaughn had left, Iris came quietly out of the front door. He saw her enter a Hill Street car, and followed easily enough in a taxi, stopped when she did, took note of each place she entered. His further plan of accompanying her home was interfered with by her meeting Hal, and going back with him on the same car line. In the afternoon, nothing.

But Tuesday evening she came out again, with her cousin, and they went to a nearby picture palace, while the ardent Augustus kept them in sight, returning to his post after seeing them go in.

He saw the various clients go in and out, noting with practiced eye the furious gesture of the one man, whom he did not recognize. He was not displeased. "He'll get it in the neck, one of these days," he muttered to himself. Red-eyed but determined, he drew on a thermos bottle of strong coffee, he watched the night through, and only near daylight did he install one of his assistants to take his place while he went to regale himself with a Turkish bath and fresh raiment and a good breakfast, before calling for his bride.

When turned out of the house at about ten-fifteen Wednesday morning, Mr. Crasher was in a most unenviable frame of mind. His only possible chance at either girl or money was wholly out of reach. If some danger to himself was gone as well, he was too harshly disappointed to remember it. It did occur to him, irrelevantly, that the man he had stationed in the alley had not reported, but this he dismissed with a grunt—what did that matter now!

Sullenly enough he returned to his lodgings, removed the unusual gaieties from his attire, indeed removed it all and went to bed, first seeking aid to oblivion from a pint flask. But he was out by supper time, eating a hearty meal and studying the evening papers with care. They held nothing that he did not know, but he followed carefully the description of the various weapons, the slim sharp knife with its slightly carved horn handle, the small strong cord sunk so tight in the neck as to be hardly visible; the long bruise on the head from front to back— "Evidently given from behind" said the astute reporter. Crasher grinned drily as he visualized the alternative—an assailant leaning over the desk from in front to deliver that blow, and agreed with the writer.

"I got to get busy," was his conclusion. The man placed in the alley still failed to reappear, and no one in his range had seen him.

"Better follow that up by daylight," determined Mr. Crasher, and betook himself next morning to the first place entered by Iris on Tuesday, explaining to the salesman that he was "looking up a case," and flashing an impressive badge to support his authority, he asked what had been purchased by a pretty girl who had come in about ten o'clock in the morning the day before. "Slim little thing," he added, "nervous too, and in a hurry."

Getting his information without difficulty, he pursued the same tactics at the other places Iris had visited, and was so well satisfied with the results that he returned to his lodgings and his bed.

Thursday morning found him early in the alley behind the Smith place, fraternizing with the officers there, and trying to pick up additional details about the secondary murder of Carlo, of which he had been reading in the morning papers. He examined the footprints and other marks with a practiced eye.

"Must have been loafing about here some time," he hazarded. "Somebody looked over the fence and beaned him, and then chucked him over another one. He's no great loss. Joe White croaked him, I guess. Got any line on those runaways yet?"

The officers were willing to discuss the evident facts amiably enough, but had no information to give and were chary of opinions as to what steps were being taken. The highly involved murder inside the house held most of their attention, and they became involved in quite a discussion as to which attack came first, and also as to whether one homicidal maniac had piled horror upon horror, or several persons had joined the orgy. As to the alley affair, they came to easy agreement as to who did it, but considerable question as to what the man was hanging around for.

"Carlo was hired to watch for somebody, that's possible," Crasher generously suggested.

"Safe enough so far, Gus," agreed the more saturnine of the two policemen, while the more cheerful one hazarded a guess that he might have been waiting to meet the maid—"She was a looker I understand."

Mr. Crasher encouraged this view. "And then the man, Joe, came out and put a stop to it—quite likely, Flannigan, quite likely." He strolled away, his hands in his pockets, and betook himself straightaway to the quarters of Mr. Davis the police surgeon, whom he greeted affably enough—"Busy, Tom?"

"Quite busy, Mr. Crasher. Anything I can do for you?"

"I'm interested in this Multi-Murder, like everybody else. All comes down to the poison, I suppose—if any. Can you give me a tip?"

"I can, but why should I? The evidence will come out in the inquest, also in the trial."

"Oh sure, we'll know all about it by Christmas! But I want to know right off, part of my business. I was pretty close to Wade Vaughn, Tom, and I'm out to find who bumped him. If there wasn't poison it's anybody's game. If it was we've got one person to find."

"I've no business to tell you—and you've no business to ask, but if you'll keep it under your hat and not give me away—you may look for one person." He leaned toward him and whispered, "Strychnia!"

Mr. Crasher nodded sagaciously. "I suspicioned when I saw that empty glass. Smelt funny, tasted funny. He used to sit there of an evening, toss off a drink, take a nap, toss off another, as jolly as you please. Clients used to come in of an evening, too. I suppose you got the bullet out. What caliber?"

"A thirty-eight," said Davis.

"He had a lot of pretty private business. Well, I'm much obliged for the tip, Tom. Do as much for you some day," said Crasher, departing.

Mr. Davis looked after him with an enigmatic expression.

"I don't doubt you would, Gus, don't doubt it a bit," and he returned to his report.

Mr. Crasher's visit of inquiry in the lane had been noted by the inquiring eyes of Jim Hunt, and his call on Mr. Davis had been attended by the same observer, who took advantage of it to buy chocolate and oranges at a nearby stand, and subsequently followed his quarry in a strictly unostentatious manner, to a remote and unattractive pawn shop in a suspicious neighborhood. From here Mr. Crasher's steps led in devious and peculiar ways, in and out of various unsavory backyards and among ash cans and barrels of waste material.

Presently he secured what he was after, namely two tomato cans. Jim, lurking in the distance, saw him wrap them in newspaper and set off for the subway, into which he promptly followed. "Set a sleuth to catch a sleuth," chuckled Jim to himself as he settled down behind his newspaper, a keen eye out for any move toward leaving.

It was a very remote and woodsy spot where Mr. Crasher finally seemed content. He had strolled thereto as gradually as any gentleman of the road looking for a quiet place to lunch, and having established himself did indeed proceed to lunch, dragging a thick sandwich from his pocket, and a doughnut or two; also a companionable flask.

Then was Jim pleased with his foresight and glad of the sportsman's chocolate and the juicy fruit. So the two detectives lunched in rural quiet, Crasher alert, watching, but quite unconscious of his neighbor.

Having eaten he rose and strolled about a little, while Jim lay low in his leafy hollow by the stump of a big tree. Apparently satisfied, Mr. Crasher moved over to a stone culvert bridging what had been a brook, and against its solid expanse he set up one of his tomato cans on a stick. Retiring to an easy distance he produced a pistol equipped with a competent silencer, and proceeded to perforate the unhappy can most thoroughly, then serving the other one in like manner.

Jim grinned to himself contentedly. "A thirty-eight I'll bet my bottom dollar, and very well thought out, Augustus."

Satisfied with his marksmanship, Mr. Crasher presently took himself off, and Jim let him go in peace, somewhat later returning to the city where he sought out the murky little pawnshop. A show of authority produced the admission that the morning's purchase was what he thought.

A friendly call on Mr. Davis followed, and the two compared notes with satisfaction. "And what'll he do now, Jim?"

"Plant 'em, plant 'em sure, and he'll produce a witness to swear he saw and heard the practicing. Yes sir!"

"Plant 'em where?"

"Smith house, of course—house and yard. It's the only place I'm watching. I'll be there tonight, *not* with bells on. See you Saturday if not sooner. And thanks awfully for a little lying."

Home went Jim, for a quiet supper and a nap. Bessie would report in the evening.

Then was Jim pleased with his foresight, and glad of the juicy fruit.*

An Inside View

"**B**eer," said Bessie, "Near-beer and crackers, cheese or what have you—anything, Jim, I'm starved"—and she stretched herself luxuriously on the sofa, tossing her little blonde wig across the room.

He brought her a tray, well filled with whatever he could find. "Don't they feed the 'help' in your new place? Better come back to the old one."

"Mrs. Warner let me off as soon as their dinner was on; guess they wanted to talk without anybody 'round. She said to eat first, but I preferred to take a chance on a bite at home, with you."

She ate hungrily, while he watched her with affectionate interest. "Guess you've had quite a day of it, old girl."

"Day!" she protested. "Two days, three days, a week! Six forty-five P.M.—and I left my happy little home at six thirty A.M.! Busy day!" But it was not very long before she sat up briskly, with the opening declaration, "I've found the fork!"

"The fork? What fork? Did that family own but one fork and then lose it?"

"And you a detective! Jim Hunt, you'd rather be funny than solve mysteries. The fork that went with the knife, of course! Same handle, perfectly good fork, but no knife to match. Just look at it—you've seen the knife." And she produced from her hand-bag what seemed evidently the mate to the bloody game-carver found in the victim's neck.

"An inside job for one attack," Jim agreed with her. "Valuable bit of evidence, my dear girl. Go to the head. But begin at the beginning and 'tell me all.'"

"Sure. I'm bursting with it. And the best comes last! Well, I rang the front door bell as meek as Moses, at about six forty-five. The boy let me in. A nice boy, Jim, a very nice boy—I've lost a piece of my heart to him at once."

"Never mind," said Jim unsympathetically. "It'll grow again. Nice boy let you in—"

"Yes, and showed me to the kitchen. He was quite cordial. Evidently Dr. Akers had wised them up—"

"Long familiarity with crime has wonderfully enriched your vocabulary, Bess."

"Hasn't it! Crime and newspaper work. Well, he showed me the ropes, said they had breakfast at eight, usually so and so, and retired upstairs again. Whereat I employed the next half hour in swiftly examining the whole lower floor, with occasional rat-tlings in kitchen and dining room to indicate proper industry. I'm a fast worker, you know, Jim."

"I do indeed. I found that out when you married me—" but his impertinence was smothered with a fat sofa pillow violently applied. Forcing room to breathe he bleated, "Take it all back! Apologize! Took me years to win you—*years*!"

Somewhat breathless, she continued, "I got them a good breakfast, some of your pet muffins, and the bacon just right, coffee that was good to the last drop, etc. They liked it all right. Just the boy and girl down, he took up a tray to his mother, fixed it himself and didn't forget a thing. Very nice boy." Jim grunted.

"And Iris is too lovely for anything. Why when I think of that little blush-rose bud being handed over to Gus Crasher!—"

"A charming plan," Jim agreed. "Puts one a little out of sympathy with the corpse, doesn't it."

"Sympathy! Why Jim, in spite of the shock and the anxiety and the possible danger—they are quite smart enough to think of that—these young people were positively gay! They tried not to show it but I could see them try. And when I was in the kitchen I could hear them giggle and say, 'Hush!' By and by I was taken up to talk with Mrs. Warner . . . "

She was silent for some moments, so that Jim grew impatient.

"Well? What did you think of her?"

"I don't know what to say," admitted Bessie. "She's—wonderful; she was kind, very kind—said Dr. Akers told her I was an old friend of his and only willing to step in like this in exceptional cases, trustworthy, and able to take full charge of the house if she wished. She had me sit down and we had a conference as to the management."

"'We are naturally unsettled,' she said, 'and I do not know in the least what our circumstances will be. Iris is quite competent to do the upstairs work for awhile, Hal will help with anything heavy. Do you think you can get along alone, with a woman to come in once a week perhaps?'

"So we arranged for our little black Jenny to come as laundress, she'll say nothing to anybody if I tell her not to—"

"Double negative makes a positive," murmured Jim, and ducked.

Bessie went on, loftily ignoring him. "Then I suggested that chains be put on all outside doors. 'There are reporters that are worse than detectives,' I said, 'as you've probably found out, and if they simply can't get in it will be much easier than trying to get them out.' She thought that was an excellent idea and sent Hal to get some at once; we had them on by nine o'clock. Before that I had turned off several, speaking from a window."

"Didn't any of them know you Bess?"

"In this 'transformation'? No sir. My complexion is different too, though you don't appear to notice it."

"I *thought* you looked funny," he admitted. "So you went back on your old profession entirely."

"I did. I was there to protect that family—and to find out things for myself. When the delivery men brought in the food supplies one of them was a reporter, that little red-head from the *Star* remember? But Hal threw him out just as easy! Nice boy, Hal."

"There'll be another murder if you don't stop dwelling on the perfections of that husky lad," grumbled Jim. "Do go ahead. Tell me more of Mrs. Warner."

"I'll tell you one thing you would never have dreamed. That poor little one-eyed cripple is a magnificent housekeeper."

"In a wheel chair?"

"Yes sir, in a wheel chair. Brains, my dear, not legs. She told me where everything was from garret to cellar. Of course the girl or Hal can keep her posted, but she has it all in her head. She knew how much there was of each thing in the closet, and what to do about the ice and milk and everything."

Bessie was beaming with professional enthusiasm. "I complimented her on her thoroughness and she seemed pleased. 'It's my business,' she said, and 'I hate waste and—incapacity.' Said she used to have trouble with servants forgetting things, but that a capable housekeeper could handle that easily enough. She had one [of] those tin lists hung up in the kitchen, with red buttons that you move when anything's out, and an even fuller list on her desk. Then when the cook came up in the morning she'd check off each item, and if the cook had forgotten she'd have to go downstairs and see; that made her careful. This runaway cook seems to have been a good one, but a moron couldn't have escaped that list. As to cleanness—that woman would run her wheel chair out into the kitchen and pantry, look into the refrigerator and the breadbox—it *smelled* clean."

"All very interesting," remarked Jim, "and I suppose business is rare in housekeepers—luckily mine has it. But I fail to see the bearing on 'the case in hand.' What's your impression of her—her character?"

"Good," said Bessie, slowly. "I'm sure she's good. Those children wouldn't love her so if she wasn't. But good people do strange things sometimes, as we both know. And I confess it does not seem to me much of a crime to remove that man . . . If he was the benevolent person described, taking care of them all, and even half-way decent, they'd show some sorrow."

"Akers bears you out in that, and he's been their doctor for years. Go on, sister, do."

"It's hard to form impressions of Mrs. Warner," she continued, "on account of her face, poor dear. One eye covered, and the other with the lid pulled down—and that dreadful scar twisting the mouth so. No, one can't get much from the face. She has the most eloquent hands, quick, graceful, tending to gesture or to grip on the arms of her chair, and singularly strong. But mostly she kept them still in her lap, perfectly still. I should say Jim, that she's been schooling herself for a long time to be quiet, not to show her feelings. And that she was under a strain now, a great strain. She was too quiet, Jim, too controlled, it's not natural."

"Ho-ho! Who laughed at me when I said she was under a strain? Isn't it perfectly natural for any woman to show strain, with a peculiarly horrid murder right in the house?" he demanded.

"Yes, I know, but somehow—well, never mind hunches. I've got something better than that. I've made a clear plan of the house, regular blue print, see? Here's that side door, the little square entry with the doors into his room and the dining room and the coat closet at the back end. Here's a china closet opening from the dining room, with a small sink in it. Over the sink used to be a slide into Vaughn's office, as if that was the dining room once. It was all papered over on that side."

"I saw all that; go on, do."

"Did you notice the big picture in the front room that came down as far as the top of that slide?"

"Yes. I remember there was one."

"And you saw that on the closet side the slide was boarded up, a chunk of plank that filled it even with the wall?"

"Yes—I think so."

"Well, Mr. Detective, that chunk comes out!"

"I didn't make an exhaustive examination, but I thought it was nailed in."

"It was, once. But those nails are nothing but heads now.

With a knife blade to start it the whole thing comes out."

"What made you think of trying?"

"My conscientious use of a dust cloth, Jim. I was dusting the frame of that picture and I happened to notice a sort of streak in the paper below it, close under the edge, hardly visible, a long level crack."

"Well paper does crack sometimes, Bess."

"Yes, I know it does, and this looked all right except that it was so straight. So I measured the distance and found it was at the top of that slide. Then I poked about a bit and out came the plank, and then I saw daylight."

"Physical or metaphorical?"

"Both. Jim—anyone in that closet with eyes close to the crack could see everything going on in that front room, except on the side nearest of course. See Vaughn's desk and whatever went on around it. Yes sir!"

Jim whistled. "So any one of the servants for instance could have had a pretty clear idea of what that home office business was. How about hearing?"

"Hear almost as well as if they were in there, regular sounding board, that thin slide, plus the crack."

"Mmmm yes. That might account for all the attacks coming together. Reasons discovered for getting busy—by anybody, Bess—the other people in the house as well as the servants."

"Yes, or one of those clients if he got in unnoticed and slipped into the dining room. Jim! Didn't your old lady say the man who looked like Crasher had a key to that door?"

"She certainly did, my dear."

"Well, listen to this, very interesting, I call it. You know that empty house across Field Street? It's not so empty as it appears."

"The dickens you say!"

"I do indeed. Several dickenses. When I was not otherwise engaged, and the folks were, I snooped about all I could. Went upstairs, with a nice excuse ready if they caught me at it, which fortunately no one did, and viewed the country round. Also I visited the garden. Anything might happen in that big bushy place. It's a long yard you know. I was peering over the fence down by the back gate; there's a box by that big syringa bush where I could step up and see over the fence, all quiet along the lane, policeman at each end. But when I turned my head and looked down the alley beyond Field Street I saw a man walking unobtrusively toward me."

"As in the movies," suggested Jim, and gave a vivid imitation of the slink-dodge and look-back method followed by the screen sleuth.

"That's the stuff," she admired, "but this man couldn't have been a real honest-to-goodness sleuth, for he walked quietly along just as anybody would, and turned into a gate."

"Don't see anything in that, Mrs. Detective."

"You don't, do you? Well, you will. The gate was that of the empty house opposite, and the man was Augustus Crasher."

"Oho! As handy as that! Now before you go any further I must produce my news about that crafty gentleman—you'll be pleased!"

Whereat he related in full the tale of his doings since leaving her in the morning, with the careful marksmanship of the rural wanderer he was watching.

"I didn't follow him back again; there's no place for him to plant that stuff but the old house and garden. I'll go back with you and we'll keep watch tonight. That is, you go back properly with your key, and I'll get in from the next yard, near the house—you be at the back door and let me in."

"And what is he hanging about in that house for? Looked as if he lived there—let himself in with a key."

"Well he didn't do any murdering, anyhow. His game was to keep Vaughn alive. I never saw a man look more annoyed than he did over that body. With a burst of sheer ratiocination, as the servants are gone, we must conclude that he is watching the family!"

"Without the least claim to brilliant deduction I had reached the same remarkable conclusion," jeered Bessie.

"He's undoubtedly a villain, and undoubtedly 'balked' in the completest manner," pursued Jim. "He's out for blood. He'll try to implicate Hal Warner, or even Iris—lover turned to hate, and all that sort of thing."

"Or even Mrs. Warner," Bess added.

"Any or all of them," he solemnly agreed. "We must keep our eyes on Augustus; he'll bear watching. But we mustn't interfere with him, just give him all the rope he wants."

"And then give him some more that he don't want. Yes I suppose they are following up Mrs. Warner's tip about the servants?"

"No doubt. I don't take much stock in it myself. It's too easy. At the most that would only cover three of the attacks."

"And the other two?"

"Yes, the other two, Bess. More especially one of 'em, the poison. We mustn't forget that all these killings come back to the poison; the others are supererogatory."

"Long experience with crime has enriched *your* vocabulary, seems to me," she scoffed. "But you're dead right. And we have not only to find out who did it, but to prevent Crasher from settling his little grudge by saddling it onto somebody who didn't.

My interest is mainly centered on that man. I hope we'll find enough to break him . . . But now Mr. James G. Hunt, prepare for a Surprise! What do you think I've found? And swiped. And risked my reputation as an honest servant girl by bringing home with me?"

She proceeded to undo a flat package, and laid on the table a typewritten paper of some thickness.

"She left the panel open a crack—careless, now he's gone I suppose. Anyway when I went up to get my things, they being all at dinner, I slipped in to have a look around her room, and noticed it. A little wall safe, over the mantlepiece, secret spring if you please. I poked about carefully and found it, seeing where it was likely to be. I left the door shut, and put my trust in Providence that she will not look for this before tomorrow's lunch. It's a record, Jim, of the goings on in that house. I've not had time to more than see that. Now then, sit up close and we'll read it."

* * * * *

The Record

10:30 A.M. July 11th 1921. My name is Jacqueline
Warner. I am thirty-one years old. Here I sit in my
wheel chair, with my crippled feet and my twisted
face, helpless, and completely in the power of Wade
Vaughn, my brother-in-law. We are living in the old
house; I have the room that was mother's once, and
afterward father's, and I have found his small typewriter and a lot of paper, in the window seat. Wade
doesn't know about it. And today I have found
father's wall-safe, a secret panel thing, quite
secure. So I am going to write an account of this
man and what he has done to us. It will be well hidden there, and some day I will tell Hal how to open
it. If I die here he can read this and see why I
stood it...

   We can't get out. He's got us in a trap. I'm helpless to earn a living for myself and two children,
helpless and hideous. And I could be cured, Dr. Akers
tells me, my feet and my face too—almost, with this
wonderful facial surgery they use now, but that would
cost money, and Wade has it all. When I asked to have

it done, humiliated myself and begged, urged that if I were straightened out I could earn enough to pay him back, he said I was sufficiently useful to him as I was, and more likely to stay! Like the Chinese women...

And there he sits in my father's chair at the table, at my father's desk in the study, drinking my father's old whiskey, master of the house, and of all the money—and of us...

That means my boy Hal, my sister's daughter Iris, and my poor self. For their sakes I must keep my head, keep up their spirits, hold on and bear it till Hal's through college if possible—if nothing happens to Iris meanwhile.

After Hal has his education we can clear out, even if we lose all our pitiful inheritance, starve together if need be, but be free of him.

I have hunted and hunted, hoping that father might have made another will before he died, but I can't find a word. What I have found is this little wall-safe with some money, five hundred dollars plus $14.70 in a purse, and this I'm going to keep hidden, so that if we have to go quickly we could live on it for a while.

Now that I have a safe hiding place I'm going to make a record of what he has done to us, partly because it may be legally useful, if he ever is brought to justice, but mainly as a "release" as they call it now, to get [it] off my mind. I'll tell Hal, but I won't worry Iris, dear child. She is far happier in not knowing about him.

Now to begin at the beginning of our troubles, being born!

There were two sisters of us, Iris, who is dead, and I. We loved each other dearly, and were so happy together that we could put up with father's queernesses. He was a peculiar man, strict, domineering, with antiquated notions about the education of girls, and particularly as to obedience. We were trained to mind like whipped dogs.

Poor mother couldn't stand it; she died when we were little children. I can just remember how pale and thin she looked that last time I saw her, and how frightened. She held us both tight in her arms, especially little Iris, and she told me, in a whisper, her eyes on the door for fear father would come in—to be good to my sister, to take care of her—to love her—love her—love her! I guess she died for lack of love, poor mother. Iris didn't need to be told; she loved everybody, even father.

I didn't. I was a stubborn rebellious little thing, but soon found out it was no use rebelling against him while I was a child. He had us educated at home, governesses, tutors and so on, an excellent education, but no freedom and no companionship or society. It's no wonder we were so devoted to each other. He was afraid of the influence of "the modern girl," and did his best to bring us up fifty years behind the times. Still he could not keep out all books and papers—we could read!

I wanted to go to college, but I might as well have asked for a trip to the moon. I wanted desperately to be an actress, but that I knew better than to mention. We could study at home, in lines he thought suitable, and we did, mostly languages.

We lived here in this old house which had belonged to father's family for generations. It's built up all about us now, but there is still quite a garden, for Brooklyn. It is on the corner of Field and Grove Streets; the names show what the place was like when first built on.

I was about nineteen and Iris near eighteen when Wade Vaughn came into the picture. We never knew much about father's business, something to do with real

estate I think; he was considered rich, and had quite
a few lawsuits. Mr. Vaughn was a very successful
lawyer, a youngish man, about thirty I guess—he
seemed old to us. He was inclined to be stout, even
then; he had a thick red mouth and small hard eyes.
We despised him.

But father seemed to like him immensely, had him
at the house all the time. He had won some difficult
case for him I believe, and was retained as a sort
of general adviser. He agreed with father in all his
opinions, flattered and pleased him, and he tried
very hard to make up to us girls, but we couldn't
bear him. Pretty soon he wanted to marry Iris—my
little sister!

He went to father first, which delighted him of
course; he quite approved. But when Wade proposed she
refused him. Poor little blue-eyed child—she had a
shivering dislike of him, used to say he made her
feel creepy. No wonder!

Then father issued his ultimatum, gave her his
direct command that she must marry Wade Vaughn. I
don't suppose Iris had ever disobeyed him in her
life, nor I since I was six. And I doubt if she could
have held out against him even at eighteen but for
one thing—in spite of all the restrictions with which
she was surrounded she had managed to fall in love.

The man was our new minister, Sydney Booth, very
young for the position, but already a noted preach-
er. I think father suspected him somewhat, his
pastoral calls were rather frequent, but one chaper-
on-housekeeper liked him and I fancy she did not
mention all of them. At any rate Iris had lost her
heart to him completely, and it gave her strength to
resist Wade Vaughn.

I helped of course. I told her she was legally of
age now and had a right to marry whom she pleased,
and that it was wrong, dead wrong, to marry a man she

didn't love at all. So we took our fate in our hands and ran away. I shall never forget the splendid feeling of being free! We were heroically willing to starve by inches, but vowed we would never go back.

Iris was saved any real privation because Sydney promptly married her. He tried his pious best to make friends with father and reconcile him to us, but when father was angry an enraged rhinoceros would have been more easily appeased. He vowed he would never see either of us again, and that we should not touch a cent of his money—he was most insulting to Sydney about that, called him a pious fraud, a fortune hunter, talked about priests and women—when Sydney came back from that meeting and told us about it he was far too angry for a Christian, let alone a minister. However he and Iris were very happy, and little Iris was born, almost as lovely as her mother she grew to be.

Meanwhile I had my troubles, but I did manage to get on the stage, and there I met Haldane Warner, an English actor, and married him. He was a fine actor and finer man—in many ways. Our baby was born before Iris, my boy Hal. He is about perfect.

Before I go on with the dreadful part of this story I want to thankfully acknowledge nine years of considerable happiness. That is more than some people ever have. Sydney, Iris said, was an angel; they did seem perfectly happy together. I had my wonderful boy, and my chosen profession, and experience.

※　※　※　※　※

It was Hal's tenth birthday, and all of us were celebrating by a long drive in Sydney's big car. I never knew what caused the accident. Only the children escaped unhurt. Haldane and Sydney were killed. Iris was so utterly overcome by shock as almost to

lose her mind, and I was a senseless hideous cripple... There was no one who could describe what happened, only Hal told of a big car coming fast—it
must have gone away fast too!

My father was notified. He had said he would never
see us again so he sent Wade Vaughn to attend to the
wreckage. He took us all to his house. I had concussion of the brain beside my other injuries and was
unconscious for many days.

When I first came to myself there was Iris by my
side, so delighted to have me know her that she was
almost like herself again. There was my boy struggling not to cry for joy because his mother was
awake, and little Iris, who did cry and cling to us
both. Of course I was weak and queer, and was just
beginning to ask what had happened when Wade Vaughn
sauntered in.

He stood there and looked at me and smiled. I didn't
know then how my face looked, that it was hurt so
dreadfully. He has a wide slow tight smile, like a
Roman emperor who has devised a new method of tor-
ture and is trying it on his pet enemy...

"We must not excite her, Iris," he said, "it will
delay her recovery. You may be quite easy in your
mind Jacqueline. There was an automobile accident.
The children are unhurt as you see, but Mr. Warner
and Mr. Booth were both killed, and you are consid-
erably cut up. But I have married Iris and will take
care of all of you so you need not worry."

My recovery was delayed, by many weeks of varying
delirium. Whenever I did remember that dreadful
announcement scene, I thought it was part of the
vague horrors I was drowned in. But there came a time
when I felt that my mind was really my own again...

There sat Iris by my bed, with a book in her lap
but not reading. Her eyes were fixed unseeingly, her
sweet mouth quivered now and then, and big slow tears

ran down one at a time. I watched her silently for a moment, and then that scene came back and I knew it was true. But this time I did not go off. I thought, "Here is my sister. If this awful thing is true she needs me more than ever. I must keep steady."

So I made a little movement, and when she turned I was smiling quietly up at her. Then she was in my arms, crying and trying not to for my sake. I held her and soothed her, told her not to worry, that I was going to get well and would take care of her, and she was comforted a little.

As days passed I gradually got hold of the facts. Hal told me what he could remember of the accident, and of their coming to this house, and that Vaughn had really married Aunt Iris.

"How soon?" I asked him, and he said, "Right away—that is, in a week or two I guess."

It was. Within a fortnight. Of course she wasn't responsible. Her mind was a blank with irregular patches of memory, all unrelated. She was always such a loving dependent little thing. He told her anything he wanted to, that for my sake and the children's sake and to please her father she should marry him. When she had a moment's memory of Sydney he told her that he had been dead for a long time and that now her duty was to the children and her poor crippled sister, that if she married him he would keep me and take care of me—I got it out of her bit by bit, never hinting at any blame. He took her to the city hall, got the license, they were married by the mayor, and Iris no more responsible than a baby. He explained to people that he did it in order to take care of her, and got credit for devoted affection and benevolence. That is the kind of a man Wade Vaughn is. It was a long while before I was clearheaded enough to get it all straight, and fully realize our position.

My poor head had been so battered it was almost fatal. But for the children I wish it had been...

Iris did not know at all what she had done, nor realize her loss. She was long in that vague crushed condition and sometimes talked as if Sydney was still alive.

So I lay there and faced the facts. The fact of my disfigurement and cripplement was a large one. When at last I got hold of a mirror it was [a] shock. The windshield I suppose; I was on the front seat. My sight was not affected, but what a pair of eyes! The worst one I wear a patch over when not alone. And a big red shrunken scar on one cheek that pulls up the mouth in half a grin.

No woman likes to be hideous, nor man either, I suppose. There I was, pretty well cut off from any hope of independence. At least it seemed so at first. There was my boy. The important thing for him was a decent home and an education. There were no near relations on the English side. As to my loss—my injury, my profession—I shut that door inside, shut it hard on hopelessness.

Here was my darling sister who had been my care since I was a mere child myself. Never had she needed me as she did now. If she was to live, to recover her mind, to be a mother to little Iris, I must stay with her and be strong and wise. I thought it all out and saw that I must, as the older novelists used to say, "dissemble," and keep friends with Vaughn.

One day when I was fairly well, first sitting up in my chair, he strolled in and proceeded to make the position clear to me in his own thorough way.

"I know you don't like me, Jacqueline, never did. But that does not interfere with my pleasure in keeping you here. I can talk freely to you; you are more intelligent than Iris, even when she is quite herself."

I kept still, listening. My expression did not matter.

"It is sadly evident that you are in no shape to earn a decent living for yourself and your boy, even if you wished to leave your sister. She, being my wife, I shall of course take care of, and her child-- Sydney Booth's child." At this he smiled a little, that wide slow smile, and I saw he was watching my hands, that were gripping so tightly on the arms of my chair.

"Now I am also prepared to take care of you and your child, on terms, Jacqueline, on terms. I have brought you a copy of your father's will. You may keep it awhile and study it, so you can see how little you can have to look forward to in that direction. A very determined man, your father. He left it with me in case of accident--you may not have heard that he has gone abroad?"

I had not. How should I?

"He made a previous will, soon after you and your sister so offended him by your disobedience, leaving some of his property to me and some to various charities. But after I married Iris, and assumed the care of you and your son, I represented to him that he ought at least to contribute to the support and education of his grandchildren. This is the result.

"I don't wish you to feel under any coercion, my dear Jacqueline. You are perfectly free to take your boy and leave if you prefer. Or you may write to any of your friends and see if they are willing to undertake your support--a rather unattractive cripple, and a small boy, with a devoted brother-in-law quite willing to keep you both."

I was still keeping quiet. It was deadly clear that there was no way out, at present.

"Now if you remain I have no doubt that you will be extremely useful in the house. Iris, I regret to say, is frequently not quite herself, as you have probably remarked. So I shall ask you to take the care of the house off her hands; you are I believe quite competent for work of that sort. The terms I spoke of are merely like those made by your father in that will, and apply to you and the boy. Merely obedience. Think it over, my dear sister, think it over."

He went off and left me with that iniquitous will; and I did think it over.

The Will and My Sister

I do not believe that my father, pig-headed and domineering as he was, could have made a will like that,
alone. I can hardly believe that he would have let
Wade pull him into it. Either Wade forged the signature, or he substituted this for another and father
signed it unknowingly. But here it was, and here I
was, and father out of the country, and my sister
needing me--what could I do?

It began with all the solemn terminology, revoked
all previous wills, left a paltry little bequest to
dear old Jane and Peter, who had been with us ever
since I could remember. Then he spoke of his daughters, of their disobedience and desertion, and left
us each an income of three hundred dollars a year.
And he a rich man!

It did not take much arithmetic to see that this
was a mere concession to prevent an attempt to break
the will. Three hundred dollars! Dear Iris was beyond
want, but for me there was no escape. It went on.

"But since my daughter Iris is now married to the
husband I had chosen for her, my trusted friend Wade

Vaughn, and since he has undertaken the care of my two grandchildren and my daughter Jacqueline who is unable to support herself, I give, devise, and bequeath to the said Wade Vaughn the sum of sixty thousand dollars, in trust, nevertheless, to hold the same and to pay over the income or such part thereof as in his sole discretion he shall think fit for the maintenance and education of my two grandchildren during their respective minorities. When either of my grandchildren shall reach the age of twenty [he is] to pay over to such grandchild the sum of five thousand dollars. If my granddaughter Iris shall marry before reaching the age of twenty-one with the consent of the said Wade Vaughn, then I direct that the sum of fifty thousand dollars of the said trust fund be paid to her husband. Otherwise, on her marriage, or her attaining the age of twenty-one, whichever event shall first occur, the said fifty thousand dollars shall be paid to the First Presbyterian Church of Brooklyn, a domestic corporation.

If either of my said grandchildren prove rebellious or disobedient during the continuance of the trust, according to the judgement of said Wade Vaughn, such grandchild shall forfeit all right to any part of the income or principal of said trust fund.

All the rest residue and remainder of my property I leave to said Wade Vaughn and his heirs forever."

※　　※　　※　　※　　※

I copied it, to keep and have to look at if ever any of us were tempted to be "rebellious or disobedient." Think of it! We were in slavery, pure and simple! And he the sole judge of our obedience. If he chose to say that those children were "rebellious" he could turn them out of doors and keep what little they had for himself.

And he gave it to me to "think over"!

Two little children, they had a right to a decent home, to an education, and my poor sister who needed me so desperately.

The main point was that there was no alternative. If I took Hal and left, what could I do for him? Who would take us in? None of my good friends in the profession had the settled home, or the means even if they had the benevolence. And Wade quite willing to take care of us. No, there was no alternative.

"No time for hysterics, Jack!" I told myself. "You are confronting a condition and not a theory. Most of the human race lived in slavery all through history, and we're here yet. This means a period of-- considerable unpleasantness, but not forever! Years pass. As soon as Hal is able to earn a living he can escape, but he must have his education. In ten years or so he ought to be through college. Ten years!..."

So when he strolled in again and asked me if I'd decided, I just told him that I had no choice, and I would be very glad to take the care of the house off my sister.

"I don't doubt you will make an excellent housekeeper, Jacqueline," he said. "But remember the condition, submissive and obedient."

"You and father seem of one mind as to obedience," I remarked.

"We are" he said, with that little chuckle I hate so. "We are both of us fond of it. He was not able to enforce it however, and I am." Then he came and sat down by me and put his arm around me.

"Give me a kiss, my dear sister," he said, "a nice crooked kiss."

There was no way out. I took the job and am here yet, his housekeeper, "submissive and obedient." To dear Iris I told nothing of course; her trouble was far too great to add one straw. With her I was cheer-

ful and comforting as I could manage to be, making
much of how glad I was to be with her, even though
it choked me--how kind Wade was to let me stay and
to care for Hal.

With little Iris there was never any trouble. She
was naturally good, like her mother, and soon understood that for her mother's sake, and for "poor Aunt
Jack's"--(that blessed child used to put up her little pink hand and softly stroke my scar and say,
"Poor Auntie! Poor Auntie!")--she must mind her "new
papa." He insisted on her calling him papa; I think
it was the very hardest thing she had to do, for she
had loved her father dearly.

For Hal it was far harder. He was more like me, by
no means naturally submissive. But he was a reason-
able child, and had always been treated reasonably.
I talked it over with him almost as if he had been
a man.

"I know you don't like Uncle Wade much, and neither do I. But you see, my dear, we just can't help
ourselves," I said. "Mother's all smashed up so she
can't earn a living, and nobody would take us in
while we have this relation who is willing to keep
us--you can see that." He nodded gravely.

"Then there's this queer will of your grandfather's. I've told you how much he thought of obedience,
and how my sister and I disobeyed him. Now he's fixed
it so that you children must be obedient or lose your
inheritance. It wouldn't matter so much about having
the money, but it does matter that you should be well
educated and able to take care of mother by and by."

He understood. We made a kind of game of it. I
read to him of men who had been imprisoned by their
enemies, enslaved, made galley slaves even, and yet
survived, escaped in time. And we'd pretend that this
was The Cruel Uncle, or an Ogre or an Enchanter, and
that we were in his power for so many years.

"How many mama?"

"Till you are through college, son."

That looked like forever to him. But I showed him that we had each other, and dear Aunt Iris, and his little cousin that he was so fond of, and that all he had to do was to be a little extra good--and he was.

Then I braced myself to my part of the job, to make it as easy as possible for the child. I must never complain to him of anything his Uncle did. I must never let him feel how I felt--he must not sympathize too much with his mother nor suspect the difficulties of my position.

When things went hard with him, and they often did--Wade Vaughn was not a pleasant parent--then I'd have to go over the Cruel Enchanter story again, and brace him up. I invented a system of medals and decorations for him, rewards of merit for being especially good, all very private between ourselves. We kept a little calendar, also private, crossing off the days and weeks and months and years as they slowly passed.

When the first year was really gone, counting from Hal's birthday, we had a little celebration in my room, while Wade was downtown of course. My sister did not remember what that day stood for, to her, and I didn't want Hal to lose all his birthdays because of that awful one. So there was a cake for him and little presents, and when we two were alone I pinned on a sort of Maltese cross of gilded cardboard, marked "Stout Fella!" from a story he was extremely fond of.

He soon realized that the better he got on in school the sooner he could go to college, the sooner be free. And I made all sorts of lovely plans for him to have in mind, about what we were going to do when he was grown up and taking care of me...

I feared at first that Wade would drive the boy

to disobedience so as to turn him out and get the money for himself, but pretty soon I saw that he loved power better than money. It was tyrannizing over us that he loved; he had no idea of losing us. So I took heart of grace and settled to my task.

Health, that was the first thing. I must live and keep strong. My looks I must simply accept and forget. But air and exercise--for a cripple, that called for ingenuity. My feet were practically useless, but my arms and hands and trunk muscles were all right. Also one can do things with leg muscles while lying down. With a determined purpose, patience and time, it is wonderful how much may be done in such training. It was another secret between me and Hal; he was immensely proud of the things I learned to do.

As for air, a corner room with four windows allows for plenty, and I had the morning sun, too. With that and careful eating, I managed to avoid many of the ill effects of loss of walking.

The housekeeping was a life-saver, too. Wade was for strict economy, but his experience with previous household management made him fairly liberal in his allowance. I had a straight business talk with him, showed him a tentative budget, and started in.

In my wheel chair I could investigate everything. Once in order I kept the whole house in mind easily enough. I inventoried the linen, china, silver and kitchen ware, just like a store-keeper's stocktaking, and so with the supplies.

I studied dietary, learned about "balanced rations," "essential vitamins" and all that. With such good things as oranges and tomatoes shown to be advantageous, it was not difficult to please and benefit at the same time. And I learned a lot about cooking too, and did some.

※　　※　　※　　※　　※

We stayed two years in Wade's house, during which time he killed my sister.

I don't mean with an axe, nothing so crude, nothing against the law--not he! He loved her, as such a man loves; that is he desired her avidly, and now she was his. But he hated her because she did not love him and had loved Sydney Booth.

She did yet, poor thing, when she remembered. But as fast as she began to recover something of her nervous poise, her normal mind, the sharp realization of what she had done, of the utter helplessness of all of us, would throw her back again. If he had not married her--if father could have taken us in and let me help her struggle back to life--little Iris might have her mother yet...

I doubt if even my self control could have held out much longer in the face of his treatment of her. Such little things for small torments--such big ones underlying! I could always tell when she had been remembering Sydney. The vague trouble in her eyes would change to sharp anguish, her gentle submissiveness to Wade turn to an irresistible shrinking from him.

Then Wade would smile that slow satisfied smile of his, call her to him, hold her and pet her...

His passion for power was much stronger than his love for her. And even his love was cruel. He fretted her constantly in petty ways, made fun of her "absentmindedness," teased her. She had a little nervous cough, poor dear, always had a sensitive throat, and when she was troubled in her mind it was worse. We could hear her coming downstairs, "ahem, a-ahem" and she would cough before speaking, apologetically.

He hated it, declared it got on his nerves (Wade's nerves!), and was always urging her to control it; made her keep cough drops on hand and use them. Of course the more he fussed about it the more nervous she was and the more she coughed.

He fussed about her clothes too, wanted her always to wear bright colors. I think he dimly felt as if she was trying to wear mourning for Sydney, but she had always quiet tastes, liked little soft grey things and clinging scarves and laces. He insisted on hard bright fashionable dresses [in] the latest style. Iris was very beautiful, with those clear-cut perfect features that never grow old. I suppose he was proud of her, as men are, and wanted to show her off as bright and happy with him.

There was a soft black and white silk scarf she was very fond of. But anything black he wouldn't stand. He made fun of it, said she looked like an Aubrey Beardsley* in it, told her not to wear it, and she would put it away--and then forget--she forgot so much, and put it on again.

I have tried to convince myself that Wade Vaughn is a human creature like the rest of us. That after all he isn't much more domineering than father was. That a man thinks he has a right to manage his own wife. That maybe he did make her marry him so that he could take care of her. That perhaps my own mind was somewhat joggled and I was exaggerating things. So I held on and did my best to keep my sister--sane.

She rushed into my room one night, in her little foolish lacy nightdress with tiny ribbon rosebuds on it--he was always buying her things he thought pretty. She was at her worst, that meant at her best, her mind clear and remembering everything, and then the dreadful sense of her position. She was all shivering and sobbing--with that pathetic little cough too.

"Oh Jack! Jack! I can't! I can't! Keep me! Hide me!"

She wasn't rational of course. She knew well enough I could not save her.

He came in after her, turning up the light and standing there in his handsome bathrobe, looking at us.

"My dear wife," he said, "I think you are still intelligent enough to realize that your nervous condition has its dangers. If you care to remain at home with your sister and your child you must be calmer, more naturally affectionate, more obedient. If you make any noise or disturbance of any sort I am sure that an examining physician would quite agree with me that--restraint was necessary, and seclusion. You need sleep my dear. Come back to bed."

The next day she was "gone" again, that dull patient look, very submissive, and all dressed out in gay stylish things. She followed him to the door and kissed him when he left for the day. All the morning she sat around in my room as usual, pretending to read, pretending to sew, but her eyes would get big and vague and she'd just sit there looking at nothing.

I couldn't amuse her or get her to talk. Even little Iris, with all her cunning ways, couldn't rouse her. In the afternoon she said she would try to sleep, and not to disturb her, please. She stood there by my door as if asking to be excused, passing her hand over [her] eyes. "I think I didn't sleep much last [night], so if you don't mind, Jack dear--"

Gentle and kind and sweet--my little sister!

When he arrived that afternoon I sat by my open door, and when he came charging up to find her I told him she wanted to rest, begged him not to disturb her--at which he merely laughed. He found the door locked, and no answer when he knocked, no answer when he called and shouted, so he burst in.

I was just behind him, in my chair, horribly afraid, and there she was, limp and staring. She had hanged herself with that black and white silk scarf...

He tore her down, tried to rouse her, sent for the

nearest doctor, but though she had been dead only a little while, was hardly cold yet, it was enough.

I sat like a stone and watched him. I kept saying over to myself, "Hal and Iris," "Hal and Iris," "Hal and Iris." That was all I could hold to.

He was frantically determined to have her revived, demanded a pulmotor,* upbraided the doctor. When he had to accept the fact that she was gone he stood there looking at that still body, with the oddest expression. There was grief, but something else I could not define at first, a thwarted air, a sort of puzzled disappointment--did you ever take a mouse away from a cat, kill it, and give it back again?

As he was going out he saw that scarf on the floor, picked it up and fiercely tore it in pieces, in shreds, put it in the grate and burned it. Then he left me alone with my sister.

Her face had settled now into its natural beauty, those clear lovely lines of brow and nose and chin; her very bones were beautiful. I held her cold little hand and talked to her softly. "You can trust me, Iris. Mother did. She told me to love you, and love you, and love you, and I have. I do. I always will. And now I'll love little Iris and take care of her--at any cost, sister--at any cost!"

✻   ✻   ✻   ✻   ✻

All this was in Wade's house, before we came here.

Father was abroad somewhere. Wade had charge of his affairs, and may have known where he was; we didn't. I cannot pretend to any real affection for father, ever, and after he had handed us over to that man to govern I felt sheer resentment.

But it was rather a shock when he came home and died so suddenly. It was not long after Iris's escape from life. He turned up unexpectedly at his house late one night, and rang and rang. When old Peter came down there he was in a huddled heap on the steps, and unable to speak. Peter and Jane between them got him upstairs and put him to bed, called Dr. Akers and summoned Wade.

I never saw him--Wade said it would only distress him to see me--and I couldn't go anyway, unless I was carried! They told me afterwards, Jane and Peter, that he was conscious and restless, and that his eyes kept asking for something, watching the door. But Wade had provided a competent nurse, two of them in fact, for night and day, and they would not allow the servants in the room.

He did not linger long. The house like everything else was left to Wade and after a little he moved over there. I think he was only too glad to leave his own and discharge the servants who remembered Iris.

"We are going back to your old home, Jacqueline," he told me. "I shall continue to support and educate the children and you will continue to manage my household. You do very well at it; you are economical and efficient. I am fortunate in having so competent a housekeeper, and one so unfailingly obedient." And he patted my head, and kissed me... A horrible moving-picture kiss.

I thought of that Browning's "Revery in a Spanish Cloister"*--Gr-r-r! "If hate killed men, Brother Lawrence."

So I became his housekeeper in good earnest. He let me have this room on account of the speaking tube to the kitchen, lucky for me. If he had dreamed of what else it had this would not have been written. It did give me some pleasure to be back in the old home except for missing my sister so! I was glad of Jane and Peter too, but not for long. Wade turned them off, with that shockingly small legacy left them in the will--I wonder if father could have made it?

UNPUNISHED

The poor old dears were surprised and hurt. They told me he had always said they should be taken care of. I cried to see them go, old and poor, but all I could do was to give them as many of father's clothes as I could find. They were sorrier for me, I think, than I was for them--and they had reason.

Then Wade installed new servants, but they never stay long; he is so over-bearing. He grew more hateful than ever, having no wife to dominate. Dinner is the worst, breakfast and lunch I have in my room, the children have to breakfast with him, but at dinner he brings me down in his arms--well he knows how I hate to have him touch me and plants me there opposite him. And particularly insists on conversation, light and amusing conversation.

The thing is like a nightmare. Any outsider sees nothing but a rather genial man, benevolently taking care of his wife's relations. He brings friends home to dinner sometimes, and they seem favorably impressed. The children do behave well--they have to! And so do I--I have to. And there he sits in father's chair, with his little chuckle, while I converse brightly and the children are like little puppets out of a book of etiquette--it is like a play--a dreadful weary play that has no curtain.

The Ear of Dionysus

June 1924

If I wrote nothing else I certainly ought to keep a record of that marvelous boy of mine. He is fifteen now. It has been a long slow hard pull, and he has been simply wonderful. I've been very thankful for my experience on the stage, and for some natural talent as well, I suppose, for our life here is steady acting. But from his father too, Hal must have inherited a special gift; he certainly could make a name on the stage. We two can sometimes almost enjoy our "double life," we do it so well. Smart as Wade is I don't think he dreams that a boy could so disguise his real temper and inclinations, and behave like a lamb, year in and year out.

His affection for his little cousin helps very much; she is a lamb by nature, and seldom gives even Wade any cause for offense. We sometimes plan, Hal and I, impossible schemes of escape, of triumph over the Wicked Uncle.

"No use, Motherkin," he says. "We'll never get ahead of him till I'm grown up. Gosh! It's forever!"

"It is, Hal, it's a lifetime," I agreed. "Ten years at your age is a lifetime. But it's half gone dear boy, and the years do move a little faster, don't they?"

"Not much," he gloomed. "But I'm used to the trick now. I'll stick it out all right. And thanks to you, mother dear, I'm well ahead in school. Guess I'll be the youngest freshman! And when I get through--he won't even see our dust! He couldn't have us arrested, could he?"

"No, not if he has no reason to suspect anything. But I tell you Hal, if he thought, if he dreamed of any such plan on our part, it would be quite on the cards for him to--'frame you' somehow. But if you keep on being docile, I guess we're safe. Iris is no risk at all, till she gets to the marrying age."

"Iris is too good to be true," Hal declared. "It's lucky she doesn't know all we know; she never could stand it if she did. And as to marrying, I mean to marry her myself of course."

This fine plan I did not oppose; it was a long way off.

"She's a perfect darling," I agreed with him. "But it's you who are doing the impossible, Hal. I never in my life heard of a boy of your age, a child when you began, keeping up such a continuous piece of acting and doing it so well."

I always tried to make him feel that I fully appreciated his efforts, but he waved it aside. "O shoh, mother. Any kid's good behavior is acting; they all have to do it more or less. It's just that I'm so fixed that I have to be good all the time, worse luck!"

One anchor to windward* I tried to prepare, since I found the typewriter. I meant to perfect myself in its use, and surely if I could do nothing else I could do typing at home, if we ever escaped. Also

I've had Hal get me a shorthand book, the one most used now, and I'm learning that. I'm going to teach it to Iris too. Then we could both earn our livings while Hal was getting started. But I do want to hold on till he gets through college.

August 1924

I have another friend, Dr. Ross Akers. At first I was shy of him because he was Wade's doctor. But he was wonderful with Iris when she was ill, Hal liked him tremendously, and by and by I found out that he was by no means fond of Wade, but seemed in some way bound to him.

He was father's doctor it appeared, after we left home, but he's a young man yet, not over thirty-six I should say.

He is tremendously anxious to have me properly mended, but Wade won't pay for it, and Ross is not a surgeon. He seems to somehow appreciate the difficulties of our position; as I said I got him to go and find out about that will for me. It is legally established, all right. His sympathy is a great comfort. He comes to see me now and then, and if Wade knows, he doesn't object.

Mrs. Todd and Dr. Akers are all the friends I have. I am thankful for both of them, especially for Ross Akers.

September 1925

Now I have something to write down that is well worth while! Something to thank that astonishing father of mine for. And particularly thank him for not telling Wade; apparently he never trusted anybody all the way.

I found it quite by accident, sitting there and waiting for a telephone connection and playing with the standard.* "They don't an--" said central, and I happened to turn something on the standard, and central was cut off and I could hear the cook talking in the kitchen! I listened in amazement, and while I was turning it back and forth to see how it worked I heard the maid setting [the] room beneath me in order, Vaughn's study.

Now I have something to take notes about! Now I shall find out perhaps why he sees so many clients in the evening. Mrs. Todd, dear soul, has told me of these people stealing in at the side door sometimes. And I've heard the vague sound of voices below me.

Shall I tell Hal? He has a right to all the interest and excitement there is to be found in our position. But suppose I find out something really criminal? After all he's only sixteen. I'd better not.

I'm so thankful for the shorthand! Iris and I are both proficient now. We've read aloud to each other and scribbled away--she will do nicely if she has to take a position. And now besides our personal experiences with this dreadful man I may be able to get hold of something really criminal, that is really actionable; there is plenty of crime that gets no legal recognition!

It's no crime, under the law, to torment two children and a helpless woman as he does. He knows I hate to have him touch me, and insists on carrying me up and downstairs in his arms, and kissing me! Talk about Judas! He doles out the pocket money of the children and insists that they keep an account of every cent, tell him exactly what they have done with it. If they forget anything he subtracts that much from the next week's allowance.

We are all kept close enough. The housekeeping is my responsibility and it is lucky for me that I know how to do it economically. One reason the servants do not stay is his keeping such a close watch on expenses. My three hundred helps out with what he allows for the children's clothes; he knows I have

95

to do that and means to have me, so that I cannot save anything.

Often, very often, I have felt that we must break away, but I cannot imperil the children's prospects, poor as they are, unless it is more terribly necessary. And Hal's college--he has a right to that. Four more years, if we can bear it!

I wish I had a first-class psychologist and criminalist to discuss him with. As an amateur I should label him as first an egomaniac--he thinks of no one whatever but himself. Second as a sadist, he takes definite pleasure in hurting people. But the very strongest is love of power, just power for its own sake.

Why even with little Iris, who is always sweet and submissive and does not know enough of his doings to hate him, he simply delights to tease her, torment her to tears, shame her to blushes with his talk--I think he does it partly to rouse Hal to rebellion, but so far that amazing boy has held out. He has an understanding with Iris about it. She is old enough to appreciate the position, and help a good deal. So when Wade teases her and she is on the verge of tears, Hal makes fun of her too, calls her "cry-baby" and spoils the game.

I have wondered much about the man's purpose in life. He never has said anything about his early life, anything that could be followed up and found out, that is. He's been here since 1907 or 1908. No family connections that we heard of. He makes plenty of money apparently, and has all of father's.

At first I wondered why he should trouble himself to keep us at all; it would be quite easy to force us into "rebellion" and turn us out of doors. But I concluded that it is the desire to have a family about him, and the credit for benevolence. People knew about the will and think he is doing better by us than he is compelled to.

He brings people to dinner at times, though he well knows what it means to me to show my poor face to strangers. But I carry it off as bravely as may be--I have to!--and the children are wonders.

I think it is partly that, and partly the sheer delight in our position. He couldn't have anyone else in such complete submission, all the time. Two nice children to order about, and a woman.

He has sent Iris to a good school, but she is too shy, too poorly dressed and too unhappy at home to have made many friends.

Hal had gone to the public schools, and had a boy's good time while out of the house at any rate. And he has made splendid progress. I've coached him all I could, kept him well ahead. If he can shorten his college years it may be very necessary.

We three are very happy together, which Wade cannot help, but he does his best to tease Hal into some outbreak. He'll do it too some day I'm afraid for the boy's affection for his lovely little cousin grows steadily.

But we talk it over together, Iris fully understanding that for all our sakes we must bear everything till Hal is through college. We try to comfort ourselves with the child's rhyme--"Sticks and stones will break my bones, but faces and names don't hurt me."

"It's a pity if I can't stand a little teasing!" the dear girl protests. "We have enough to eat and wear, and our beds to sleep in. We are healthy enough. It's just unpleasant. Think of those poor Russians, what they had to stand--and do yet!"

She doesn't know, Hal doesn't know, what I know now.

A good deal of business goes on in that room below mine. A good deal of money is paid. Part of the income is from money lent, lent under sharp necessity at exorbitant rates of interest, and collected ruthlessly. But most of it [is] worse than that; it is blackmail.

Practicing criminal law evidently gives a man opportunities. Wade has a henchman, a private detective, named Augustus Crasher. He used to be on the force but was dropped, for good reason I imagine. He is a coarse harsh man, but clever at his trade. They have worked together for years, and by and by I found why he was so meek and serviceable with Wade. Wade's specialty is having "the goods" as Crasher calls it, on people. He has evidence of some dirty work of Crasher's, something that would "break him" and "send him up." They had a sort of quarrel one day and Wade reminded him of it in no uncertain terms. But he has no desire to do it; the man is too useful to him, and he simply delights in the power he holds.

Between them they have accumulated a good deal of evidence against ever so many people, some rich and important people, some good ones with just one thing to cover up, and they have to pay him to keep still about it. They come stealing in, mostly in the evening and pay tribute. He sits there and simply revels in their helplessness. That's all he lends money for, as far as I can see, just to get people in his power. I cannot follow all he does with his tools and victims, but it runs into local politics, and investments; he makes money out of it, increasingly.

The safety of his position is that these people are his clients; the money he calls payment for professional services; they come to see him privately as clients; who can show any harm in that? I can, Wade Vaughn! But I mustn't move until I have definite criminal charges, names, cases, something that will stand up against even his trained ability.

Meanwhile I take notes, gritting my teeth over his calm cruelty. And when he has the whip hand over a

woman, and she comes here to pay him--I have to put
the telephone down and pray for strength to hold out
till Hal is graduated.

I have found out why my dear Dr. Akers is so--
amenable to Wade. It has puzzled me all along. I
could see he didn't like him, and Wade treated him
with that chuckling air of friendliness I've seen so
often. Now I know the whole story, and if anything
could make me hate him worse than I did it is this.

Ross was one of those brilliant young doctors who
make a name very early. He is one among these rational
progressive physicians who do not believe in letting
hideously deformed babies live, or in refusing the
supplications of people sure to die and suffering
horribly who beg to be put out of their misery. Very
early in his practice he was suspected of killing a
patient, a very dear friend of his, who was slowly
and hopelessly dying in constant agony.

How any man can keep his courage, his patience,
his cheery good will as Ross has done I can not
understand. One day when he came to see me, and Wade
had not come home yet, I determined to give him at
least the chance of someone to speak to about it. I
told him of my "Ears," of my notes, and asked his
advice as to whether I had enough to bring any sort
of action against Wade.

He read the whole thing so far as I had typed it,
and laid down the papers, little white dents showing in
his face, he was holding his jaws so tight together.

"Not one thing!" he said. "Not one. There isn't
one of these people who would dare to come out
against him. And look at your notes! What does he
ask for? Payment for 'professional services' every
time. All they do is to beg off--and call him names--
he merely assures that he is only charging for his
services and if they do not like it they had better
try another lawyer."

"Ross," I said softly. "Would it make it any easier to talk to me about your own trouble--I heard that too."

It was a relief to him. He told me all about it, and showed me how solid Wade was with his evidence. "There isn't a jury alive that wouldn't convict me, Jack. That dictograph stuff alone would smash me professionally. I could prove blackmail perhaps, but it wouldn't save my position."

But it is a great deal to have someone of my own age, and a man of understanding and sympathy to discuss things with. He says it's an immense relief to have someone he can free his mind to. So there's that much light in our darkness.

_____

June 1926

There is a new interest in our house, a new instance of Wade's methods. He has brought in three new servants, first two women, and a few months later a man. Norah Brown is the name given by the cook. Her daughter, who is chambermaid and so on, is Nellie Brown. They both seem somewhat "above their station" as people say, especially the daughter. We are very friendly; they are most kind to me and sympathetic, we chat quite a little, but they never tell me anything about themselves.

What I've learned is from their talk in the kitchen, which I hear so mysteriously, and occasionally a bit from Wade's room.

The woman is Italian, though born in this country, in California I gather. She married a young Irishman and came to New York with him; Nellie was born here. He died when she was a young girl, and they had a hard time for a while. They are both handsome, but Nellie is the beauty, with the dark intensity of her mother's people, and her father's blue eyes--and "the come hither" in them.

She fell in love, it appears, fiercely, desperately, with a man somewhat older and much richer, but she would not give in to him without marriage, so he married her--but was frequently away on various business excuses. Then she found out that he was already married. There was a furious quarrel, he knocked Nellie down--right before her mother-- between them they killed him. Each of them claims to have done it; I don't believe they really know. It is pathetic to hear each one reassuring the other. But they were not tried.

This is another case of Wade's success as a criminal lawyer. He got hold of the case before the inquest, heard their story and told them what to say. Then he produced not only witnesses but a man who confessed he had done it, and who was properly convicted. Singularly enough he got away before reaching Ossining.*

The lawyer's bill is now being collected. He has it all arranged to bring out other witnesses to show how he had been deceived and to send them both for life. He says the chair, but I don't believe that. But they are in utter fear of him, each for the other's sake, and he has what he likes best, more people utterly in his power.

The mother is an excellent cook, and helps Nellie with her work. Between them they keep us very comfortable. But I feel as if we were living on a volcano.

Then he brought in the man, Joe White. I didn't believe any of their names were the real ones, and soon found out I was right. Joe was evidently of a better class. He was well born and well educated, but wild, as often happens. He was in the war, with a good record, but came back no steadier for the experience. There was some bootlegging I think, and a long period of knocking about.

Finally he was caught in a gambling house row, drunk, quarrelling, a man killed, and Joe accused. It is possible he did it, he does not really know, being drunk. But Wade defended him, got him off, and he and Crasher saved out evidence that would incriminate him on another charge, a worse one. It makes me dizzy the way these two make a definite business of framing people.

And here is Wade taking out his pay in service, service from a man much more of a gentleman than he is, and proud as a Spaniard. It is like a Roman general with his victims chained to his chariot wheels. Imagine it, this high-spirited man, who has been an army officer, and is now a chauffeur-butler-valet to Wade Vaughn!

No wonder he seems bitter and queer. It is dangerous too, of course, and I believe Wade positively likes it. I heard them once when Joe was stung to fury and fairly threatened him. Wade only laughed.

"That's the business risk I take," he said. "You are the captive of my bow and of my spear, Joe, and of course you don't like it. It makes life exciting to feel how gladly you would cut my throat any minute. But remember that your dossier is in safe hands, and that if I were gone you would be quite at the mercy of men who would by no means offer you a good safe berth--in service. Besides, if I were bumped off, these poor women in the kitchen would be no safer than you."

He has a stronger hold on Joe now than even the fear of death.

Poor Nellie! That helpless furious miserable child! There must be some way to get these people out of his clutches. He holds the three of them in the hollow of his hand, the mother and daughter each by love for the other as well as fear for themselves, and Joe--Joe has fallen in love with Nellie.

The Screw

I am afraid!...

This cannot go on--we must give up--after all this long terrible effort we must break away before Hal is graduated. We can't wait any longer on account of Iris, brave little Iris! She hasn't told me, but I heard.

It is Monday night, Sept. 2nd., 1928. On Wednesday morning she is to be--we must get away at any cost... There's no money but what's left of that hidden nest egg of mine--I've <u>had</u> to use some of it from time to time. What can we do? Where can we go? and my face-- to show it to strangers!

Steady, Jack, steady! You haven't stood this thing for nine years to give out now. This has to be met... First I'll finish this record, bring it up to date, with this last enormity...

It has been a busy day in that spider-web down-stairs. Wade has been at home all the afternoon, tak-ing tribute. Several "clients" called and paid him money. He makes them bring it in cash. I often hear him counting it. One man was hard pressed; extra expenses at home, sickness in the family, he begged for release.

No use of course. Wade told him that he was really his protector. "Why my dear sir," he said cheerfully, "if I didn't hold my hand you wouldn't have any home to pay for. Just consider it as ground rent. You can manage it somehow." He paid.

One man was violent, raged, threatened. Wade sat back in his chair, I could hear it squeak, with that hideous contented little chuckle. "No use making a spectacle of yourself," he said. "It's amusing, but a waste of time. Hand it over." He handed it over. One was a woman...

Then Ross Akers came, by the side door. He must have walked, I didn't hear a car. And he did not ask for me at all. Wade suffers from hay fever, and it appeared he was going to try inoculation; he has never mentioned it to us. Ross had a payment to make too, and though he did not beg, he did suggest that without repudiating their agreement Wade should allow him to retain a larger proportion of his own earnings. The girls were growing up, he urged, and it looked strange for him to have an increasing practice with no commensurate increase in income.

Wade seemed amused. "You do so much unpaid work, my dear fellow, and rich people are so slow in paying their bills. However I do think that if you cut more of a splurge you might enlarge your practice still further to our mutual benefit. Suppose I cut off say five hundred dollars and you take a better office. Now get on with your vegetable garden." Ross thanked him. Thanked him!

It is hard to choose among Wade Vaughn's wickednesses, but the way he has crushed down that splendid man, holding him by his devotion to his family, and only a poor sort of half-family at that, is as devilish as any.

Joe was the next one. I was proud of him. Perfectly controlled, no recriminations, just a business proposition.

"Mr. Vaughn," he said, "I have served you for some years. I trust I have given satisfaction, sir?"

"Perfectly, Joe, perfectly. A little sulky at times, but always respectful, and most efficient. I couldn't do without you, really."

"I am hoping that you will, sir. If you will allow me to leave you and go to work for myself, I will undertake to pay you the hire of another servant, and an increasing amount over that as I get on. In the course of a few years I am sure I could make it well worth your while, sir."

"Nothing doing, Joe. My income is good enough, and there are some things I like better than money, as you may have observed. It gives me more pleasure to see a ten thousand dollar man blacking my boots and putting in my studs, handing my soup and cleaning my silver, than I should get from that much more money."

Joe kept cool, and made a quiet but moving appeal as man to man. He told him that he and Nellie wished to be married, that they were both competent and strong, that as free earners he was sure they could make it well worth his while to let them go.

"What, take my Nellie too?" demanded Wade. As if he didn't perfectly know they were in love with each other. "Oh no, Joe. You are asking too much. You'll be taking my excellent cook next! But I'll be liberal with you. If you and Nellie want to be married, do so by all means! Nothing more stable than a pair of married servants. You shall grow old in my service. And I'll leave you something in my will."

Joe went out without [a] word, and Wade sat there, chuckling. Norah was next. She had no such cool command as the man. She cried and sobbed, she begged him on her knees, thumping down melodramatically, for her daughter's sake. "For the poor child that's had so much trouble, sir! You wouldn't rob her of this one chance of happiness, sir! In the name of the Holy Virgin have a heart, Mr. Vaughn, have a heart!"

He was very short with Norah, and very clear. "No use for the sob stuff, not a bit. Get this through your thick head for good and all--you and Nellie either stay in my house as servants, or you both go to the chair. If those two wish to be married, let them, but they stay in my service."

And then Nellie, struggling hard to be calm, to hold her voice steady, begging hard for her happiness and Joe's, for freedom. She even made a pathetic appeal to his heart--Wade's heart! "If I've been of any use and comfort to you! Sir--if you have ever cared for me at all--" and then that little chuckle.

That she could not stand. She lost her temper, an Irish-Italian temper--and began to charge him with all manner of things. He moved his chair back-- "Stop," he said. She stopped. "Come here!" I judge she came, for he presently went on, "Sit still, my dear. Now understand that you three people are absolutely helpless. You might be willing to be electrocuted, might prefer it to your present position."

"I would!" she interpolated, fiercely.

"Exactly," he went on, "Quite likely. But you do not want to send your mother to the chair, nor Joe... Very well, keep quiet and take your medicine."

Some time later Crasher called. He rang the front door bell. Iris was downstairs and she opened the door. I heard a sort of scuffle in the hall, and then Iris ran upstairs, but she did not come to me, went to her own room. I kept on listening.

That man Crasher, that coarse heavy cruel man, wants to marry Iris Booth, my little Iris! He told

Wade so, asked his consent. Wade played with him awhile, like a lazy tiger. "I'm afraid you've been reading the will of Grandpa Smith, Gus?"

"I have read it, of course, I know about the property end of it providing you're agreeable, but you'd have to give it to anybody she married with your consent. I don't believe anybody'd make a better bargain with you than I will. And if she don't marry you don't get any of it."

"Very well reasoned, Gus. Quite astute, but it doesn't go far enough. As to bargaining, I've got you where I want you as it is; you are very useful to me, and I to you in a negative way. So why should I give my pretty little niece to you? Or any of the money due her husband?"

"I'd marry her if she hadn't any money," Crasher protested. "I'm crazy about her. I never thought I'd fall so hard for any Jane."

"I'm afraid your passion is not reciprocated, Augustus. It even strikes me that she does not like you."

"She doesn't," he agreed grimly. "But I don't care for that. If I can get hold of her I'll take care of that. I'll learn her!"

"But she's such a child, Gus; and you are nearer forty than thirty, twice her age, I should judge."

"That's no obstacle; it's an attraction. I'm--I tell you I'm nuts on her! I've got to have her."

"Why not get her to elope with you--you say you don't care for the money?"

"She wouldn't marry me of her own free will, I've sense enough to know that. I tried to grab a kiss just now, and she bounced away as if I was a snake! But you can make her! And if you'll make her I'll split on the bonus."

"I see," said Wade slowly. "You appreciate her soft fresh youth; you'd like to hold that slim little body in your arms, and kiss her when she couldn't bounce away."

"Damn you, Wade, stop talking about it. I'll split on any terms you like--I want the girl."

"A very proper feeling, disinterested personal affection. Yes, yes. And you say you would marry her if she hadn't a cent?"

"I would," said Crasher, stoutly. "I'd marry her today. I don't know but I'd be willing to pay for the privilege," and he laughed harshly. "Is it a go, Vaughn?"

"You shall have her, Gus, not today, but day after tomorrow, Wednesday morning. And you shall pay for the privilege--but you won't lose anything. You can't lose what you never had, Gus. Without my consent, yes, and some force to execute it, you never would get the girl or the money--that's clear. With my consent, you get the girl, with all her endearing young charms, Gus, but you don't get the money-- you give it back to me."

There was a sort of stunned silence. Then Crasher: "You mean to say you'd hog it all?"

"Why not Gus? There is many a man I should prefer to you for a step-son-in-law, men who would be a credit to the family, and of some further assistance to me perhaps. Now I can't get anything more out of you than I do now, except that you are more likely than a better man to agree to this little bargain. So you have only to choose between no money and no girl, or no money but a charming bride on Wednesday. If your feelings are as warm as you say, it ought not to take you long."

It didn't. In his beastly way Crasher is in love with Iris, and my unspeakable brother-in-law is going to give her to him, unless we can escape... He came out in the hall and called her down. The poor child went to him, and I kept on listening. "Iris, my dear, you have always been a good and obedient daughter."

"I have tried to be Papa."

"I hope you will continue to be so. You are old enough to be married now, and I have chosen a husband for you, Mr. Crasher."

She gave a little muffled scream--"Oh no, Papa! Oh no! You can't mean it! You can't!"

"I can and I do, my dear. I have very good reasons for my choice."

"But I don't love him Papa! I can't bear him--I can't!"

"You'll get over that, my dear. You will have to bear him, you'll get used to him. Perhaps in time you will even love him. As a step to it go now and give him a kiss."

The lesser brute went out after that, and the greater one applied the screw to that sweet child with as little feeling as if she had been hateful to him. Her tears, her pathetic appeals, her promises to be good, to do anything else, everything else, if only he would let her off from this--and I upstairs, helpless, but listening to get it all--and only one day's grace!

He was gentle enough to her, held her in his lap I judge, which she always hated, but he showed her how she must do this thing.

"Suppose I disobey you, Papa--give up the old money and everything--suppose I won't do it, just won't--you can't make me."

"No, I can't make you, by force, but I will tell you what will happen if you disobey me. Listen carefully, for there is no avoiding these consequences. If you do not go to the city hall with Mr. Crasher Wednesday morning, you not only lose your future share of your grandfather's estate, but I shall give Hal a command which he will refuse--something to hurt his mother perhaps, something he would not do, and being disobedient, he will lose his share too. Then I shall turn him and your Aunt Jack out of doors, at once. Hal will have to leave college and go to work at whatever he can do. He will find it hard to support his mother, to say nothing of you.

"Furthermore, as another painful consequence, I will foreclose the mortgage I hold on Dr. Akers's house, and break up his business as well. I have criminal charges against him--I can put him in prison. I can do it. He will find it hard to keep those three feeble females of his, and can't possibly help you.

"On the other hand, if you forget your likes and dislikes and marry Mr. Crasher like a good girl, you may be more or less unhappy at first; women often are. But I shall have to pay over quite a sizeable fortune, and if you are a satisfactory wife to him he may let you do a lot for your aunt and Hal with money. So you see it is merely a question between your doing something you don't want to and the misfortune of several people you are fond of."

"But you are doing it Papa! The misfortunes would be from you, you needn't be so--so cruel!"

"I told you I had good reasons for your doing this thing, Iris. And cruel or not the consequences of your refusal will be as I have said." I heard the poor child sobbing softly. Then in a small voice she said, "Very well, Papa," and left the room.

She did not come to me. She does not wish me to know. She will make that hideous marriage rather than bring pain and loss on the people she loves. Wednesday at ten he is coming. One day's grace. What can I do?...

Iris has told Hal. She did not mean to do it, but he got it out of her. In his horror, supposing she could love that man, she owned it was under a threat--

told him everything. He brought her to me, frantic.

"Let's go, mother, now, tonight! I'll take care of you, somehow. Confound college! Plenty of men have got along without it, got rich, too. You shan't do it, Iris, you shan't! Why you darling I'm going to marry you myself as soon as I'm of age, you know that!"

She raised her tear-stained face and looked at him, then ran into his arms. He looked so glad and daring and triumphant, and she so safe--for a moment. Then she remembered, drew herself away, looked at me despairingly.

"Hal's right, dear," I told her. "You shall not do it." Then we began to think, to plan. We thought of Dr. Akers first, of course, and then we all remembered that he would be ruined too.

"It's a dreadful thing but it has to be faced," I told them. "He is a man; he'll stand it somehow. We have got to get out and take care of ourselves--just us."

Now I'm glad of this little typewriter--and that Iris is so good with it, and her shorthand. I showed them my little nest-egg, told them how I found it. It's enough to keep us till Hal gets a job, and Iris. Nobody would have my face in an office, but I can get copying to do at home--sewing--anything. I'm sorry enough about Hal's losing his college, but he'd better be a stevedore than have Iris do this thing...

Tuesday. I've seen Ross. He says he'll have to leave the country. There's a cousin of his stepmother's it appears, who is perfectly able to care for her but has stoutly refused. "I'll leave the family on his doorstep!" he said. Dear Ross! But he said he wouldn't go till he knew our address. I'm worried about him...

Hal has found a place for us to go to, only two

CHARLOTTE PERKINS GILMAN

rooms. It will have to do for now. And we'll clear
out early tomorrow, before that man comes...

    I suppose this is the end of this record. I must-
n't forget to pack it. But it's safer behind this
panel till the last minute.

    Tomorrow we'll be free--free!

Jacqueline Warner

Various Efforts

Bessie straightened the pages neatly, replaced them in the folder, [then] the stout envelope, and sat quite still, looking at the opposite wall. Jim was still too.

"I'm not sorry I took it," she said presently; "and I'm mighty glad we're on this job! Any remarks?"

"I regret that Mr. Vaughn is dead, that's all," he answered; "so I cannot have the pleasure of killing him. Of all sub-human criminals!"

"Augustus Crasher is not dead! Yet!" said Bessie ominously. "Are you coming back with me?"

"I'll join you at the back door, via the next yard, at eleven forty-five sharp."

She was there much earlier, letting herself in at the side door, and showed a light in her room for some fifteen minutes afterward. Then, waiting by the back door in the dark, only by the closest listening did she hear Jim's faint scratch and let him in. Her bedroom was locked, the key in her pocket. They left off the chain on the side door, and bestowed themselves in the big parlors, watching the back and front stairs. Enough light came through the fanlight and narrow side windows by the front door to show anything moving. After an hour or so they heard the faintest of stealthy steps, and visioned a dim figure moving slowly and soundlessly up the back stairs. The outline was recognizable, thick shoulders, thick legs, thick neck.

As softly they crept after him, peering through the balusters when their heads were above the level of the second floor. The figure stood by Hal's door, still as if listening. With imperceptible motion and no faintest sound he opened the door. Bessie thought of what she had read of elephants, so huge, so noiseless when they chose. A diffused light from a partly clouded moon made it possible for them to follow his movements.

He stood first by the bed, listening to the boy's regular breathing, then moved like a thick ghost to the tall old wardrobe and drew a chair beside it. He reached up over the top but made no sound. Descending as silently he went to the heavily ornamented black walnut bureau, and crouched before it, pulling out, by careful inches, the thin lowest drawer.

As he rose the two observers stealthily withdrew down the front stairs, and watched their visitor let himself out by the side door as he had come. Then they raced up softly to Bessie's room, from which they had a clear view of the garden.

"You go to sleep, young lady," her husband urged in a whisper. "I'll watch for a while and toward morning you can spell me."

"I will if he don't come in a minute," said she in his ear. "But he won't want to sit up all night either—you see."

So two heads peered over the sill, and kept the long dim garden in view. It was not very long before a movement was visible at the lower end; a heavy figure slipped in over the back fence and moved along to a shadowy corner.

Jim could not wait. "You sit here," he breathed. "I can get out there without his hearing," and he slipped away into the garden, melting from shadow to shadow so imperceptibly that his wife's keenly watchful eyes could hardly follow him. He had made himself quite familiar with the ground, and slipped along among the over-grown shrubs; he could plainly see the marksman of the morning carefully burying his targets.

He dug with a large trowel and Jim admired his forethought—"Not so conspicuous as a spade, smart boy!" he thought. The big man squatted and dug, tucked in his tomato cans, covered them smoothly and sprinkled a few leaves over the place. He even risked a moment's view with a low-held small light, and seemed pleased with the result. So he straightened his knees with evident relief, and eased himself over the fence as softly as he had got in.

The two watchers agreed that nothing more was to be expected that night, and held a whispered conference in Bessie's room on the third floor.

"It's a simple device, too easy, melodramatic." Jim protested. "Who does he think is going to fall for stuff like that!"

"Most anybody—that didn't know better. I've a sort of notion of what he'll try to do with his plant. You stay here till morning my dear—they'll not know but what you came then, and we'll see what we shall see."

This being arranged with mutual satisfaction, he remained concealed in the morning, and as soon as Hal had gone down to breakfast, Jim slipped into his room and looked on the top of that wardrobe. He did not disturb the dust, nor do more than lift the pistol with gloved fingers and note its caliber. Thirty-eight. He laughed.

*   *   *   *   *

"You'd better see me," urged Mr. Crasher at the phone Friday morning. "I've got some information about your cousin that will come out pretty raw at the inquest—I think you'd better hear it first. I'm round here at Liggetts*—I'll be at the door in five minutes, and you let me in. You needn't worry his mother about it; she wouldn't thank you. What say?"

Iris did not know what to say. She hated to see the man, to have any words with him, even for a moment. But she knew he was dangerous. If Hal were there—but Hal had gone out. Mr. Crasher made sure of that before he telephoned. "He can't kill me," thought Iris. "I'll have Betty* within call"—so she very reluctantly agreed to let him in.

Once admitted he marched upstairs at once to Hal's room, the girl protesting vainly. "There's a bit of evidence that ought to turn up in that room," he told her, "and if you and I find it without anybody else knowing the better it will be for the young man."

Uncertain as to what it was best to do she followed quietly and watched him make a swift and thorough search. She had no idea of the speed with which a trained hand can go through a room, closet, drawers, suitcases, everything. He poked under every piece of furniture, and finished by standing on a chair and passing his hand along the tops of pictures and doorcasings.

When he came to the old wardrobe he put a hassock on the

chair and peered over. "I thought so," he remarked with coarse triumph, and took down a pistol. This he stood weighing in his hand, and still looking further. Surely he had examined everything. Suddenly he made a dive for the shallow extra drawer at the base of the heavy old walnut bureau, and from the farthest corner produced a box of cartridges. "Now we can talk business, Miss Iris," he stated with decision, and led the way downstairs again.

Being busily occupied he had naturally not noticed the pair of keen eyes which had watched him from the hall while he made these discoveries; still less was he conscious of their regard from the narrow crack under the picture frame.

He seated himself heavily in the desk chair and waved the girl to another.

"Now young lady, my point is this. I want to marry you. You do not want to marry me, I know that, but maybe you'd rather than to see that handsome young cousin of yours go to the chair."

Iris wet her lips; her hands felt hot and dry. She said nothing.

"You see *some*body shot your stepfather. That's certain. This morning I dug up in the garden back here a couple o' tin cans all riddled with bullet holes, target practice, and then hidden! And I've a witness to testify that he was going through the alley and heard a sort of popping—you'll observe there's a silencer on this pistol, Miss Iris—and he looked over the fence and saw young Warner practicing away like a good one. Saw him bury the cans too; that's how I knew where to look. Now here's the gat,* and here's one box of shells, minus one round, and the thing's been fired once—here's an empty shell—see?

"Now being a lady I dare say you don't know much about evidence but I know a lot about it, and there's enough here to send a man to the chair, p.d.q. Very well. I've a fair proposition to make. If you marry me I will suppress all this evidence. It's nothing to me whether he did it or not. And I swear I'll make you a good husband," he added huskily.

Iris was shivering. She knew far better than he, how Hal had felt toward his uncle. Her mind was confused by the very number of attacks. Aunt Jack had begged her not to try to unravel it, to just wait for what the inquest might bring forth.

"He wouldn't!" she protested. "He couldn't! It's wicked of you to say so."

"I'm not saying so," Crasher patiently explained. "It's these things that say so, and they talk pretty loud. The court will not feel as you do about him, you know. This is Friday and tomorrow's the inquest. But if you are Mrs. Crasher they can't find any evidence against him—there won't be any."

It was only four days since the girl had forced herself to consider this hateful marriage as a sacrifice to save her family, only two days since the dreadful discovery of her stepfather's death had freed her from that nightmare. She felt oddly submerged in an old fashioned melodrama. Her native common sense warned her not to be—what was it Hal called it?—"buffaloed." But there was Mr. Crasher in the flesh, eying her as if he read her thoughts.

"I know it's a pretty raw deal to drive you into this, but I want you enough to do worse things. I never was so crazy about a girl in my life. I won't kill you, Iris. And as for the boy, you know even if they don't convict him it will spoil his career all right. Pretty poor lookout for a young man who's been up for murder."

She wavered. To high-minded youth there is a certain allurement in sacrifice, high spirited youth, and sacrifice for one's best loved is almost irresistible. But before she committed herself her cousin burst in to the room and stood with clenched fists looking from one to the other.

"Shall I throw him out Iris?" he asked quietly.

"Oh no, Hal—no! Wait, please. I must speak to him myself."

"You'd better not say another word to him, Iris. Come Mr. Crasher, you are not wanted in this house."

"You'd better keep a civil tongue in your head young man! I've got the goods on you all right. It's up to your cousin here whether I send you up river or not. Clear out till we've finished our little talk."

But Hal calmly seated himself, "What's he mean Iris? Let's see the cards. What's he got on me?"

"I've got *this*! And this!" said Crasher, suddenly producing the revolver and shells. "And Miss Iris here saw me find 'em in your room. Also I've found those nice targets you was popping at in the yard. It'll be a cold day for you when these are brought up against you."

Iris looked at him eagerly, anxiously, but Hal stretched out his long legs and burst into cheerful laughter.

"Oh Iris—did you let him fool you with that stuff! In the first place it's a plant, every bit of it. But what's more to the purpose it doesn't matter who shot a dead man—he must have taken on the poison first."

"Poison?" Iris stood with her hand to her throat, pale, startled, while Crasher watched her narrowly.

"Sure he was poisoned! Don't you read the papers, kid?"

"No—Aunt Jack thought I'd better not."

"Well there's no doubt about it, Iris. Poison was in the whiskey; he must have taken it before he was dead, so there's only one murderer to discover, and that's not the one with the pistol! Good morning Mr. Crasher."

But it was now Mr. Crasher's turn to stretch himself comfortably and gaze at them both across the desk.

"You're quite right, young man, quite right, but you'll be very sorry you mentioned it. It seemed to me a neater thing to reach this young lady through her natural interest in you, and protect her completely from a poisoning charge."

Hal shot up fiercely, but Iris held him back—"Wait, wait Hal—hear what he has to say!" She sank back, huddled small and pale in her big chair, and watched with a sick fascination the small hot eyes of the big man at the desk.

"I'll show you my case," said he, slowly. "You wanted the cards on the table, young feller. Here they are. On Monday your late Uncle Mr. Vaughn arranged with this young lady that she was to marry me. She didn't like the idea—I know that; I'm no lady's man. But he used considerable pressure. Very well; on Tuesday morning this young lady went shopping. She visited four drugstores in succession, and in each one of them she bought a bottle of strychnia. On Tuesday evening she went to the pictures with you. Perhaps you remember she had to excuse herself for a few moments?"

Hal started, gave a frightened desperate look at Iris. She was holding tight to the arms of her chair. "It was to get my cough drops, Hal! I told you I had to get them," she eagerly explained.

"She ran home for her cough drops," Crasher went on smoothly. "They must have been kept on her uncle's desk. For when I first looked things over here's what I found on that desk—" and he showed them a half-ticket to the picture palace, dated on the previous Tuesday.

"I *did* come for cough drops, Hal. I did! And they *were* in his room, I left them there that awful Monday when he tried to make me marry that awful man! He was asleep, I came in and got them, they were right here on this corner—and put them in my little bag—the ticket must have dropped out somehow."

"All correct I don't doubt, Miss Iris, but how about the strychnia? Did that somehow drop out, too?"

"I didn't! I didn't!" she protested quiveringly, "I got it for myself! Hal! I was going to marry him to keep you all from being turned out of doors—but I didn't have to live afterward. You've got to believe me!"

Hal patted her hand reassuringly. "Sure I believe you, Iris." He turned to Mr. Crasher.

"And your proposition is—?"

"Same as before. She marries me, and I quash this evidence. Nobody else has got anything on her. She'll be safe."

"Otherwise you propose to send her to the chair?"

"Straight!" replied Mr. Crasher.

"And a much better place," said a quiet voice in the door. It was Jim. "I always did admire your forthright methods, Gus," he went on. "But I strongly advise the young lady here to say no— and put her trust in Providence. Meantime I think we can confer about this terrible fix we're in more comfortably without you."

Mr. Crasher rose menacingly.

"What is your answer, Miss Iris?" he demanded.

"No," she breathed.

"You can turn me out of this house, Jim Hunt," he said grimly, "but you can't turn me out of the inquest—nor the court room." And he took himself off.

Then they sought Aunt Jack, and regaled her with Mr.

Crasher's discomfiture.

It was a very tearful and agitated Iris who told them all her pathetic little story, how she had had no difficulty in getting the strychnia; she had bought it before for her aunt who sometimes used it as a stimulant. "I didn't know how much it would take, so I got a lot. I meant to mash them all up together, make a paste and just eat it. I wasn't going to live with that man."

"But you were going to marry him to save my neck just now, you little burnt offering you!" cried Hal, and they told about the discoveries made by this industrious lover.

"Pretty coarse work," Jim commented. "He could have picked up a dozen of those tickets outside the door. I've known him to do better. But he hadn't much time, and he was mainly trying to bamboozle this child. Miss Iris, don't you ever marry anybody unless you very much want to. And not always then!" he added cheerfully. "Now let's have a good talk and a clear slate for the inquest tomorrow."

But Iris was still alarmed. "But won't he? Can't he?"

"He won't and he can't do anything to hurt you my dear child," Jim told her in his most fatherly manner. "And as for Hal here, he couldn't have hurt a dead man even if that had been his pistol."

Then Jim prefaced any further remarks by offering to make a confession. "Do you like your new maid?" he asked with entire irrelevance.

"Like her? We love her on two days' experience," replied Aunt Jack. "She's no servant; she's a friend in need." Hal and Iris quite agreed in this good opinion, and Jim grinned delightedly. To their surprise he applied his mouth to the speaking tube, cheerfully calling, "Oh Bess! Come on up!" and when that young lady hurriedly appeared he presented her with a triumphant, "Meet Mrs. James Hunt!"

"I hope I've given satisfaction," Bessie modestly remarked.

"You see you had to have somebody," Jim went on. "This child thought of it herself—being a housekeeper. And we wanted to have an eye on the enemy night and day. Lucky we did too!"

"I knew you were nice, anyhow," Aunt Jack assured her, "And so did I," put in Iris. Hal wagged his head sadly.

"Too good to be true! We never shall see those muffins again!" but he shook hands with her warmly. She promised him one more lot tomorrow.

"As Jim says, it's lucky we did, Mrs. Warner," and they told her of last night's vigil and what they had seen.

"It was a hasty job," Jim said rather apologetically. "But he was pressed for time. He'll bring out a good story tomorrow—but ours will be stronger."

It is not to be supposed that the long arm of the law remained inert while Mr. Crasher pursued his private ends and Mr. Hunt pursued Mr. Crasher. The autopsy was conducted with the utmost thoroughness by Mr. Davis and his associates, and a report prepared for the inquest.

Mr. Clargis had more than one interview with Mrs. Warner, striving to discover something further as to the possible plans of the obviously implicated servants, whose successful disappearance remained completely baffling. It is true that a careful combing of the waterfront resulted in an account of three men seen in a small power boat belonging to a more or less suspicious character known among his friends as Bugs, but this entomological character, being questioned, was disarmingly willing to testify.

"Sure I took three dagos to the *Chimborazo*," he cheerfully admitted. "They was in a hell of a hurry to connect with that boat and put up good money if I'd make it for 'em. What size was they? Why various sizes, I didn't notice much. One was taller than the other two, I know that. We caught her all right, but there was a lot of chatter before they let 'em on board, charged 'em high, I guess."

A wireless was sent after the *Chimborazo*, but the captain was incensed at suspicions cast upon his passengers. Some warm remarks were exchanged, and he was told to have these three men looked over and he'd find that two of them were women. "And we'll be waiting for 'em when you land, Captain—the joke's on you."

"I will not insult my passengers," he protested, but was told that he'd better insult them pretty quick—and wire the results, of which nothing had been heard so far.

Mr. Crasher, not unwilling to stand in with the authorities, came forward with a considerable amount of information about the missing three. He referred to the cases of some years back, in which Mr. Vaughn had succeeded in saving them from serious charges.

"I thought at the time he was wrong, but Vaughn was a good lawyer, none better, and he got 'em off. Then when I wasn't workin' I kind of followed up the evidence, and in my judgement all of them birds was booked for the chair. And maybe he knew it too, and held it over 'em. It looked kinda funny, all three of them settling down as servants, not at all the kind of work that big fella'd a taken to—of his own will.

"Well, here's the stuff, and if he had it up his sleeve all the time and they knew it, there's motive enough. There's no manner of doubt to my mind that Joe White cleaned out that safe, and did his share of the murdering."

But however much additional guilt might be placed at the door of those three departed ones, it served not at all to bring them to light. No utmost inquiry at any train, boat or ticket office roused the faint memory of any such passengers, more especially as the inquirers could not say if they came together, singly, or as one couple and another alone.

Various persons did come forward with vivid remembrance of having seen just such people at the appropriate time, but nothing came of all their kind suggestions.

"Twelve hours start, and not the slightest idea of where they'd put for," said Crasher, who refused to be impressed with the pursuit of the *Chimborazo* passengers. In which indifference he was presently justified, for a belated marconigram* presently informed the New York police: "Those three men are all men, and all pretty mad."

With praiseworthy persistence they were waited for and watched in Rio de Janeiro later, but remained unquestionably men just the same.

Meanwhile attention was concentrated on Mrs. Warner's evidence as to the threatening man, the angry woman, the alleged blackmailing business. Careful examination was made of Mr. Vaughn's books and files at the office, and among such of his clients as were known to the police there were several who furnished excellent opportunity for blackmail. His clerk, Mr. Isaacs, a keen quiet man with a close-lipped mouth, could give little information. At least he did give little.

"Mr. Vaughn kept his business to himself, mostly. In the big cases every one could see what he did, but he had a lot of private business with various clients of which I know absolutely nothing. I dare say much of this was carried on in his house—I have no knowledge of that."

No will was discovered, and no provable relatives appeared. Deeper investigation showed that Mr. Vaughn had come to New York in 1907, and made a sudden reputation by rescuing an important client from a most damaging charge, following which success came others, and visible prosperity. But none of his legal acquaintances or clients seemed to know anything of him personally. Whereat the investigators concluded that perhaps Mr. Vaughn had been Mr. Something else, somewhere else, and that if his business was largely blackmail he had been successful in leaving no evidence of it.

His property remained, a fairly comfortable fortune, securely invested, but as an individual he had sunk without trace.

An Informer

It was a Friday evening. Bessie Hunt had again slipped home to compare notes once more with Jim.

"It's a relief to get out of that house," she proclaimed, "and be able to walk easy and talk out loud. Secret ears are worse than secret passages I think. I like investigation, but I hate creeping around."

"Nevertheless, you are a pretty good creeper, my dear. Anything more turned up?"

"The lawyer was there in the afternoon. Seems to be a good one."

"Yes, Anderson's square as they make 'em. Could you follow the talk?"

"Easy as pie. The young folks were in the front parlor. Hal brought his mother down and she saw him in Vaughn's room."

"Good nerve!"

"I'll say so! She doesn't know that I know anything about her "ears," and further she doesn't know about the eyes-and-ears in that disused pantry, where I was. So I took it all in. But not any light on the Who problem. She was perfectly frank with the man, told him what she told us, nearly, about Crasher and all. Asked him a lot about inquests and how much they would be obliged to tell.

"You see she was still trying to shield Iris. But he was quite firm about it. Told her that it was very poor policy to conceal anything which bore on the case. Dr. Akers had posted him pretty thoroughly; it was clear where his sympathies were.

"She said he need not be afraid of shocking her, that she saw perfectly well that every member of the household would be suspected, including herself, and wished to be advised carefully about her testimony.

"'You have only to answer the questions asked,' he told her. 'An inquest is not a trial. Tell the truth and show no desire to conceal anything.'

"'There is so much truth to tell'; she was still anxious. But he switched off to the property side of it, asked if she was not interested in their financial prospects.

"'We are not relations, any of us,' she said, 'and he was not likely to have made a will in our favor! I did not suppose we had any financial prospects.'

"So then he went into it at great length, told her how he had gone over the will carefully, and that the small income due the young people from their grandfather's bequest would still be paid to them. 'The court will appoint a trustee,' he explained, 'and on reaching majority each will receive the small capital.' And he asked if she had 'any other resources.'

"She told him of their plans, how she and Iris had secretly fitted themselves to stenography and typewriting. 'We were going away you know—Iris could undoubtedly have got a position, and I was going to take work at home, if I could get it. Hal was going to work of course. Now with nine hundred dollars a year among us it will be easier.'"

"Think of it, Jim!" Bessie stopped to exclaim. "Nine hundred dollars for that dear woman and those children! And all her father's fortune waiting for Vaughn's relatives!"

"He was very nice about it. Said he thought perhaps he might put some work in her way, might even find something for Hal, and she was grateful and interested of course.

"But she harked back to her testimony.

"'We were all going to leave that morning, rooms engaged. Hal knows the taxi he ordered, all perfectly above board. Will it help to tell that?'

"'Much better [to] tell a thing than to have it found out,' he advised. Said he was very glad she understood the position they were in. 'You can hardly escape the "motive and opportunity" suspicion. But after all there were six of you in the house, all with motive and opportunity, and from what I learn of Mr. Vaughn's business there were plenty more with motives at least, and it did not seem difficult to make opportunity. I cannot understand how so acute a man could expose himself as he did . . . '

"Then they talked some psychology, and about criminals always having some sort of screw loose. She told him she thought Vaughn was a 'sadist,' whatever that is."

"'Sadist,' my innocent young friend, named for a vicious old party, Marquis de Sade*—who got more satisfaction out of hurting women than making love to them. Vaughn seems to have enjoyed both at once."

"Hideous!" said Bessie. "Moral disease seems to me as disgusting as skin disease. Why the plain murderers and thieves we are so hot after seem like mere naughty children besides this kind of pervert."

"Quite so," said Jim drily, "and since at present the pervert is excused on account of his disease they seem to be rapidly increasing. But you did not gather anything on the case?"

"Not a thing. I got 'em a good dinner and left early. Dr. Akers was there; they'll be all right for a while. Now what have you got?"

"Heaps and heaps, my dear. Startling revelations! Sinister facts! Honestly, I have some new stuff. After Crasher's fiasco this morning I wasn't afraid of his doing anything more till he brings out his evidence, and I'm certainly not afraid of that. So I came home to get a little sleep. How about you, Bess? Did you get a nap today?"

"Forty winks or so. But I'll sleep tonight; Crasher's shot his bolt. Are you coming over?"

"I am that; you go to bed and I'll keep an eye on things. Well, I'd barely got home when the bell rang, and up comes a shabby little man with a story to tell. And who do you think he was, Mrs. Sleuth?"

"Give it up—don't waste time. Who was he?"

"Carlo's brother. Angelo or Mario or something. Yes'm. Back in sunny Italy they'd been boys together and all that sort of thing. Really seemed fond of him. By profession they were both pretty much alike it appears, small rascals, willing to do most anything, within reason, for good money. But they object to being killed it seems, and this one objects to having his brother get killed and nothing done about it.

"He'd been to see Crasher, had tried to collect what was due the dead one, and Crasher was in a horrid temper, wouldn't give him a cent, threatened him, and so on; threw him out, hurt him some. So the little weasel comes to me, with much more up his sleeve than Gus had any idea of. If he had he'd have paid him quick!

"Well, here's the gist of it. You see such a business as Vaughn's had to use these spies and informers. Vaughn used Crasher and Crasher used the lesser lights. Outside of those super-criminals you read about, who hold the absolute loyalty of hundreds of assistants by direful revenge on any squealer, there's no safety in it. The strength of a chain's in its weakest link, and some of these gentry are pretty weak. Look at the line, Bess. Vaughn had the dope on his victims, and used Crasher to do the dirty work. He deputed it, had to, and the small fry had the dope on him. Risky business.

"You remember when old man Smith came home—paralysed?"

Bessie looked up sharply. "Yes?"

"Well he was paralysed with a blackjack! Not on his doorstep—a long way from there. He took a cab when he left the steamer, the cab was driven by this gentleman, and presently another man got in, and a little later another. By and by they got out, the two last, and carried out Mr. Smith. They laid him in the gutter, his head banged against the curb, and all cleared out."

"How did he know it was Mr. Smith?"

"Gave him his name and address when he took the cab, of course."

"Oh yes, stupid of me. Where did they leave him?"

"North end of Central Park somewhere, he wasn't sure. And Bess—this was as much as a week before the old fellow got home . . ."

"Where does Crasher come in?"

"He was one of the two men who got into the cab."

"But Jim, if Crasher knew that this fellow was in on that job he'd never have dared—"

"Exactly. He didn't know. The cab-driver was supposed to be Carlo. Carlo was sick and sent his brother. Crasher never knew he had a brother. See?"

"Were they twins?"

"No, but pretty much of a size and general appearance. And it was night."

"Does he know who the other man was?"

"He thinks he does. A good gun-man, but crazy to get back to Italy. Crasher sent him, paid him high to stay away. But he found life too dull or something. Anyhow he's back again, but hiding, afraid Crasher'll know he's here, and our little friend is onto him. They are from the same town—another thing Crasher didn't know, so our boy chummed up with him, asking questions about folks back there.

"Then Carlo turns up in the morgue, and nothing done about it. So Emilio tells his friend about Carlo, and what he thinks of Augustus, and his friend unbosoms himself as to the same, they exchange confidences about that taxi-cab affair, and they make vows of vengeance. But both are careful persons, they know the limitations of their position, so Paolo comes to me. How about it?"

Bessie was looking at him with shining eyes. "Gorgeous!" she breathed. "Simply gorgeous. Especially your grip on the gentleman's name! And back of Crasher I seem to see the fine Italian hand of our esteemed friend the corpse."

Jim quite agreed with her. "Yes, it looks so to me. Here's the old man, persuaded to make that awful will."

"If he did make it!"

"Yes, if he did make it. Anyhow he's been travelling awhile and maybe had a change of heart. Maybe he meant to come back and look into things for himself. As he evidently wasn't wanted I agree with your suggestion as to the will. No, sir! Wade Vaughn didn't want to have him inquiring round. He was too comfortably fixed.

"So via the ever useful Crasher and an accommodating cabman the old gentleman is picked up as soon as he lands, and—attended to. Doubtless they went through him efficiently. No identification, no letters, money, passport, notebooks—anything. Just one more victim of the crime wave. Policemen picked him up, took him to Bellevue or somewhere, never regained consciousness—"

"Hold on, hold on," interposed his wife. "After a while he did recover consciousness and somehow got as far as his house before he collapsed. If he came to in a hospital he'd have told 'em who he was. And they'd never have let him out in that shape."

"Ye-es. There are some difficulties. But we can follow it up. Let's see—it's nine or ten years back. Have to do some hunting in hospital records."

"Did your Beppo or Marco or whatever he is get the name of the steamer?"

"No, he wasn't that smart," Jim admitted ruefully. "Wasn't sure about the date either."

"Never mind. Mrs. Warner can give us the time of his arrival at the house and we can go back of that and look at passenger lists of incoming steamers, can't we? Then you'll know just what date to inquire about in the hospitals."

"Yes! And forty-'leven* hospitals, each with any number of unconscious old gentlemen! We'd better try police stations too; they'd have thought he was drunk."

"How do you know he was unconscious when found, Jim?"

"He was when they left him—for dead. But see here—Guido may be wrong about that week. The old fellow may have pulled himself together and toddled home that same night!"

Bess considered this a moment but dismissed it as immaterial. "We can tell when we get the steamer arrival. Plenty of work, young man. But it can wait till after the inquest; have to I guess."

He agreed with her on this, with intense gravity. "Since that ceremony begins at ten tomorrow I think your sagacious observation is correct my dear." After he was properly punished for this impertinence, they set themselves in good earnest to compare impressions.

"Where do you stand now, Bessie—as to the family? You've had them under observation for two days."

"Ye-es. But you see it is a very difficult family to observe. They appear to be good actors all of them—had to be, under Vaughn! There's no grief, that's sure, which is nothing against them, and no pretence of it, which is something for them. As for any part in the murder—it looks worst for Iris of course."

"Don't you fret about Iris," Jim told her. "If he tries that pistol stunt we'll discredit him so completely that he can't make any impression afterward. And Davis told me I needn't worry about anything he might attempt in the poison line. But what does your feminine intuition tell you about these folks?"

"I should say Iris couldn't have done it. And Hal couldn't have done it. That's how I *feel*. But I may be wrong at that. Ten years of living with that man, under him, must have done something to anybody's character!"

"Well. You seem reluctant to approach the lady of the house."

"I am reluctant. I will first dismiss the servants, with the general suggestion that each one of them may have had a share in it or that any one of them may have deliberately added murder to murder, just piled it on, to relieve their minds! Do you realize the maid's position, Jim? And that the cook was her mother? And that Joe was in love with her? Also that there was some connection with previous crime for all three of them? Furthermore, if they did, I don't blame them a particle!"

"You've lost your moral sense, my poor girl. Don't you know murder is a crime?"

"That's all very pretty, Jim, but there isn't a crime in the calendar to equal that man's slow cruelty. And his use of his power over those poor "clients" of his! He was worse than Jack the Ripper."

"Granting that, which brings us to consider those clients, what do you think about them?"

"I think it is very likely that some of them were implicated. And as before I don't blame them if they were!"

"Shocking!" said Jim, "simply shocking! And now perhaps you will bring yourself to give me your opinion of Mrs. Warner."

"Mrs. Warner is one of the most wonderful women I ever saw," began Bessie slowly. "Do you remember Jean Valjean,* who trained his muscles so that he could climb up the corner of a room?"

"Yes," her husband answered, smiling. "But I never believed

it. Do you think she can?"

"Mentally, she can. She gives me the impression of incredible strength of character. Like—like—you've read of those savages who are tortured to death and never make a whimper? Or what was his name? That old Roman who burned his hand off to show what Romans were like?"

"Mmm! Yes. Mucius Scaevola.* I never believed that either."

"You have to believe in Mrs. Warner anyhow. Now just *think*. She'd evidently worshipped that sister of hers, and Vaughn—we can see a little of how he must have treated her, and she killed herself. Here is this woman, widowed, crippled, disfigured, disinherited, and the only person on earth to look out for those two children. Even if she could have escaped with them, any sort of court would have given them back to him—what could she bring against him—that would hold? And being sane, and brave, and conscientious, she couldn't take her sister's way out—she couldn't leave the children. She had to take her medicine, and Jim—I don't dare think too closely of what she had to stand..."

He nodded, grimly, his mouth in a hard line. "Quite so, Bess."

"I had a little talk with Iris, now and then. I'd say a word of admiration about her aunt, and she'd show what she thought of her, almost worship. But she's too well bred to chat with the maid; most of what I got was by listening. Both she and Hal have a feeling toward her that is beyond anything I ever met before. And they can't imagine the half of it I fancy. Jim—"

"Yes dear?"

"I'm not reconstructing the crime. I'm reconstructing the virtue. First she would have to conceal from the children her own feelings. She was alone mind you, unable to get out to see anyone, seems to have had no friends but Mrs. Todd. She had to school herself to be "submissive and obedient" to that—devil, which was enough, but she had also to help the children to be submissive and obedient too! She couldn't complain, she had no confidant, she had no sure hope even—he might turn them all out whenever he chose! But she hung on. Year after year she could count on achieving one more of a decent home and a good education for them. It was hard enough for them; I don't see how that high-spirited boy ever stuck it out, but she made it possible. If she'd ever let on to him how things really were he'd have broken out before now!"

"Perhaps he did, at last."

"Perhaps. But Jim—do you see something of how hard it is to judge possibilities about Mrs. Warner?"

"I do indeed," he assured her. "What she has done is so colossal that a murder or two—if thrown in—would not have shaken her."

"That's it exactly! You take an ordinary woman and if she has to chloroform a kitten she is all white and wretched—upset. But that tortured savage of mine—did he kill an enemy or so? It wouldn't have altered his state of mind at all."

"Then you think it is possible—?"

"I think it is possible. I think it would have been more than justifiable. But I don't think she did it."

"Why not? On account of her being crippled?"

"No. But on account of their being off for good that morning. If they were all going to be free, at last, why complicate matters."

Jim was not so well satisfied. "That may have been a blind. To reassure the young folks. Let's see—something had to be done quick, to save Iris. If they left as planned the boy would have had to quit college and go to work—might set him back for life. She and Iris would have to work at their typing. No money but their earnings and her three hundred dollars. Two rooms, light housekeeping outside of working hours."

"All of which was heaven compared to what they'd been standing," she insisted. "Besides you are too gloomy. A stenog ought to get twenty a week, easy, I did, and twenty-five later. The boy should have covered another twenty and Mrs. Warner ten at least, as well as her income—why that's fifty a week! Plenty of families live on less."

"But with Vaughn removed there's six hundred more."

"Shame on you, Jim! Even a detective can't suspect Mrs. Warner of killing a man for six hundred dollars a year."

"Doesn't look likely," he admitted.

"Besides she didn't know about the six hundred."

"How do you know she didn't?"

"Because if she had, and had been as unscrupulous as you cruelly suggest, she'd have done it long ago!" triumphed Bessie.

"Might have waited as long as she could on account of the boy, and then when they had [to] leave on account of Iris—non-sense!" he said irritably. "We are not a bit nearer as to who did anything!"

"We are not. There's too much of it. Too many people involved. I've read lots of stories about one man committing many murders, but never a one about many murderers combining on one victim!"

"You ought to be in bed, Bessikins! Come on, I'll go over with you."

"You are right," she agreed. "You can stay, be ready for tomorrow." They found Mrs. Warner was still up and wished to see them. She was much impressed to learn that Bessie was her husband's professional assistant. "And a good one," he boasted. "Meet the firm, Hunt and Hunt, Private Detectives. And your very good friends."

"I have at least to thank you for a most pleasing and efficient assistant," Mrs. Warner answered. "And am I to understand that this amiable young lady has been detecting all over the house— discovering all our secrets?"

"She has indeed, and to some purpose."

"Jim was here too, nights," Bessie explained. "I let him in. And it was lucky we were on hand, for Mr. Crasher has been up to his little tricks."

"We thought you'd be interested to get it all clear in your mind before tomorrow. It will be less startling at times." And both took turns or interrupted each other, giving her a full account of what they had seen in yard and house.

Her air of relief was unmistakable. "Then he can't drag us in, not successfully?"

"Not an inch," said Jim. "He'll try it; we are keeping dark just to let him, and then he will be so completely discredited that it will be all up with his business. And what is more—Bessie, my masculine intuition tells me that Mrs. Warner will sleep the better if we tell her all we really have got on Crasher."

"If that man can be—removed from the scene it will give me more comfort than any sedative you can offer," she at once agreed.

She listened eagerly to the story of Emilio, nodding her head slowly as they proceeded. "I have wondered much about my poor father's miserable home-coming. I did not love him, but he was old and alone, and to die speechless like that—! Old Jane told me he seemed to long to tell her something, but after Mr. Vaughn took charge there was no chance."

"Do you know where those servants are now, Mrs. Warner?"

"No, I have not the least idea. I wish I had."

"Perhaps we can find them," Bessie suggested.

"No, my dear. The firm is engaged at once to follow the trail. What is more important is Mr. Crasher's trail. I'm so glad you told me this. He is too dangerous a man to be at large."

Jim asked if she could give them the date of her father's return.

"Not at all accurately," she slowly admitted. "But his death was in the papers—"

"Of course!" Jim was crestfallen. "And we can look up [the] steamer list before that."

"Wait a moment," said Mrs. Warner, "will you see if Mrs. Todd's light is still burning?"

It was, and the 'phone brought prompt reply.

"Bed? No. Why should I be in bed. I'm all wrought up thinking of the doings tomorrow. It's mighty nice of your Strong Arm Squad to undertake to tote me over."

"They'll love to. And it must be very early before the crowds come. Will you come to breakfast?"

"I'll be delighted, my dear, delighted. I don't know how long it is since I've been out to a meal!"

"Mrs. Todd—can you remember the date of my father's return?"

"If I don't my diary will," squeaked the 'phone, "Wait a second." They waited several, and presently heard, "Here 'tis," and she gave the date. "What you goin' to do with it my dear?"

"I'll tell you all about it when there's anything to tell. It's just a 'lead' for my nice detective."

"He is nice," chirped the old lady. "Give him my compliments! Good night."

Mrs. Warner hung up the 'phone and turned to them with a cordial smile. She gave a hand to each. "Thank you so much for coming. I feel that I have two real friends in you young people. You'll stay won't you, Mr. Hunt? This admirable young lady of yours will take care of you. Go and feed him, my dear. And if you don't mind, I'd like a cup of cocoa myself. She makes the best cocoa I ever tasted," she added, and Bessie ran off happily.

"I hated to impose on you," Jim explained, "but it seemed wiser to have a totally unsuspected person in the house. She has been really useful, too."

"Useful! She's been invaluable. Not only super-efficient, but understanding! I don't know what I should have done without her. She was quite right about the difficulty of getting new people in at such a time . . . Goodnight. I shall sleep, thanks to you both."

The Inquest

The large double parlors of the Smith house were packed to bursting on Saturday morning at ten.*

But for determined policemen on front steps, side gate, alley gate, and guarding the long fence, there would not have been standing room anywhere in the house or yard; as it was a disappointed crowd stood on the side walk, and milled around on Field Street and in the alley, quite in vain.

It was generally held that such a fascinating investigation should have been carried on in the largest hall in town, but the authorities thought otherwise. Sufficient space was roped in the farther room for the coroner, the jury, the reporter's table, and the important witnesses.

The family, with Dr. Akers, sat near the coroner, also Jim Hunt and Mrs. Hunt, the last named no longer in cap and apron but looking alertly pretty in "plain clothes"—not too plain.

Tom Davis was close to the Hunts, and exchanged some words with them from time to time. Mr. Crasher, with a grim look on his heavy face, placed himself with Clargis and Flannigan.

Of all present none wore so eager and delighted an aspect as Mrs. Todd. Immensely overjoyed was she at her unlooked-for outing. Hal and Jim Hunt had brought her over, chair and all, long before the crowd arrived, and there she sat by Mrs. Warner's side, holding her hand, and whispering so persistently that she had to be repeatedly called to order.

It was inevitable that all eyes centered on poor Mrs. Warner, as some thought of her, with sympathetic glances. Others, looking for a murderer in every one concerned, studied her scarred face relentlessly. It was difficult, however, to read much in a black patch and twisted mouth, save that the more suspicious deemed her expression "sinister."

"It's a shame!" whispered Mrs. Todd, fiercely. "They ought to be ashamed of themselves—staring so." Yet she had been surreptitiously staring herself, ever since arriving, trying to make out in this sad wreck the features of the good looking girl she remembered.

"Sh," murmured Mrs. Warner. "Don't mind, dear. I don't." And to herself she thought, as she had over and over since Wednesday morning, "He's gone! He's gone! Nothing else matters. We are *free*." They were all strengthened to bear this unpleasant inquisition by agreeable thoughts. As Hal had said at their early cheerful breakfast, "If they don't hang us, mother, we are all right!"

Their long training served them well on this occasion, and the three showed no undue cheerfulness or any other expression save that of close attention.

143

The coroner, Mr. Michael Martin, however, gave every sign of satisfaction. He liked his position, enjoyed making searching inquiries, what he considered artful inquiries, and squeezing a witness's information out of him as if he was a tube of toothpaste.

The present subject of inquiry he found unusually fascinating, and was proud indeed that he had the privilege of presiding at the very first inquest on a "multi-murder."

"D'ye see, my dear," he had told his wife that morning, "It's not to find what killed the man once, which is hard enough, but to find what killed him four times—five times there's some that hints! It's a most amazing case."

He had read every word he could find about it for two days, and felt himself equal to any amount of horrifying disclosure.

The jury were duly impanelled; they and he filed solemnly out to the still room upstairs and "viewed the body," and all were settled again in their places.

The first person to be examined was Mrs. Warner. Her chair was rolled forward a little. Everyone's attention was fixed on the marred face, the black patch, the hands holding so tightly the arms of her chair.

"When did you last see Mr. Vaughn alive, Mrs. Warner?"

"At dinner, Tuesday evening."

"And where did he go after that?"

"To his office."

"And where did you go?"

"My son carried me upstairs to my room."

"You saw nothing further of Mr. Vaughn that night?"

"No."

"Did you hear anything further?"

"Yes."

"What did you hear?"

"I heard a loud voice in his office."

"At what time?"

"At nearly seven o'clock."

"Was it usual for Mr. Vaughn to have callers in his home?"

"It was."

Mr. Martin consulted his notes. He was in no hurry and had evidently arranged a certain order of exercises in his mind.

"Now will you please tell us exactly what happened Wednesday morning?" A soft stir ran through the rooms. People leaned forward, tried to hear better. She told the story calmly.

"My niece Iris and my son Hal came to my room at a little before eight. She was in some alarm because on going down to see about breakfast she found there was no breakfast and looking for the cook she found the kitchen empty and clean. Then my son came down and they went to look for them—there were three servants, the cook, Norah Brown, her daughter Nellie Brown, our maid, and a man. Not one of them was to be found. Their rooms were empty and clean; the beds had not been slept in. So they came to tell me. I told them to get some breakfast quickly, and perhaps Mr. Vaughn would not be down till later. He never wished to be called for breakfast, but came down between eight and half-past.

"We ate ours and waited, but he did not come, and there was no sound from his room. Then we got worried, the strange sudden disappearance of the servants, and this delay, so I had Hal go and knock on his bedroom door. There was no answer. He called and hammered—no answer. Then I grew really alarmed and telephoned Dr. Akers."

"Why Dr. Akers?"

"He was Mr. Vaughn's physician, our family physician and good friend. I told him I was afraid, and that perhaps he'd better bring someone—he came, and brought Mr. Hunt."

"What did you mean by 'someone'?"

"I meant someone in authority, a policeman perhaps; I was worried."

"Had you any reason to suspect foul play?"

"The disappearance of all three servants—the locked door— the silence."

"That will do for the moment, Mrs. Warner. Dr. Ross Akers—" Dr. Akers came forward, quietly yet with an air of professional importance.

"You are the physician regularly employed by this family, Dr. Akers?"

"For many years. I attended Mr. Smith in his last illness, Mr. Vaughn from time to time, also Mrs. Warner and the children."

"Will you give us your account of what happened Wednesday morning?"

"I was having my breakfast as usual. My friend Mr. Hunt dropped in at about eight fifteen to ask me a technical question or two about a case he was interested in. My telephone rang and Mrs. Warner called me up. She was anxious, alarmed, begged me to come at once, and added that perhaps I'd better bring someone with me. I told her that Jim Hunt was there and I'd bring him if that would ease her mind any."

"Had you any reason to think that Mrs. Warner's alarm was justified?"

"Not until I learned of the absence of the servants."

"At what time did you arrive at the house?"

"Not until nearly nine. We were delayed by the traffic. I

found the family much alarmed by that time as was natural. With Hal's assistance we found a key that opened Mr. Vaughn's bedroom door. There was no one there; the bed had not been slept in. The other door of the room was locked on the inside."

The coroner made a special note of this careful locking of an empty room. "Go on Dr. Akers."

"Then we approached the door of his room downstairs. This was locked, leaving the key in the lock. At this moment the bell rang. I was near the door and opened it. Mr. Crasher promptly forced his way in, and insisted on remaining, against the protest of the family." Mr. Crasher was seen to start forward as if to speak, but thought better of it, and Dr. Akers continued.

"He claimed that he had an engagement with Miss Iris, which she denied. Meanwhile Hal Warner brought some slender pliers, and with some difficulty the key was turned and the door opened. We were confronted by the dead body of Mr. Vaughn, sitting at his desk. Mr. Hunt and I went in, also Mr. Crasher, and made a cursory examination. There was a severe bruise on top of his head, a bullet wound in the right temple, a thin cord tight around the neck, and a slender knife thrust down to the hilt inside the collar bone."

Though all present were quite familiar with these facts from profuse newspaper descriptions there was an indrawn breath of horror at this cooly given list, especially when at a look from the coroner Mr. Clargis came forward and laid on the table the identical cord and knife.

"Miss Iris became hysterical," Dr. Akers continued. "I urged her to go upstairs—went with her, and Hal carried his mother. It was a ghastly sight for women. Mrs. Warner kept her head. She told me to tell Mr. Hunt that she wished to engage him as a detective, and sent word for Mr. Crasher to leave the house. This he was loath to do, but there were three of us . . . "

"Very well, Dr. Akers. That will do. Mr. James Hunt."

Mr. Hunt took the stand with a calm and noncommital air. He corroborated Dr. Akers's story in every detail, adding that as soon as the ladies were gone and Mr. Crasher induced to leave, that he had at once notified the police.

"What do you mean by 'induced to leave?'"

"The lady of the house sent word for him to go, and he refused. So Mr. Warner, Dr. Akers and I—insisted."

"Do you mean you used force?"

"No, your honor, but we—seemed likely to, and he left."

"What did you do before the police came?"

"I looked around a bit. When the ladies went upstairs I had already given a hasty examination of Mr. Vaughn's room, Mr. Crasher doing the same, and now I took a look around the premises, taking great care to disturb nothing. The servants' rooms were cleaned out completely; they left nothing whatever. The kitchen was in order except for getting breakfast—it was a very neat getaway. I found nothing whatever to build on.

"Then I had some talk with Mrs. Warner, getting details about the servants and so on, till the officers arrived."

"That will do for the present, Mr. Hunt. Mr. Thomas Davis."

Mr. Davis testified that he was the police surgeon, that he had arrived at nine-forty Wednesday morning, found the body of Mr. Vaughn and examined it. That deceased had received at least four visible injuries, already described, sufficient to have caused death. That he judged death to have occurred some ten or twelve hours before, and that Dr. Akers, physician to the deceased, had concurred in this opinion.

"Can you give no closer opinion as to the hour of the attack—or attacks?"

"It was probably twelve hours or more earlier, but this was but a hasty examination. Since the autopsy I do not hesitate to say all of twelve to thirteen."

"And this first examination was made at nine forty. Mr. Vaughn then was killed at about eight forty Tuesday evening?"

"Yes your honor, between eight and nine, I should say."

The audience felt that at last they were getting somewhere. All the reporters carefully set down the hour of death. Mr. Martin seemed well pleased with the unfolding of the story under his searching and connected questions. He allowed Mr. Davis at his request to defer the full account of the later autopsy as he much preferred to keep on with his sequence of events that fateful morning.

Messrs. Clargis, Flannigan and Moore told of receiving notification of the case at nine twenty-five, and arriving at the house at nine forty, that they had found the body as described, that Mr. Davis had made his examination and left, having other pressing duties that morning. That they had then proceeded to examine those present, beginning with Dr. Akers. Mr. Martin stated that he preferred to question the family directly and would ask Mr. Clargis to describe their further investigations.

Mr. Clargis, giving his official status as the others had done, repeated briefly the finding of the body and its various wounds, the last with some unction. "The most thoroughly murdered man I ever saw your honor. After the questions were over we set to work at searching the premises, beginning with the office or study where the body was. Whoever did that job knew their business, your honor. There wasn't a fingermark on anything, even the glass he had been drinking out of and the decanter he had lifted—wiped clean!"

Again the listeners stirred with enthusiasm. Here was competence.

"Both doors had been locked; the key to the other one was gone. There were four windows, all unfastened, and on the east side one was open. There was a safe in the corner, and no fingermarks on that either—it had been wiped clean as a whistle. We had no means to force it at the time, but continued our search. When we came to the grate, it had an iron front placed in it, covering the whole space. We got this out without difficulty, and there was a heap of ashes, with a sort of a note on top of it."

Breathless attention, eager straining forward to see and hear.

"What do you mean by 'a sort of a note?'"

"Just a rough scrap of paper your honor. It was printed on with a soft pencil, and said, 'Vaughn's private business is closed out.'"

"Vaughn's private business!" repeated the coroner slowly, and made a note of it. One of the press men hastily jotted it down as a good headline.

"Proceed, Mr. Clargis."

Whereat Mr. Clargis proceeded with great detail to recount the careful search of the whole house, with no results bearing on the matter in hand. "Except that it was clear that the departure of the three servants was a prearranged job, your honor. And the last thing they did was to *dust*!"

"Dust? What do you mean?"

"Exactly that, your honor. They'd gone over everything with a cloth. There wasn't a fingerprint on a door, on a chair, on a dish—so far as we've been able to find yet."

This was felt by all present as sealing the fate of those servants—when caught. The coroner was struck by it at once.

"I suppose, Mr. Clargis, that measures have been taken to secure the runaways?"

Mr. Clargis smiled. "First thing that was done of course. Everything that the police of New York know how to do is being done, you may be sure." He then gave a detailed account of his examination of the yard, accompanied by Flannigan, Moore and Hunt. "Not a thing did we find till we got to the gate into the alley, and there was a footprint or two, at the side, up to a box that stood there by standing on which we could see over the fence. Outside we found marks of someone standing around near the gate, also the same footprints as inside. Following these we came to the lot next but one on the west, and inside that fence, behind some lilac bushes, was the dead body of a man."

This second corpse awakened some stir of interest, but the coroner refused to be impressed. He soon elicited the information as to his identity, and that he seemed to have died from a blow on the head similar in appearance to that on the head of Mr. Vaughn, and that he had been dead at least eight hours. The yard in which the body was found belonged to Mr. P. R. Hudson, and that gentleman was the next witness.

He seemed incensed at being brought into any connection with the crime, and volubly protested an utter lack of knowledge of the matter.

"I was out of the house pretty much all night, Mr. Coroner, and here's four friends of mine will back me up in that!"

The four friends all agreed with Mr. Hudson that they had spent the night playing poker at their club, till near daylight, going somewhat farther to state, "and when we brought him home he was in no condition to commit a murder. All we could do to get him to bed; he was dead to the world."

Mrs. P. R. Hudson, [a] square-build elderly woman, with a determined jaw, gave definite corroboration as to the hour of her husband's return, the nature of his condition, and the fact that after being put to bed he had remained there.

"He left home about eight o'clock Wednesday evening, your honor. Said he might be a little late, and not to wait for him. But I waited! He came home at five o'clock in the morning! He never did such a thing before, and I can promise you he never will again!"

Judging by her expression, and that of Mr. Hudson, this promise was reliable, and the heartless spectators seemed to derive pleasure from the thought. She continued firmly.

"So your dead man must have been dead five or six hours before my husband got home, and whoever has been dropping corpses in our back yard, we are not responsible."

It occurred to some that Mrs. Hudson was a more likely suspect than her husband, but Mr. Martin did not pursue the investigation in that direction. He leaned back in his chair and ran over his notes.

"This inquest is not upon the body found in the yard of Mr. Hudson," he announced, "save and except as this secondary murder, if we may call it so, may have been committed by the same hand as that which struck down Mr. Vaughn."

Indeed no one was much interested in the incidental decease of Mr. Carlo, now lying in the morgue for anyone to see. He had only been killed once, and was apparently not missed.

Further Information

After a careful examination and rearrangement of his papers, Mr. Martin settled himself firmly in his chair and again called on Mrs. Warner.

"Now Mrs. Warner, will you tell us of your personal relations with your brother-in-law, of his attitude toward the young people, toward the servants. Whatever has connection with this tragedy."

The witness was again wheeled forward. Bessie brought a glass of water and set it on the table within her reach. The coroner added, "You had better give your entire acquaintance with the deceased, as briefly as convenient."

The jury settled themselves to listen with a hopeful interest. There was an eager feeling throughout the crowded room that this was going to be exciting.

"Mr. Vaughn came here in 1907, from the west I think. He

won some important case my father was interested in; father seemed to like him very much, brought him to the house often, made a friend of him. He wished to marry my sister Iris—she hated him. We ran away, my sister and I. A little later we were both married . . . I to Mr. Haldane Warner, my sister to Rev. Sydney A. Booth.

"There was an automobile accident—all of us were riding together. My husband and Iris's husband were killed. I was hurt, as you see. My sister was so overcome by the shock as almost to lose her mind; she was quite irresponsible. I was unconscious for many days. When I came to myself I was in Wade Vaughn's house—and he had married my sister."

"This was within a short time?"

"Within two weeks."

"Was your sister—in her right mind?"

"She was not. She had lucid intervals, but then the memory of what she had lost rushed over her, and the horror of her position, and she broke down again."

"What do you mean by the horror of her position?"

"She had always had a strong repugnance for Mr. Vaughn."

"Was he kind to her?"

"He was—more than affectionate."

"You felt that she was not happy?"

"As soon as her mind was really clear she committed suicide."

All this sad tale had been fully recounted in the newspapers, with ample invention to support lack of knowledge, but the brief cold story told by her sister sent a shiver through the crowd.

"Was your father living at the time of the accident?"

"He was, but he had said he would never see us again, and left Mr. Vaughn to attend to us. When he married Iris, which had been so strongly urged by my father, he made a will, which is I think known to the public."

It was. It had been widely discussed.

"When your sister died you felt it your duty to remain and take care of your little niece as well as your son?"

"I had no choice. In my condition I could not earn enough to support them. Also the scanty bequests left them dependent absolutely on the pleasure of Mr. Vaughn. And no friend would have been willing to take us so long as he stood ready to give us his support."

"Why do you think he was willing to care for an invalid and two children? He has been credited with real benevolence for doing so?"

"I have never been sure of his reasons. One was perhaps the credit you have just mentioned. One perhaps that he was at liberty to use what he chose from the trust fund of sixty thousand dollars for the maintenance of the children—and used very little, on them. Another perhaps that I kept his house efficiently, without a salary. A fourth I am sure of; it was the obedience clause in that will. He had in us three utterly helpless people, obliged to obey his slightest word, and he delighted in it."

"Do you mean that he took advantage of it? Was he cruel to you?"

Mrs. Warner smiled her crooked smile. "Not with blows."

"In what way then?"

"In a constant petty tyranny over all of us, in the most arbitrary exaction of that 'obedience.' Even for a sweet and submissive little girl it was difficult, [and] terribly difficult for a growing boy."

"And for you?" Mr. Martin showed a touch of genuine sympathy. "Tell me, Mrs. Warner, could not something have been done for your injuries with modern surgery?"

"Certainly there could have been. But it would have been expensive and Mr. Vaughn did not think it necessary. He said I was sufficiently useful to him as it was."

A wave of repugnance swept through the listening crowd. The coroner consulted his notes again.

"After your father's death Mr. Vaughn moved into this house?"

"Yes, it belonged to him, with the rest of the property."

"And you were given the room which had been your father's?"

"And my mother's when she was alive. He gave it to me because of the speaking tube to the kitchen and upstairs telephone. In using these I discovered a mechanical trick of my father's by which he could listen to conversation in the study below, or in the kitchen."

This was news. The reporters wrote furiously, people leaned forward eagerly, the jury looked at one another. Pencil artists made rapid sketches of the speaker, of her son and Iris.

"And you made use of this device?"

"I did."

"Will you tell us something of what you overheard, so far as it may have a bearing on the tragedy."

"I learned that Mr. Vaughn was in the habit of receiving clients in the study, which he used as an office. These visitors generally came in the evening. As I listened it became apparent that most of them came to pay him money as the price of silence. He was a blackmailer."

Here was news with a vengeance. This prominent successful

lawyer, this man hitherto supposed to have so benevolently supported three dependents—a blackmailer!

"This is a serious charge, Mrs. Warner. You are very sure?"

"I am absolutely sure. In some cases he held mortgages, or had made loans, and he collected his money relentlessly; but generally it was blackmail. Through his professional sources and with the help of a private detective employed for the purpose, he gathered damaging facts about people, and they paid him to keep silent."

"Can you tell us the name of this detective?"

"Certainly I can. It was Augustus Crasher."

Mr. Crasher had shown considerable uneasiness since she had first mentioned those "ears"; evidently he had been running over in his mind what she might have heard implicating him, but after all, he seemed to decide, there is no crime in being a private detective. So when his name was mentioned he showed no surprise, or any other emotion.

The coroner made no comment, but continued. "This inquiry is not as to the nature of Mr. Vaughn's business except as it may have a bearing on the murder—the murders. Was there anything which you heard which might lead you to fear retaliation on the part of any of his—"

"Victims? There was indeed. Some were furious, abusive, often threatening."

"Did Mr. Vaughn seem alarmed?"

"Not in the least. He seemed to fairly enjoy it. It was the same pleasure he took in the helplessness of his family. He liked to have them wriggle, totally unable to escape. Last Tuesday evening—" as the fatal date was mentioned the breathless interest of the hearers deepened "—there were three particularly unhappy clients.

"The first, who came before seven, was very angry and threatening. He said, 'Have you never thought, Wade Vaughn, that you may go too far for once, and get yours!'

"'I've often thought of it' he said. 'It's quite exciting. But you are not the man to do anything like that. You make too much noise to be dangerous. Better pay up and trot along.' He did."

"Do you know how much they paid?"

"No, but it was cash; he always insisted on that. He used to count it, at least there'd be a pause, and then he'd say 'correct' or 'OK,' and give them a receipt—'For professional services. On account.' He did that Tuesday night. The man read it over, aloud.

"'You are at liberty to show it,' Mr. Vaughn said. 'And if people think my charges are a little high, and wonder why you pay so much, you can tell them if you wish.' And he gave that little chuckle of his."

"What time was this?"

"Still early, a little after seven. We have dinner at six, and then Mr. Vaughn used to go to his desk and sit there. He had his whiskey by him, and would take some now and then, toss it off the way men do, and take naps, just doze in his chair."

"How do you know these details?" inquired the coroner.

"Sometimes he would insist on my spending the evening with him. He'd carry me in there and I'd have to stay till he took me upstairs . . . "

"And who else that night?"

"The next was a quiet man I had not heard before, quiet but bitter. He called him a blackmailer and threatened to have the law on him. Mr. Vaughn only laughed, remarking, 'The law, my dear fellow, is my business. You are my client and I am merely collecting for professional services. What you call me is quite immaterial so long as you pay.' This man was pretty desperate, too. He changed his tone, swore he could not pay, that he hadn't the money. Mr. Vaughn told him he knew how he could find it, same as he did before. He said, 'You clear out now and come back with the money, or it's goodbye to home and family for quite a stretch.' There was a silence, and then the man said, low and quiet, I could hardly hear him, 'Very well. I will come back.' And he left."

A little thrill stirred the more excitable among the listeners. Had he come back that night?

"And the third, Mrs. Warner?"

"The third was a woman."

"And you listened?"

"Usually I did not when it was a woman . . . This time I did. She was a new visitor. She had a slight foreign accent, and was more excited, more dramatic than most. She took it hard. But he had her absolutely and she'd been obliged to sell her jewels to buy him off. It wasn't enough at that; he insisted on her bringing more. She protested, she begged and prayed, she said she had no way of getting any more. And he told her—"

"Yes, Mrs. Warner? What did he tell her?"

"He told her, 'As handsome a woman as you are, my dear, with as many friends, can always find ways of getting money.'"

If any in that audience had retained a spark of sympathy with the late Mr. Vaughn they relinquished it then.

"And then—?"

"She answered, 'Hell hath no fury like a woman scorned.'*

"He replied, 'I am glad you are reading the English classics, my dear.' And chuckled."

159

There was a cheerful activity among those of the reporters whose papers stressed "the sex motif." They seemed to scent dark scenes in the office of Mr. Vaughn.

"It would be your opinion that there was reason in Mr. Vaughn's dealing to account for attempts at murder?"

"More than reason."

Again the coroner ran over the page of notes he had prepared for his examination. "And now Mrs. Warner, will you tell us all you can about these three servants who have so suddenly disappeared."

"The two women, mother and daughter, Norah Brown and Nellie Brown, came to us about two years ago. Mrs. Brown was a satisfactory servant, though gloomy. The girl Nellie was excitable, and often seemed unhappy, but did her work well. Joe White, the man-servant, came some months later.

"He was quite a superior person, had been in the army overseas, was evidently educated. He seemed to hate his position, though filling it with elaborate accuracy."

"Just what was his position?"

"Whatever Mr. Vaughn chose to demand of him. He waited on table, drove the car, worked in the garden, and acted as body servant."

"And what did you learn about these people?"

"The same story. Mr. Vaughn had them in his power. He had got them off from some criminal charges—I do not know whether they were guilty or not—but he held some sort of evidence against them, so strong that they were in danger of life-imprisonment or the chair. To save their lives they must accept his terms, and as they could not pay him in money he took it out in service."

"You make out a terrible case against your brother-in-law, Mrs. Warner."

"I do. And the results have been terrible."

"You heard nothing which indicated the intention to—murder?"

"Nothing direct, from any of them. But a sufficient hatred."

"Did you hear anything as to plans for escape?"

"Only what I have already told the police." She repeated the proposed arrangement, apparently leading to escape by power-boat and steamer. Mr. Clargis was then called and rather disgustedly told of their efforts to follow up this clue.

"If the lady heard 'em right, and I don't doubt she did, your honor, they must have changed their minds altogether. There was three who got off in that boat, but not this lot."

Sketches were made of Mr. Clargis' disappointed countenance. The busy press men saw admirable comedy in the captain's reluctant examination of the three men.

After Mrs. Warner's withdrawal from the foreground the extreme excitability of Mrs. Todd became so marked that she was next summoned, and was brought forward in a twitter of pleasurable emotion.

"First time I've been out of my house for ten years, Judge," she cheerfully began. "It's a real treat!"

Mr. Martin surveyed her appreciatively. "We are glad to have your assistance, Mrs. Todd. Now will you be good enough to tell us what you know of the comings and goings about Mr. Vaughn's office in the evenings immediately preceding this melancholy event."

"Not so melancholy either, to my mind," she chirped. "If ever a man needed killing it was that one."

"Not opinions, if you please, Mrs. Todd, just facts. I understand you have amused yourself by keeping a pretty close watch on this corner."

"I certainly have, your Worship. And pretty goings on there's been! A decent man does his business downtown and leaves it there. But this one had all manner of visitors at all hours of the night. I'm a poor sleeper, Judge, and when I can't sleep I don't try to, I sit up and take notice. My window is right on the corner, I'm thankful to say. I can see four ways up and down. And there's a street lamp."

"What sort of visitors have you noticed?"

"All sorts. Rich and poor, mostly rich. Men and women, mostly men. Women stayed the longest. Whichever it was they came alone, and did not want to be recognized. Some in big limousines, used to stop farther down where it wasn't so light, and then come stealing up. Some came to the front door, but most to the side. They'd pop in at the gate and knock, knock softly too, even when the window was open I could hardly hear it—and my ears are good, your Honor. Some of 'em sneaked up Field Street, out of the alley; some came down Field—from the car-line I guess."

"Was there anyone you could recognize?"

"Mostly not. All of 'em kind of pulled their hats down, men, that is; women couldn't pull theirs down any more'n they are—unless they covered their shins! They just hunched their collars a bit more and ducked their heads. There was one man used to come pretty often, seemed to have a key to the side door." She lifted her head and peered sharply about the room, suddenly pointing a withered finger at Mr. Crasher. "That's him!"

All eyes were directed at the heavy visage of that disinterested sleuth, but he showed no surprise nor alarm. Those who sketched him, however, put in whatever expression they saw fit.

"Did you ever see anything, Mrs. Todd, which would lead you to believe there was any danger to Mr. Vaughn from any of these people?"

"Some of 'em seemed pretty much worked up," opined the old lady. "Last Tuesday evening there was two that looked real excited. One was a big well-dressed man, came to the front door, early, came out early, too. He stood on the top step a minute, stiff as could be, and then turned square round and shook his fists at the door. The next man was quiet enough, and quick enough too! And then there was a woman—Mrs. Warner's told you about them all. This was a slim graceful thing, a lot of fur on. She'd been in there some time. Came out with a kind of a rush, stood there a minute with her face in her hands, and then stretched her arms up wide, as if she was calling on Heaven, the way they do in plays. Nothing happened. She scuttled off down Grove Street to where her car was."

"Did you hear on Tuesday evening, the sound of a shot?"

"I thought there was a kind of a pop, once, but there are so many cars popping here and there that I didn't pay much attention. But I saw one man that must have sneaked up from the alley, by the back yard, and along the fence inside. It was just before nine. He got in that side window that was open, and came out the same way, and ducked behind the fence again. Didn't stay but a minute."

"Do you think the noise you heard, as of a shot, was during his visit?"

"I'm sorry your Worship, I didn't notice at all. It wasn't

much of a noise."

Mrs. Todd was released, though evidently willing to hold forth much longer. She commanded warm approval from the audience, and was to be delighted next day by having her picture in the papers.

Hal Warner next took the chair, with a resolute look, and gave his account of what happened Wednesday morning.

"Were you fond of your uncle?" asked the coroner.

"No sir."

"Why not?" The boy looked at his mother, and at Iris.

"He was tyrannical—and enjoyed it."

"Was he unkind? Cruel?"

"Not—physically. He punished us children, mostly me, but it wasn't that. It was just—we couldn't call our souls our own."

"Was he unkind to your mother?"

"It wasn't a—visible unkindness, sir. He just—she had to do everything, *everything,* exactly as he said. It wasn't natural." The boy showed a good deal of emotion, in spite of evident efforts at restraint, and all was eagerly noted by the reporters.

But nothing was added to what had been already elicited, and the coroner called for Miss Iris Booth. Iris held her head very firmly. She was pale, but determined.

"Miss Iris, have you anything to add to what your aunt and cousin have told us as to Wednesday morning?"

"It all happened just as they said, and Dr. Akers said, and Mr. Hunt. Hal and I came down first and found no breakfast and the servants gone. We got some coffee and eggs and toast and took it up to Aunt Jack, and we had ours downstairs. Then Auntie got worried, and so did we, and she sent for Mr. Akers. Do I have to tell it all over?"

"What can you tell us about this engagement with Mr. Crasher?"

"Is that—necessary? Must I?"

"I think you had better. It may have some bearing on this matter."

The girl was flushed now; her eyes were in her lap. "Papa was going to make me marry him."

"Make you marry him? How could he make you?"

"It was that will. We had to mind or he could keep all the money for himself. Grandpa left it all in his hands you know. And he said that unless I married Mr. Crasher, right away, he would turn us all out of doors. And, and Dr. Akers, too. He had a mortgage on Dr. Akers' house he said. And he said if I did marry him I should have my share of the money and I could do things for Aunt Jack and Hal . . . There didn't seem to be anything else to do . . . "

"Quite mediaeval," observed the coroner drily. "Mrs. Warner, do you know anything of this bargain?"

"I know all about it," replied that lady drily. "I heard it made."

"You did not mention it in your testimony."

"No, your Honor. You told me this inquiry was not in to the nature of Mr. Vaughn's business except as it had a bearing on the murder."

"Quite true, Mrs. Warner. But this may have some bearing. Will you tell us what you know of this matter."

Iris retired and Mrs. Warner came forward again.

"This man Crasher was in constant association with Mr. Vaughn, who seemed to have a hold over him as he had with the others. I do not know in what relation. He was frequently at the house, and within the last year had been quite offensive in attentions to my niece. She could not bear him, but though she complained to her stepfather he would not stop it.

"Then last Monday afternoon I heard Mr. Vaughn and Mr. Crasher make the following agreement. Mr. Crasher expressed himself as desperately in love with my niece. Mr. Vaughn taunted him with only wanting her money. Crasher admitted that that was his first idea, but that now he was 'crazy about her' and would marry her if she hadn't a cent.

"Mr. Vaughn took him at his word. 'There isn't the slightest possibility of her marrying you unless I make her' he told him, and then demanded that if he gave him the girl he was to return him the money—all of it. This was a blow to Mr. Crasher, but Mr. Vaughn gave that little chuckle of his and put it to him clearly. 'Girl and no money, Crasher, or no girl and no money—see?' Mr. Crasher was sufficiently 'crazy about her' to accept the terms, and then Mr. Vaughn called in Iris and—applied pressure. Including the statement of how she was to have her own money!"

Mrs. Warner was silent. The packed audience breathed deep, and whispered fiercely. The coroner adjourned the inquiry until two P.M.

The Inquest Continued

Mrs. Todd refused to go home, though Hal and Mr. Hunt were quite willing to carry her.

"Jack Warner you've simply got to feed me. I haven't had such an outing in years—and years! And to think that all my observations have come in so useful. *Do* you think it was the woman or the man that did it? Or just the servants? Or somebody else? And I don't see any extreme sympathy for the corpse, do you?"

The amiable colored helper secured by Bessie Hunt had prepared sufficient lunch for them, and in the comparative retirement of a well locked dining room, with policemen protecting the hall and stairs, the family ate and rested. Mr. Hunt was with them, and Bessie, now owning her duplicity and being gratefully accepted as a friend. Dr. Akers stayed too. And before it was time to return to the parlors, Mr. Davis dropped in to confer with Mr. Hunt.

Mrs. Todd listened to all the talk with keen bright eyes and many vigorous nods and flashing smiles. "It's the nicest murder I ever heard of," said she.

Iris was particularly excited at the last bit of duplicity on the part of her stepfather. "And to think that I might have done it! I really might have! Why didn't you tell me right away, Auntie!"

"Dear child, so much has happened you don't remember some of it. You weren't going to marry him; we were all running away Wednesday morning, if this hadn't interfered. We had enough to think about."

At two o'clock they were all back in their places. Some of the crowd had stayed, lunch or no lunch. Others had pushed in when space was left. The rooms were fuller than before if that were possible. The coroner looked over his notes, and called, "Mr. Augustus Crasher!"

Mr. Crasher came forward and settled solidly into the chair as one with plenty to say.

"Mr. Crasher, did you make the bargain described with Mr. Vaughn?"

"I did, and I ain't ashamed of it. He was a hard man and out for the kale, but I hadn't the ghost of a chance with the girl without his authority, and I wanted her more than the money."

"And you were willing to—buy her?"

"I was willing to do anything to get her—then."

"Why do you say 'then,' has your feeling changed?"

"It has to some degree; I know more'n I did."

"You have some evidence to offer in regard to this murder?"

"I sure have."

"Proceed, Mr. Crasher."

Mr. Crasher proceeded, slowly and with care. "After I had

this understanding with Mr. Vaughn I was worried for fear the girl would get out of it some way, run away or some trick or other. I'm used to watching people and I made use of that empty house on the other side of Field Street, and watched this one. Also I had a man in the alley to see she didn't get off that way, that man Carlo. You know what happened to him."

"Have you any idea of his assailant?"

"I have no knowledge, but it might have been Joe White when he was making his getaway, or it might ha' been—no I've no idea. I was just watching to make sure of my girl. But there was something Carlo told me the day before they got him that has some bearing on this case. He was loafing out there in the alley and he heard a sort of soft popping in the yard here. So he peeked over the fence careful, so's not to be seen, and there was this young man here," he turned and indicated Hal Warner, "shooting at a tomato can."

Hal started up with a fierce denial, but the coroner waved him back.

"This was at what time, Mr. Crasher?"

"It was Tuesday morning."

"Have you any other evidence as to this shooting? Anyone else who heard it? We can hardly accept alleged testimony from a dead man."

"No, I thought you wouldn't, but that's what he said. There was a silencer on the pistol; it didn't make much noise. Well this dead man told me the boy peppered two cans full of holes, set 'em against the big elm down there, and then buried them under the bush in the corner. And I went down there later and dug 'em up. And here they are. Moore here was in the alley. He let me in and saw me do it." This Mr. Moore corroborated.

Mr. Crasher reached down and unfolded a parcel he had brought with him, and set on the table two well perforated tin cans, soiled with earth.

"You found these in the corner of this back yard?"

"I did. Early Friday morning. Then I had a hunch, after all the news about this mixed murder came out. I called up Miss Iris, here, and persuaded her to let me in. I told her she'd better on her cousin's account, and when I got in I marched up to the young man's room, Miss Iris with me, and on top of his wardrobe I found this. And in the little false drawer at the bottom of the bureau, these."

He laid on the table beside the tomato cans a thirty-eight revolver and a box of shells. The coroner examined them. The pistol was equipped with an efficient silencer. He broke out the shells; one chamber was empty. He turned toward Iris. "Miss Iris, did you go with this man and see him find these things?"

"Yes," said the girl in a very low voice.

"Why did you not mention it in your testimony."

"I did not think it was necessary," she murmured, still lower.

"Mr. Warner," said the coroner rather sharply. "What have you to say?"

"Merely that I have never had a pistol in my possession, nor used one," the boy replied firmly.

Then Jim Hunt rose in his seat and addressed the coroner. "Your Honor, if you will allow me I think I can throw some light on this part of the investigation." Crasher gave him an ugly look but stepped down and Jim took the chair.

"I was engaged as I have said, by Mrs. Warner, to keep an eye on this case, and the person who seemed to most need watching was Mr. Crasher. So while he was keeping an eye on the house I was keeping an eye on him. And here is what he did on Thursday." Followed the story of Mr. Crasher's visit to the shabby little pawn broker's, where he had purchased a pistol thirty-eight, with a silencer and several boxes of shells; of his search among the garbage barrels and salvaging of two tomato cans; of his long trip beyond Van Cortlandt Park and careful pistol practice.

"I didn't follow him home," said Jim, "for I felt pretty sure what he wanted of those cans. Now my wife is a pretty good assistant in my business, the best half of the firm, and she had volunteered to come here to help out as a servant while the family were going through this trouble, and to watch for Mr. Crasher; and I was in and out as was necessary. We kept a pretty close watch Thursday night, and left the chain off the side door—we knew Crasher had a key to that."

"How did you know?"

"I told him!" briskly interpolated Mrs. Todd. "Often I've seen him let himself in that door, evenings."

Jim smiled and went on: "Sure enough he came in late that night, and Bessie and I both followed him up. He sneaked up to Hal's room, soft as a cat, there was plenty of light to make him out, and we could see him standing on a chair over by that wardrobe, and stooping down by the bureau, not a bit of noise, and the boy sleeping as sound as you please. We let him get out as soft as he came and then we watched the garden. And sure enough it wasn't very long before we saw him, Bessie from the window, I nearer, outside; we both saw him, down by the big bush in the corner, apparently doing something down on his knees."

"How could you be sure it was he, at night?"

"There was some moonlight, and we are both familiar with

Mr. Crasher's outlines. I was quite near him. We can both swear that it was he."

Bessie bore out her husband's testimony in every respect, and was equally willing to identify the garden digger.

"What have you to say to this, Mr. Crasher?"

"I say nothing to what they say, your Honor. I stick to my story. This is no court of law. You're trying to find out what killed this man, I take it, and I say that pistol was one of the weapons." At this point Mr. Davis asked to be heard and was allowed.

"There are two little things to be considered as to the pistol, your Honor. In the first place the bullet that was taken from the head of the deceased was a forty-four caliber."

"You told me it was a thirty-eight," burst out Mr. Crasher.

"Yes I did," admitted Mr. Davis amiably. "You asked for a bit of private information ahead of time, and I wanted to see what you'd do with it. But your Honor, if this was the right sized gun, and if Mr. Warner did use it, there would be no charge against him. The man was dead before he was shot. A dead man cannot take poison."

This point had been raised in the papers at considerable length; all present were familiar with it. The coroner nodded acquiescence.

Mr. Crasher rose to his feet again.

"If your Honor will allow me to finish my testimony I can throw considerable light on the poison question."

"Continue," said the coroner drily.

"I told you I was watching this house since Monday afternoon, for fear of losing my girl."

Iris gave a shiver of disgust at the term, but listened with pale intensity. Mrs. Warner held her hand and Hal patted her shoulder reassuringly.

"Well sir, on Tuesday morning she slipped out and went downtown in the street car. I followed her in a taxi. She stopped at a drugstore and went in. I noted the place and followed her again, when she came out. She went to another drugstore, she went to four of 'em, one after another. Then she met her cousin downtown, and they went home together; I kept 'em in sight, and kept my eye on the house all the afternoon and evening.

"Tuesday evening she and her cousin went off together—to the movies. I followed 'em, and stood around outside to make sure they stayed there. And in about ten minutes out comes Miss Iris and runs home very quick and quiet—me behind her. She pops in at the side door. I watched her window; no light there. She didn't stay inside two minutes, came out and scuttled back to the picture place as fast as she could go. I thought it was funny. I saw them come home at nine, and watched the house all that night."

"Did you see the three visitors mentioned by Mrs. Todd?"

"Yes, I saw them, but didn't notice much; I was watching the young lady. Next morning I was on hand as agreed, to get my girl—and found Vaughn was dead, and she gave me the gate. I stayed to see what I could about the murder, and on Mr. Vaughn's desk I found this." He took from his pocket book and handed to the coroner half of a ticket to the picture palace on the next street. It was dated Tuesday evening. The coroner examined it and read the date aloud, which was eagerly set down by the reporters. It was passed to the jury to examine. People craned forward to see it. Iris was paler than ever and held her Aunt's hand fast in hers.

"When they put me out" said Mr. Crasher grimly. "I went home and got some sleep; I needed it. But I was out by evening, and I went to all those drugstores and made inquiries about what was bought the morning before by a pretty young thing with a shiny little hat, rather nervous. I showed my badge, and they remembered all right. Well, your Honor, she had bought the same thing at every one of those four stores—four bottles of strychnia. Wanted a plenty."

Mr. Crasher sat down. The audience crowded and pushed; they stood up and stared over one another's shoulders to see Iris, who sat like a carved figure, looking steadily down at her feet.

"Miss Iris, will you please take the stand again."

She came forward slowly and took the chair. Dr. Akers and Mr. Davis had told her it was all right, not to be frightened, but she was frightened, visibly.

"Did you buy four bottles of strychnia last Tuesday morning?"

"I did."

"For what purpose?"

"For myself. To take. I thought I had to marry that man, but as soon as I had got the money and given it to my Aunt I was going to kill myself—I couldn't bear him!" She shivered and covered her face with her hands.

"Why did you buy so much strychnia?"

"I didn't know how much was necessary, and I knew this kind was not very strong. Aunt Jack used to take it for a stimulant; that's how I knew I could get it, in the sealed bottle."

"And did you run back to the house from the movies that evening?"

"Yes sir."

"What for?"

"To get my cough drops."

"Cough drops!"

"Yes sir. I'm apt to have a little cough; my mother had it, and Papa hated it. He hated to hear anybody cough. We always had to keep cough drops about."

"Can you account for the half ticket being found on your stepfather's desk?"

"Yes sir. I went in there to get the cough drops, and put them in my little bag—I must have dropped the ticket."

"You went into Mr. Vaughn's room to get them?"

"Yes sir. You see I always carry them about, and Monday afternoon when he called me in and told me I had to marry that man, I was dreadfully excited and I coughed, and he scolded me, and I took out the box. I forgot it, left it on his desk. So when I began to cough in the theater I just ran back to get the box."

"What did he say to you?"

"He didn't say anything. He was asleep."

"You're sure he was asleep?"

"Yes sir. He often was in the evening, used to take little naps in his chair."

"You are sure he was alive then?"

"Oh yes, I could hear him breathe. I found the box just where I left it, and took one quick, for fear I should cough, and put it in my bag and ran back."

The coroner sat back in his chair and looked at her. She still kept her eyes in her lap, pleating and repleating her little tiny handkerchief. Quick pencils caught the pose; a stealthy pocket camera did the same. Mr. Crasher sat with his hands deep in his pockets, regarding her under lowering brows.

"Are you aware," asked the coroner slowly, "that of all the attacks made upon this victim, the death by poison must have come first?"

"Yes sir." This was a mere whisper.

"And that in his stomach has been found—strychnia?"

At this point Mr. Davis leaped to his feet. "I beg pardon, your Honor! That was what was given out at first, but after the full autopsy was made and the final report, it has been established that the poison found in the stomach of the deceased, and in the whiskey decanter, was arsenic."

Mr. Crasher started as if stung by a scorpion. "Damn you Davis," he cried, but the coroner beckoned to two of the officers, who came forward and stood on either side.

"Take him out," said the coroner, "but see he doesn't get away." And he was removed, protesting violently.

Before this excitement had passed and the people were still eagerly discussing the narrow escape of Iris Booth, who was crying softly on her aunt's shoulder, a letter was brought in for the coroner—"Special delivery, sir." It was clearly addressed "To the Coroner at the Inquest No. 127 Grove Street. Important and Immediate."

He turned it over slowly and read the address aloud. Opened, it contained three notes in separate envelopes, addressed simply to the Coroner, Vaughn Murder Case. The stationery was plain and ordinary, no two notes being identical.

He looked at the signatures and started in surprise, ran through the three notes, and then smoothed them out on the table before him.

"I have here," said he, "a most astounding communication, three of them in fact. These are letters from the three servants who left this house last Tuesday night. The enclosing envelope is stamped New York, twelve noon. The letters inside bear no address or date or any distinguishing mark. They are different from one another.

"I will read first the communication from the man Joe White.

"'Mr. Coroner, it occurs to me that a good job well done may make trouble for someone else, which would not be fair. This is to state that I am responsible for the smash on the head and the neat garrote. That man needed killing. I came in behind when he was sitting there, asleep I guess, and laid him out with a blackjack. Then to make all snug I fitted a little necktie, for fear he might wake up—just to make all safe. I would do it again, with pleasure. Joe White.'

"Do you know his writing, Mrs. Warner?" asked the coroner, and she readily identified it.

"The next is from the cook," he went on. "'To the Coroner. I've seen the papers, and all the guesses they are making, and I don't want anybody to carry any blame for me. Before we cleared out I slipped in where that Snake was sitting asleep, and ran a little knife into him. And I'm glad of it. Norah Brown.'

"It does seem rather a pity," remarked his Honor drily, "to have so many apparently well deserved attacks all wasted. But here at last we learn who was the real murderer—her note is very brief. 'Mr. Coroner. Don't make any mistake. I gave him the arsenic. Nellie Brown.'"

A general sigh of relief went up all over the room. Mrs. Todd sat back in her chair and laughed delightedly, patting Iris' other hand. The newspaper men began to pack up their materials; people stirred as if to start out.

"It would seem as if our inquiry had narrowed itself to a search for one person," said the coroner with evident satisfaction, "and all the other would-be slayers stand exonerated—it is no crime to kill a dead man. With this confession before you, gentlemen, it should not be difficult to bring in a verdict as to the manner of Mr. Vaughn's death, and the guilty party. What is that Mr. Davis? Are you still holding something out on us?"

"I am your Honor. I have not yet read the report of the autopsy, which may alter your views."

At this there was a sudden renewal of interest, eager, breathless. He read the careful technical account, the anatomical details as to each wound, the definite statement of the amount of arsenic found in the stomach of the deceased. It was held that although a sudden pain may have led the subject to hastily swallow the glass containing poison there had been no time for it to produce any results, as the patient had died of coronary thrombosis.

"We find, therefore, that deceased came to his death from heart disease. Signed,

Police Surgeon, Thomas R. Davis M.D.
George M. Wilson M.D.
Ross Akers M.D."

Amid a rustling discussion, an atmosphere of empty disappointment, the jury gave their verdict in accordance with this latest fact.

Mr. Martin seemed to have almost shrunk a little.

"The inquest is adjourned," said he.

Further Developments

The sense of frustration following the inquest on the most popular and complicated case of supposed murder yet known was extreme. The papers gave vivid accounts of the examination, the elimination of one suspect after another, the machinations of Mr. Crasher, now in prison awaiting trial, and the spectacular arrival of the three confessions, the guilt so fixed on pretty Nellie Brown. But even the most sensational were obliged to wind up with that dull verdict—heart disease, the most commonplace form of death.

There was no use in searching for anybody. No matter how determinedly they had tried to commit murder, not one of them had succeeded. There were, to be sure, ultra-ethical critics, who insisted that those so attempting were each and all guilty, just as guilty as if they had been successful, and should be captured and punished.

But the courts were busy enough with completely guilty murderers. They had too many criminals who were legally responsible to be greatly excited over the moral responsibility in attacking a dead man.

Wherefore the eager public, so hotly interested in the crowding confusions of the case, had to relinquish that interest, as unsatisfied as one balked in a large sneeze. Peace settled on Grove and Field Streets. No more policemen protected the house from pressing visitors; and fewer and fewer curious persons cared to pass that way.

* * * * *

Aunt Jack, Hal and Iris sat together, considering ways and means. Could they afford to remain in the old house? Had they enough among them to allow Hal to finish his college course, if his mother and cousin went to work as they intended?

The careful Mr. Anderson brought them the account of what they might expect, and the failure of his faint hopes of something better.

"If your father's will were less carefully drawn, Mrs. Warner, there might be a chance to break it, even now, but there being this definite provision, however inadequate, made for the natural heirs, and eight years having passed under the specified conditions, it would be idle to attempt it." He left them with a sense of genuine sympathy.

He was patient and thorough and kind; his bill was most moderate, but the total result left the fortune of the late J. J. Smith almost entirely the property of the late Mr. Vaughn, and waiting the discovery of his natural heirs. These, being advertised for, appeared in increasing numbers, but so far, proved unable to establish their claims.

Hal was determined to leave off studying and find work at once. "I won't have you working, mother, nor Iris either, while I putter over books. It's ridiculous. I'll get me a job right away."

"A poor investment, my boy," his mother told him. "You being our main source of income, Iris and I naturally wish to get all we can out of you! You stand a much better chance of taking care of us as you'd like to if you get as good a preparation as possible first. It is no hardship for this child to work awhile, good experience in fact, and as for me, it will be sheer pleasure to be doing something for real money, even if not much. Of course I hate to leave the old home, but we couldn't stay here on the strength of what you might earn, my dear. Or on what all three of us might earn."

So they began to plan for moving, on a basis little better than that of their attempt [to] start so few days before.

"Isn't there someone knocking?" asked Iris. There was no one in the house but themselves, and a patient visitor at the back door stood rapping in vain. Hal ran down to investigate and returned promptly. "It's an old woman, mother, says her name's Jane and she used to work here."

His mother was delighted. "Old Jane! Bless her good heart! Bring her up, Hal, do. And Iris dear, will you make a cup of tea, good strong 'kitchen tea' for the dear old thing!"

So presently a sturdy old Irish woman was crying over "Poor Miss Jack!" "And to think of you being hurt so bad all this time and nothing done about it! And my sweet Miss Iris gone so long! But little Miss Iris here is the very image of her mother. It's a lovely girl she is. And Master Hal, a man grown! You've reason to be glad and proud, Miss Jack, for all your trouble, and this horrid murder and all."

"I have indeed Jane dear. And you must tell me all about yourself and Peter—he is well I hope?"

"Yes'm, we keep our healths, thanks to the blessed saints. And he has had work a good deal of the time, and I've been able to do something by the day. But it is hard for old folks in these days."

"It was a great grief to me, Jane, that my father's will left you so little. Had I anything myself I should have made it good to you."

"I know you would, Miss Jack. It is like your kind heart. But to think of your father doing nothing for his own children! Nothing to call anything for a man with his money! But Miss Jack, I've something for you here that may do some good—and maybe not—but I brought it for you to see. When Mr. Vaughn brought us in to sign that will he had a mean grin on him, and another paper sticking out of his pocket. Maybe he fooled the old man."

She began to undo an untidy newspaper bundle fastened with a quantity of well-knotted string. "You remember the clothes of your father's you were so kind as to give us when we went away?"

Mrs. Warner remembered well, and also how carefully and how vainly she had felt in the pockets before doing so. "Yes Jane, it was all I had to give you, unfortunately, when you should have had so much more!"

"It's very useful they've been to us all these years. Peter is not a hard man on his clothes, praise be! And the things your father had were good. Miss Jack, they've outlasted a dozen of what we could get now."

She succeeded at last in unwrapping her bundle, and brought out an ancient well-worn coat.

"'Tis the one he had on the night we found him and brought him in. And a good coat it's made Peter, with a patch and a darn here and there. But just now, when I was trying to hold the lining together I came upon this—"

She showed a tiny slit of a pocket opening sideways under the facing of the front, and from it produced a small folded bit of paper, yellow and creased and worn. Mrs. Warner took it with trembling fingers, opened it carefully and spread it on her desk blotter. It was only a leaf from a doctor's prescription pad, Dr. G. R. Murdock. On it was written in pencil, weakly and crookedly, "I leave all my property to my daughters and their children." Then very faint and ragged, "J. J. Smith," and following the name of the physician as printed above, and that of a woman, Coral Saunders. Jacqueline Warner read it over; her eyes blurred with tears. She knew the writing, she saw the weakness, the tremendous effort, and felt as if at last some touch of a father's love had come to her.

"Is it a regular will, Ma'am? Is it a good one? Will you be able to get what belongs to you by means of it?" Jane was as eager as if she was the legatee.

"Jane O'Connell," said Mrs. Warner slowly, "if it is a good will, if we do get the money, I promise you that you and Peter will not have to work anymore. Jane—Jane—I always had a feeling that there *must* be another will, that my father could not have left us like that. This may change everything! But I can't tell; I mustn't hope too much. This is such a poor little scrap of paper to be so important. It's father's handwriting—and yet it's so shaky that it would be hard to swear to. Have you told anyone about it?"

"Never a one, Miss Jack. It was only this morning that I found it. And Peter out for the day."

"Can you wait awhile, Jane? I'm going to 'phone for my lawyer; if he can come he will certainly want to see you."

"I can stay till 'tis time to get his supper," said the eager Jane, not referring to the legal gentleman.

So Mrs. Warner phoned to Mr. Anderson and startled that worthy man exceedingly. "A will! You don't say so? And the woman is there? Of course I'll come over, at once."

"Please don't feel too sure," she said carefully. "It's on a mere scrap of paper, but it's signed and witnessed."

Then she called Jim Hunt, but he was not at home. She told Bess what had happened, and to ask Jim to come when he could, that it might mean a good deal of work for him.

"Now Jane, will you go down and find Iris. I asked her to get you some tea. But please don't say a word to the children about this—I can't bear to think of the disappointment it would be to them if it turns out to be useless."

"Not a word, Miss Jack, not a word. I'll be bursting with it till we know is it good or not, but I'll say nothing to anyone. I'll be below when you want me. And it's a pleasure to be in the old house again. The better part of my life I lived here, and Peter too!

"And to think of your lovely mother, that I remember so well! And her leaving you poor little orphans—and the mother you were to your sister! And she the sweetest thing that ever walked!"

"She certainly was, Jane. Everyone loved her."

"And now you're being another mother to little Miss Iris again! And how wonderful big and strong the boy has grown!

Oh Miss Jack—if I may make so bold as to ask—shall you be staying on in the old house?"

"I would if I could, but what little money we have left us would not be enough to keep it up. Of course if this is a good will—"

"And if it's not," went on the old woman, eagerly. "Wouldn't you let us come back, Peter and me? He could still be workin' out when he could get jobs, gardening and the like around here perhaps, and we'd have no rent to pay! There'd be no question of wages, Miss Jack, only what you could afford by and by. But I'd rather live here with you for nothing than anywhere else."

Whereat Mrs. Warner drew the old face nearer and kissed her.

"My dear Jane, if we stay you shall stay. It would seem like home indeed to have you about again. But I can't tell yet; I'll let you know. And now go and have your tea; I must think it out."

Feeling immensely important and hopeful Jane betook herself to her familiar kitchen, and proceeded to pour affectionate compliments on Iris till that young lady was quite overwhelmed. She diverted the stream by asking questions about her mother and aunt in childhood and youth. Hal came in and joined the party and good Mrs. O'Connell, wholly in her element, regaled them with endless stories of the Past.

She was curious too to hear all about the dreadful experiences they had been through, and Hal was quite willing to describe it.

"And with all that killing he only died by himself, after all! 'Tis the most surprising thing I ever heard of. And those runaways now, that owned they did it, will they not get after them?"

"Nothing to get after them for," the boy explained. "Even the poison didn't have time to work. That kind of heart disease goes like a shot. If it hits a man in the street he just drops in his tracks. I guess nothing but prussic acid* would have had a chance, and this was only arsenic."

"And that black villain tried to put it on you, Master Hal! With the pistol and all!"

Hal grinned. "Yes, and didn't he get it in the neck! That police surgeon knew his tricks and kidded him along in great shape. Think of his trying to drag in Iris!"

Iris shivered again at the thought of that ordeal, but Hal put his arm around her. "Cheer up Sis. He's busted up now all right. Guess he'll be shut up for some time."

*   *   *   *   *

Mr. Anderson arrived astonishingly soon, and Hal showed him upstairs rather wondering what he had come for, but the entertaining Mrs. O'Connell kept him pleasantly occupied.

"What's this you tell me?" demanded the lawyer of his client. "Another will has been discovered?"

"I hope so," she told him, with enforced quietness. "We are waiting for your opinion, somewhat anxiously!" She showed him the coat, the tiny hidden pocket, and drew out of it the bit of folded paper, with full explanation about the O'Connells and her gift.

He took it gingerly in his long fingers, opened it as carefully as she had done, and spread it before him on the desk. Slowly and attentively he read it over and over.

"Is it your father's handwriting?" he asked at length.

"Yes. I think so. I would be sure if it were not so shaky and weak. The signature is just as father used to make it—those long 'Js' with no tops to them, just the stem and loop at the bottom.

It might be a forgery, I suppose?" and she looked at him imploringly.

"No occasion for anyone to make such a forgery except you or your sister," he answered, smiling slightly, "and if you did it you certainly were in no haste to realize on it. No, I think it is a good will. The trouble is to prove it. The witnesses will have to be found, this doctor, the woman—probably a nurse. See here, has Mr. Hunt followed up that story the Italian told him?"

At this point Mr. Hunt arrived, breathless, and had to be told the whole thing over again. He stared at the shabby bit of paper with intense eagerness.

"Your father's handwriting, you say. And in your father's pocket. And didn't the old woman that was here say how his eyes were anxious?"

Mrs. O'Connell being sent for, gave a clear account of that return, and her impressions of the old man's condition. "If't had been me I'd have had his daughter brought at once, his eyes were asking, and his hand, he'd make as if he was writing, and look around. But we were turned out at once, and the nurses that man hired wouldn't let a soul into the room. Even the doctor didn't see him except when he was asleep—I heard him speak of it in the hall, goin' out, and Mr. Vaughn gave that little chuckle of his and said, 'All the less trouble for you my boy.' It's a hateful man he was, even if he is dead."

She had to return to get Peter's supper, but promised to come again soon and left her address. Mrs. Warner handed her an envelope—"just for your expenses as a witness," she said, and bade her an affectionate goodbye.

Jim asked to have the momentous bit of paper photographed at once. "I want a copy with me, to show this doc, if I find him.

That oughtn't to be much of a job, if he's in town. He can give me a line on the hospital, and the nurse too, perhaps. I'll get after it right away."

Mr. Anderson returned to his office, leaving the precious bit of paper to be photographed and then brought to him for safe-keeping. Jim placed it carefully in an envelope, and that in his innermost breast-pocket, together with a late photograph of Mr. Smith, and he and Mrs. Warner looked at each other excitedly.

"This goes with Emilio's story of your father, all right," he said. "He was picked up, taken to a hospital, and somehow per-suaded them to let him write—even if he couldn't speak. And he wrote this. And the doc and the nurse signed it. And—"

"Yes," she ruefully interpolated, "and how did he get out—in that state, and find his clothes! And get way over here!"

"Well, he did," insisted Jim. "That's certain anyway. Say, Mrs. Warner, this'll make some difference, won't it!"

"I don't dare think of it yet . . . And he'd have told me then if I could have seen him! He wanted to write, Jane says." And she spoke of the old woman's visit and her eager offer to come and work for her for nothing. "And she must be sixty-five or more! I never heard of such devotion, nowadays."

"That's the kind you read about," he admiringly agreed. "Suppose I look at your telephone book right now; maybe we can put our finger on Mr. Doctor at once."

As a piece of good luck the name was there, and being called, he agreed to see Mr. Hunt that evening.

"So there we are, as fine as a fiddle! I'll go home and tell Bess—I may, mayn't I?"

"Oh yes, I told her myself; she was most enthusiastic. Good luck to you, Mr. Hunt!"

With a hope like this in her heart it called on all the long habit of acting at the table to talk freely and gaily with the young people on no better basis than the prospect of a job. Iris, relieved of the load of compulsion under which she had spent so much of her young life, and of the shock and terror of recent days, chattered brightly of her probable employer, and enraged her cousin by threatening to find a wealthy and agreeable gentleman and triumphantly marry him!

At this wild flight of fancy from the shy girl, her aunt realized afresh that even if no more was in store for them freedom had come, and hope. They could be happy enough with that.

But she sat near the telephone that evening, waiting for news.

Bessie called her up, keen with interest, asking eager questions. She had become much attached to her temporary mistress, full of sympathy for her pathetic condition and admiration for her courage and ability. "Jim's very hopeful. He said that doctor ought to clear it up all right. And there's Emilio's story to back it up. Oh Mrs. Warner—if it is—if you get it, is it too late to have things done—surgically, I mean?"

"Don't Bessie! I daren't think of it yet. Do come and see me when you can, Mrs. Hunt."

* * * * *

When Dr. Akers came in, as he now so frequently did, she had much to tell him. He was as deeply excited over the news as she could wish.

"The main thing is you," was his comment. "The children would be off your mind and you could hie to the hospital and get re-decorated at once." Then gloomily—"I suppose, like the pure and noble gentlemen in the story books I should promptly refuse to marry you, if you get all that money."

"Mayn't I have enough to be re-decorated, as you call it? Then, if I give the rest away will you marry me?"

"Jack," said he, seriously. "I'd marry you if you hadn't a cent, if you couldn't be mended, and if you were stone blind into the bargain. As for this nobility business, that was a poor joke. What's a million or two between friends?"

Very happily they sat together, close and still, his arm around her.

"I don't care," she murmured softly, "for anything more—if I have you."

The sharp buzz of the telephone broke this contentment.

"Jim Hunt speaking. Just had a good talk with Dr. Murdock. He remembers all right. Say—is it too late for me to come over and tell you about it?"

It was certainly not too late he was told, with the added suggestion that he add cabs to subways and hurry.

Dr. Akers carried her downstairs, and they sat awhile with the young people, till Mrs. Warner sent them off to bed. Presently Jim appeared, triumphantly ushering in and duly introducing—"Dr. Murdock, and Mrs. Murdock! They've come to tell you about it." Jim was looking as pleased as if he had brought Santa Claus.

"I might add," he put it happily, "that Mrs. Murdock's maiden name was Saunders!"

Mrs. Warner received them cordially, eagerly looking from one to the other, and Mrs. Murdock plunged into the tale at once.

"I made him come over," she triumphed. "What difference does it make how late it is—when anything like this comes up.

Of course we read all about you, Mrs. Warner, awfully exciting, wasn't it! But we never dreamed we'd have a finger in the pie!"

"A pretty important finger, too," Jim contributed. "Go ahead Mrs. Murdock, tell us all about it."

She went ahead, full speed, giving them the story briskly and clearly.

"I was a nurse in that hospital when it happened. I remember just as well when that poor old man was brought in! He was too well dressed to be a drunk, and no liquor on him either. Concussion it was. He remained unconscious for ever so long, and when he came to he couldn't talk, nor move much. But his eyes were anxious, desperately anxious, and he kept trying to write—and looking at me so! Dr. Murdock happened to be going through the ward—" ("as often happened," put in that gentleman softly, but she ignored him) "—and I called him; I knew there was no time to waste. He had no paper but his sub-scription pad, I had a pencil, we propped up the old man, and he wrote that scrap of a will. Dr. Murdock seemed to take it as a joke," she added mischievously, "but I didn't. So he signed it, and we signed it and the old man seemed much relieved. I folded it up and tucked it into his pajama pocket. Then—he must have got better all at once—for that very night he disappeared."

"Most sudden recovery," Dr. Murdock added. "I never heard of anything like it. His head must have been quite clear, for he found his clothes, and was able to walk out unobserved."

"How on earth he got over here from that hospital without any money beats me," protested Jim. "Especially as he couldn't talk."

"I know one way," suggested Dr. Akers. "I had my pocket picked once, when I was a young fellow, and a long way from home. I made a desperate search and found a dime that had slipped through a little hole and settled in the hem of the coat. A thin dime would have been overlooked when they cleaned him out."

"That would have been just enough," Jim agreed. "Subway and surface. Anyhow he did it. Mrs. Warner," he rose and made a sweeping bow. "Allow me to congratulate you."

"Do you think—is it sure?" She still feared to accept the good news.

"Sure as shooting seems to me," he answered. "Owing to this happy marriage"—he grinned cordially at Dr. Murdock and his triumphantly smiling wife, "we've got both the witnesses, the date and the identification."

"I wouldn't swear to the photograph," Dr. Murdock carefully began but his wife cut him short.

"Well I would! I saw him every day, you only just that one time. I'll swear to him Mrs. Warner."

"Besides," Dr. Akers suggested, "the possession of the little will, together with his condition on reaching home seem conclusive. By the way, could you by any chance give us the exact date, Mrs. Murdock?"

"By a very special chance." She smiled at her husband. "Dr. Murdock proposed to me that evening. It was my evening off. And when I got back my patient was gone."

And as the date she gave was that of Mr. Smith's collapse on his own doorstep, there seemed no room for any further doubt.

"Ross," said Mrs. Warner. "Will you get those children—I don't believe they have gone to bed yet."

"What if they have!" he protested. "I'll get 'em up."

"Won't you telephone Bessie, Mr. Hunt, she must be anxious—while I thank these good friends." And thank them she did, against urgent disclaimers.

"Why I've done nothing at all; it's all my wife," protested Dr. Murdock, while that lady assured them that she wouldn't have missed it for worlds. "It's like a play," she delightedly explained, "like a novel, a nice novel. I never was in one before."

When Hal and Iris appeared they were promptly commissioned to produce whatever the house afforded in the way of eatables and drinkables, ably assisted by Jim Hunt, and while they all gathered around the table Aunt Jack broke the news to the young folks.

They were somewhat dazed, but Hal declared that he had smelt a mouse that afternoon. "We knew you were up to something, didn't we Iris? But say mother—are we rich now? How much did Grandfather leave?"

She did not know, but Jim Hunt knew.

"I asked Anderson this afternoon," he said. "He looked it up. Said as far as he could find out it was about three million."

A Final Verdict

"No sir!" declared Aunt Jack. "I will not marry you, my dear Ross, in a wheel chair. Nor lugged in like a babe in arms. Nor wearing a black patch. Nor grinning like a crooked Cheshire Cat.* No sir!"

"Dear Heart!" he pleaded. "*I* don't care if you're brought in on a stretcher. Do let's be married first, so that I can help through the job. It's a long fussy business, and it hurts a lot."

"No sir again! You may not care, but I do. Blessed man—I haven't been able to call my soul my own—much less my body—for nine long awful years. Now I'm going to have my own way for quite a while. Just you devote yourself to establishing your family in one place and your office in another. Build up your practice. Play about a bit. It may be in a year's time, with all your new freedom and prosperity, you will find 'anither ladye, exactly to your taste.'"*

Dr. Akers devoted himself to convincing her on that point, with considerable success, but she remained adamant on the other, and proceeded to unfold her plans.

"Firstly here are my dear old Jane and Peter, comfortably re-installed in what is more like home to them than any other place. Then there is Jane's stout niece, Mary Flynn, who will do the real work, as far as Jane will let her. And who do you suppose is going to be Lady Manager?"

He gave it up, smilingly.

"Mrs. Todd! Mrs. Todd on a handsome salary. Mrs. Todd, who has been perfectly miserable on the grudging support of that stingy nephew of hers, and who now will have a room with the morning sun in it, and the same kind of window to look out of. And Ross—I've told her about the 'ears'—and she is simply wild with delight. She can 'Stop, look and listen' to her heart's content."

"Suppose the old servants don't like her?"

"They can go off on their own, anytime; they have an annuity. It's only for a while, and all the alterations and so on will be done, too."

"And you are going to desert your children, you unnatural mother."*

"For quite a while, cruel man. Oh Ross! Don't you see? I want a wide clean space between these black years behind and the bright ones before. And I *will* be patched up as far as possible before I come to you." There was a little pause and she added, almost reluctantly, "You see, dear, there were so many horrors to put up with that I never gave much thought to my own special disaster—and now somehow it is bigger than anything else."

So the family was reestablished without her. Hal returned to his studies with new ambition, and Iris suddenly developed a thirst for instruction and took a partial college course herself. At home they found endless amusement in their new chaperon, and she bloomed like the rose in young society, lots of it, teas and lunches and dances whenever the young people could have them, and the workmen were not too dominant.

And Aunt Jack took herself off. At first to a lovely quiet southern beach accompanied by a competent and agreeable woman Dr. Akers found for her, half maid, half nurse, and there she basked in sunshine and rest, good food and pure air. Then, refreshed and strengthened, to a sanitarium, and a long period of treatment under the artistic skill of modern surgery.

She wrote to Ross Akers, but would not let him see her, nor Hal. "I shall come with my shield or on it," she wrote. "But I don't want anybody to see the stitches. How's that for a mixed metaphor!"

And by and by, when only time was needed to finish the work of art, she recalled her companion, and the two of them set off for California.

Along the fawn and purple foothills and golden mesas of that rich country, among the blossom-spread ranches, was one that sat a little back toward the hills, not large, but comfortable and prosperous. On its broad rose-hung veranda, sat in the perfumed shade a group of happy looking people, a man, his wife, a sturdy baby, and an elderly woman smiling on them all.

The man was watching the swift chase of far-off cars that slid along the distant road between them and the sea. One turned and wound along the rising grade among the hills, turned again and followed the less-travelled way that passed their ranch. While they idly watched its progress it stopped at their gate, and a lady came lightly up the path.

She was handsome and richly dressed, her smile was friend-ly and warm, she came toward them with outstretched hand, but none of them knew her.

"Are you alone?" was her odd first question, in a voice some-how familiar.

"Yes, Madam," said the man, rising politely, then with a little stiffness, a faint tinge of suspicion, "To whom have I the honor of speaking?"

She came forward and shook him warmly by the hand. Also the hand of the elder woman, who did not know how to refuse it. But the young mother she kissed, and stood smiling.

"Don't you know me, my dear Joe? And Norah and Nellie? It's no wonder—I've had my poor face mended—and my feet."

They made no sign. Nellie turned white but sat still and held her baby close. Joe was perfectly quiet in speech.

"Some mistake, Madam. My name is Henry Waters, my wife Julia; her mother Mrs. Mary Allen."

"What nice names," said Aunt Jack, calmly taking a chair. "Now my dear people. I want you to feel sure that in the first place I am wholly your friend. In the next place, as you probably read at the time, you didn't any of you kill him. In the third place *I* shouldn't blame you if you did. In the fourth place, Joe—I mean Mr. Waters—as to the money in that safe, it would have taken much more than that to make the smallest return for the injuries you suffered, to say nothing of withheld wages. In the fifth place I owe you more than thanks for your kind thought of me—when you needed every cent for yourselves." And Aunt Jack smiled at him warmly, as she recalled that envelope tucked under her door that Tuesday night, the brief note saying, "He owed you some too!" the big bills with it.

"And now my dear Henry and Mary and Julia, won't you stop being frightened and be friendly instead?"

"We were more than frightened, of you especially," he told her, "because we read about those 'ears' and wondered how much you knew—how much you would tell—it was the only weak spot. Of course I had to leave you some—he had all yours. And we all admired you so. Julia said you wouldn't tell even if you heard."

"I heard a lot, enough to know the new names and where to look for you when I was able, but all I told was of your wild rush for South America. Wasn't that a picture!" And she regaled them with details of the swift action of the police, the enraged captain of the *Chimborazo* and the more enraged passengers whom he searched.

Henry grinned delightedly. "I remember! You heard me telling mother about those three Italians making that connection—if they could. And you told them we were doing it."

"Yes. It seemed to me an excellent scent, and occupied them for a little while. Gave you more time. But your plans were wonderful, and I am rejoiced to see how well they have succeeded."

Then he told her of how they had slipped away by different roads to different places, worked honestly and steadily, communicated only through their good friend in New York, and finally came together here.

"With the savings of the three of us, and this extra we had, we got this little place. There's a mortgage, but we see our way to paying it off. And now we can really breathe!" he said, lifting his broad shoulders.

"Dear Mrs. Warner," put in Julia timidly. "Do you mean you don't think we were wicked?" Now Mrs. Warner had heard more by her ear to the kitchen than she had told anyone. "We tried to kill him, all of us. You see I was really the first; I poisoned him. Joe didn't know it of course, I was going to tell him afterwards. He told what he did. And last thing before leaving mother went—"

"I did!" said Mrs. Allen, with no sign of repentance.

"I know you did, my dear people, all of you. If ever a man deserved to be executed it was that man. You see I heard what he said to you Tuesday afternoon . . . Oh, did you read about the end of Augustus Crasher?"

Joe lifted his head sharply. "No . . ." They were all hotly interested. She told them of his arrest and trial, that he was condemned, but escaped, and crept back to his room to secure hidden papers, how Emilio had surprised him there, stabbed him and set the place on fire, destroying everything. But she did not tell him that Emilio was Carlo's brother.

Henry was thinking of that victim however. "I was awful sorry to hear that little dago in the alley was dead," he said slowly. "I just bashed him to get him out of the way—smelt his tobacco over the fence—I had no idea of killing the little guy."

"He wasn't much loss, as far as I could gather, and it was only an accident," she comforted him. "And now Crasher is gone you can feel wholly safe I am sure." They sat still, thinking of it.

"You mustn't think me a heartless monster, my friends, condoning attempted murder and casual homicide," she pursued. "But you know something of what I had to bear at the hands of that—unspeakable man! Julia knows most—" Their hands stole together in a clasp that hurt.

Julia relieved the atmosphere by offering to Mrs. Warner's open arms the best baby in the world, to which she paid due homage.

"Now tell me more about yourselves," she said, still hugging the baby. "It was such good psychology, the way you managed. I'm really proud of you. As good and useful citizens you are far better occupied than if adding to the public expense as bad and useless prisoners."

Then Henry Waters laughed. He laughed freely, happily. He was realizing that the haunting sense of danger was gone. With Crasher dead and Mrs. Warner an understanding friend, their child might grow up in happy peace.

"It was an effort in practical psychology," he agreed. "We all understood that we had to make a change in our own minds, as well as in our names and places. Steadily we set ourselves to *be* the new people and to forget the old ones. We have not talked about the past, nor thought about it. We tried as far as it was possible to ignore and gradually forget."

"We did read the papers at first," he admitted, "couldn't resist. That inquest must have been exciting."

"It was," Mrs. Warner agreed.

"It did seem disappointing," he suggested quizzically, "to do all that killing and confessing—and have it wasted!"

"Shame on you, my boy," said his mother-in-law, kindly. "We should be more than grateful to have the load off our minds forever." Then she heartily congratulated their visitor on her improved appearance. "And to think of your walking so light and easy. And your face as good as new."

"Yes, it's a blessed miracle. And so it is to have you all here, happy, prosperous and respected. Have you nice neighbors?"

"Very nice," Julia assured her. "Henry's quite looked up to; he knows more than most of them, but he doesn't show half of it. There's a prosperous little town down there with movies, a good library, and so on, pleasant people on either side of us, and we've got a car. Mother was brought up in this country, you know, further south. Perhaps now, some day, she can look up her relatives."

"Perhaps," said Mrs. Warner. "But how about names?"

"Better leave well enough alone!" Mrs. Allen remarked. "There's relative enough for me right here!"

Then Mrs. Warner told them of her own good fortune and happy prospects, to their great delight, and before she left tucked something under the baby's knitted jacket. "Put it in the bank for him," she whispered to Julia as she gave the child back to her, "for college, or anything you please."

*   *   *   *   *

Then Aunt Jack went home. She went home with a glad heart and an easy mind, and was met at the station by an eager family and a more eager lover . . . The old house smiled at her, lovely in fresh color and decoration, and old Jane took her to her heart with rapturous cries.

"It's beautiful you are, Miss Jack! As beautiful as the day! And stepping like a girl at a dance. Thanks be to all the saints!"

Mrs. Todd rejoiced beyond measure, and declared herself so much improved by her visit that she meant to travel awhile herself. Which she promptly did, with ample funds provided and Mrs. Warner's wheel chair, as well as her erstwhile nurse-companion.

Dr. Akers had established his former incubus of a stepfamily in a small flat by themselves. "I'll take care of them of course, but I don't have to live with them any more," was his position. Having never had a satisfactory home of his own since childhood he was quite willing to share in his wife's—and urged her to make it soon.

"You've made me wait forever for all this fancy work," he protested, "and I loved you well enough as you were! Now I shall be a prey to jealousy! Surely, Jack darling, there's nothing to keep us apart any longer."

This urgency was after a happy week of home-coming, of settling into the new old house, of Hal getting used to his handsome mother, and of the worshipping affection of Iris.

A slight shadow swept over her face. "You've been very patient, Ross dear. Let's talk it over after they've gone tonight—there's the bell."

"They" were the Hunts, who had been invited to a dinner of general celebration, and came with delight, eager to congratulate Aunt Jack on her amazing renewal of beauty.

Bessie held her hands and gazed and gazed. "You're fairly blushing—and no wonder. Isn't she lovely, Jim! It's just wonderful!"

Jim agreed with her. Ross Akers more than agreed with her, but she only laughed and quoted. "She'd pass very well for forty-three in the dusk with the light behind her!"*

The dinner was a gay one, a very happy one. All were delighted to hear of the prosperity and contentment of the three in California.

"That's what a criminal can never do," declared Jim dogmatically, "settle down and live like other folks. Those people were not criminals, never were. Just good folks in a horrible position. And Joe's a gentleman. The only thing he has to kick himself for is the Carlo—accident, and that was no loss after all!"

"I fear you are hardened," said Aunt Jack, "by the constant

pursuit of crime."

"Hardened, yes, and softened too. Crime! How do you measure crime? By the harm done, for one thing. By the pressure driving to it—even the law allows for that. For utter case-hardened inborn highly-developed criminality I never knew any man to equal Wade Vaughn."

They were taking their coffee in the pleasant library, soon to be Dr. Akers' office, and there was no disagreement with Mr. Hunt's opinion.

Iris set down her cup. "If you'll excuse me Aunt Jack, Hal and I have to be off now or we'll miss the overture. And if you're going to talk about—that—I'm not sorry to leave you."

The young people went gaily away, happy in each other, and in the safe bright hopes before them. Mrs. Warner watched them with a proud glad light in her eyes.

"Isn't he splendid—my boy! And Iris—she has blossomed out so she's almost as lovely as her mother."

They all agreed with her, warmly.

"They can forget," she went on. "Just in this year I can see how the horror, the dreadful pressure, has receded. It will hardly leave a mark . . . You were quite right Mr. Hunt."

"Jim," he interpolated, with his pleasant smile.

"Jim it is," she went on, "and Bessie. You saved our lives, my dear girl, coming in as you did."

"You make me feel guilty," she answered. "I was just helping Jim. And," she added honestly, "ready to suspect anybody."

"You see," Jim explained, "at first we didn't know very much about Mr. Vaughn, didn't know how he deserved far more than he got. Heart disease! Why, *good* people die of heart disease!"

"There's one thing we never did find out," said Bessie, meditatively. "That is who fired the pistol. Not that it matters—he didn't accomplish anything. But just to round out the story I'd like to know."

Dr. Akers carefully put out his cigarette. "No he didn't accomplish anything, but he showed good faith. I fired that pistol. You see I knew about Iris too, and I'd just found out the measure of his iniquity toward—"

"I was free of that back door* too," Jacqueline touched his foot.

"Thank you," remarked Bessie, calmly. "Now I'm easy in my mind."

Jim looked at him admiringly. "You certainly carried it off well, old man. I'm good on suspecting, but I'd never have thought it of you. You'd heard about this Iris arrangement—I see."

Mrs. Warner said nothing but looked at him with shining eyes, eyes that showed nothing but faith and love.

He turned to her. "You ought to know the worst of me before we are married, Jacqueline. Now's your time to drop me as a dangerous character."

"Now's my time to tell you all something you don't know," she answered steadily. "You don't any of you know what killed Wade Vaughn."

There was a stunned silence. Bessie stared with wide open eyes. Jim's narrowed as he looked. But Akers started, visibly.

"Not know! I know, I examined him. It was coronary thrombosis!"

"Yes. One cannot contradict medical testimony. But one can, sometimes, go behind it. My friends—I am going to marry this good man—if he'll have me. And we'll drop a curtain, forever, over all this bitter past. But," she smiled at Bessie, "just to settle the inquiring mind of this young lady, I'm going to show you something."

She placed them all in this room that had been Vaughn's, as close as possible to where he had sat that night, behind the big magazine covered library table which took the place of the desk, under the center light above.

"While you are waiting I'll give you something to induce the right state of mind." She brought down to them a typewritten package, laid it on the table. "When you've read it, all of it, one of you open this door and go back and sit down, just as you are now."

She shut the door into the hall and left them, sitting close, all reading together the record she had kept so long. It seemed worse now to the Hunts than in that first hasty reading.

Bessie put down the last page with a shudder, and clung to Jim. His teeth were set, his fists clenched. But Akers was white with horror. "I never knew half of it," he breathed. "She never told me. She carried all that—alone!"

"The children!" murmured Bessie. "She carried *them*. She made it a game. A *game*! A *game*!" her voice broke. "And her sister! That man!"

"I will open the door," said Jim.

The hall was dark; no light showed anywhere. They sat tense, waiting, and they heard, in the dark hall a soft descending step on the stair and a cough, a slight repeated cough. Dr. Akers gripped his chair.

There appeared in the doorway and stood looking steadily at them, not Jacqueline, but Iris her sister. Iris of the soft bright hair, the perfect features, the tender and small mouth. She wore a soft blue frock, but her color was not rosy; it was death-white. Her eyes stared dim and blank. Around her neck was tightly tied one end of a long black and white silk scarf. And she coughed again.

Bessie screamed; she couldn't help it. Dr. Akers leaped forward and caught the figure in his arms.

"Jack! Jack!" He tore off the clinging scarf, and she removed the mask, its blue gauze eyes shimmering dimly.

"Now you know," she stated quietly, "who killed Wade Vaughn."

Then to Ross Akers, who was still holding her, "How about it, Ross? Are you willing to marry a murderer?"

His answering embrace was hearty enough to convince any doubter.

"My dear girl I'd marry you if your name was Nero!* You didn't kill him. He just died of heart disease!"

"Verdict unanimous," agreed the Hunts.

Bessie was looking at the mask. "You pretty near scared me to death, anyway! Now for a penalty you've got to tell me how you did it. This is the loveliest awful thing I ever saw."

Jim interposed with a deadly calm judicial voice. "Mrs. Warner, we have read this—document. I am on my knees to you. If you had boiled him in oil, I should still be on my knees to you. I have never in my life or literature heard of such—colossal courage! Such superhuman power! Eight years of it—"

She made a little curtsy to him. "You see I was an actress once; that made it possible. And you remember how the rabbit climbed a tree? He couldn't, but he just had to! If you want to praise anybody, it's those children who did the impossible—especially Hal. It was harder on him.

"And now Mrs. Bessie I will relieve your mind as to these de-tails—and then send you home!" She looked at Ross again and smiled.

"I made a death-mask of my poor sister. She was so beautiful. I kept the little frock. And the scarf was one I had just like hers, we bought them together—he never saw it. He burned up hers. We were going away early next morning, to save Iris. All my long effort was wasted, or mostly so, Hal's education stopped, what little my father left us lost. And Ross here—" she held his hand, "was going to leave the country, a ruined man.

"Then I made up my mind to—to—at least to make him *feel* for once! I made a fitted mask from the plaster one, and painted it. It was like, oh terribly like! So I came down, with her little cough, and stood there. He had been asleep. The cough woke him and when he saw me standing there he put up his hands before his face at first—then gave a choked cry, clutched at his heart. He had just time to swallow that little glass of whiskey— that was all . . .

"He had a little notebook with the safe combination in it. I was quick—I took out all those papers of his, that he held over his victims, Ross' mortgage was one—I burnt them all, and left the note on top. Then I went upstairs . . ."

"But your poor feet!" cried Bessie.

"Yes, my poor feet. To stand there, still, that hurt! But for the rest I was pretty good at getting about on my hands and knees…"

Then Bessie hugged her close and long. "And you saved Ross, you brave darling! If they had found that stuff it would have been all up with him. To say nothing of the other victims. Jim—! Let's go home!"

They went, he bowing low to kiss the small hand of his hostess in tender admiration, and left her alone with her lover.

THE END

Textual Notes

p. 8   Reynard is the clever fox of an old German beast epic, who relies on tricks to gather information.

p. 29   Here and elsewhere in the novel, Gilman used racist language and ethnic stereotypes as she occasionally did in other writings. In her autobiography, she expressed xenophobic sentiments when she lamented that New York City, her home for twenty-two years, had become an "unnatural city where everyone is an exile, none more so than the American" (*Living* 316). See also Susan A. Lanser's essay, "Feminist Criticism, 'The Yellow Wallpaper,' and the Politics of Color in America," in *Feminist Studies,* 15:3 (Fall 1989): 415–41 and Ann J. Lane, *To Herland and Beyond: The Life and Work of Charlotte Perkins Gilman* (New York: Pantheon Books, 1990): 251-54; 295–96.

p. 35   Mrs. Todd is paraphrasing a verse from "Fit the Third: The Bakers Tale" from *The Hunting of the Snark* (1876) by British writer Lewis Carroll (1832–98). The verse reads:

> "I skip forty years," said the Baker in tears,
> "And proceed without further remark
> To the day when you took me aboard of your ship
> To help you in hunting the Snark."

p. 40   "A Council of War" is also the title of a short story Gilman published in *Forerunner* 4 (August 1913): 197–201, in which a group of women meet to devise a plan to abolish the "evil results of male rule."

p. 46   A blackjack is a small bludgeon-like weapon.

p. 48   After consulting several journalists, we believe that the abbreviation *s. a.* probably stands for "sex appeal."

p. 48   The term *space writers* probably refers to early writers of science fiction, whose tales of outer space appeared in such early pulp magazines as *Amazing Stories.*

p. 50   Abraham Henry Hummel (1850–1926) was an American criminal lawyer who was convicted of conspiracy in 1905 and imprisoned.

p. 50   Gilman is parodying Freudian psychology, "with all the flock of 'psycho-analysts,'" for which she felt deep contempt (*Living* 314).

"Always it has amazed me to see how apparently intelligent persons would permit these mind-meddlers . . . to paddle among their thoughts and feelings. . . ." (314).

p. 50   Gilman is paraphrasing Micah 7.6, which reads, in part, "A man's enemies *are* the men of his own house" (italics added).

p. 52–53   The significance of Gilman's reference to Mr. Wommick, Jr., is not clear.

p. 59   The final sentence in chapter 5 resembles another sentence that occurs some nine paragraphs earlier. In the first instance, Jim is glad that he had the foresight to bring fruit along on what could have been a long stakeout. In the second reference, however, Gilman is apparently being metaphorical. Jim is pleased that he had the foresight both to tail Crasher and to observe the pistol that Crasher is about to plant; here, the "juicy fruit" is analogous to a "juicy tidbit," since he now has the goods on Crasher.

p. 87   Aubrey Beardsley (1872–98) was a British artist and illustrator.

p. 89   A pulmotor is a device used to apply artificial respiration.

p. 90   The reference is to Robert Browning's poem, which is actually titled "Soliloquy of the Spanish Cloister," published in 1842.

p. 93   "An Anchor to Windward" was the title of a private, autobiographical essay that Gilman penned in 1882 at the age of twenty-one. The essay is a reflective examination of her desire for independence; hence, in this context, the phrase suggests a "means to independence."

p. 94   *Standard* is a now seldom-used term for *base* or *stand*.

p. 101   Ossining, New York, is the location of Sing Sing prison.

p. 116   While the meaning of Gilman's reference to Liggetts is not clear, it seems likely that she meant it to represent one of the four drugstores she alludes to in *Unpunished,* which probably would have been equipped with a phone.

p. 116   "Betty" is mentioned nowhere else in the manuscript. Perhaps Gilman meant to have Iris refer to "Bessie," who is acting as the family's maid, or perhaps "Betty" refers to Bess Hunt's "undercover" name.

p. 117   *Gat* is slang for *pistol.*

p. 129   The parenthetical comment, "I'm not sure of my spelling," was inserted into the text at this point but appears to be a notation Gilman made to herself as a reminder to verify the spelling of *Marquis de Sade.*

p. 134 Gilman is probably using the term *forty-'leven* as an informal expression of exaggeration. Such colloquial expressions are found frequently in her writings.

p. 135 Jean Valjean is the hero of French author Victor Hugo's *Les Misérables* (1862). To elude his pursuer, Javert, Valjean trains his muscles so that he can climb up walls.

p. 136 According to legend, Gaius Mucius Scaevola was a Roman hero who volunteered to assassinate Lars Porsena when he was besieging Rome in 509 B.C. Scaevola penetrated Porsena's camp and mistakenly killed Porsena's secretary. Threatened with being burned alive if he refused to divulge details of the plot, Scaevola thrust his right hand into a nearby fire and held it there until it was burned off. Impressed by Scaevola's courage, Porsena released him and negotiated peace with Rome.

p. 142 It was not standard practice to hold a coroner's inquest in a private home. As critic Lillian Robinson notes, the inquest is "held anomalously in the murder house itself." See notes to the afterword for further information on Robinson's essay.

p. 159 Gilman is paraphrasing lines from William Congreve's *The Mourning Bride* (1697), III.viii:

> "Heav'n has no rage, like love to hatred turn'd,
> Nor Hell a fury, like a woman scorn'd."

p. 186 Prussic acid is a highly poisonous acid.

p. 194 Gilman makes a second allusion to Lewis Carroll's work, in this case to one of his most memorable characters from *Alice's Adventures in Wonderland* (1865).

p. 192 Although the exact source has not been identified, Gilman was probably quoting either from an early English ballad or from a play. She was an avid reader and often attended the theater.

p. 195 This reference recalls "An Unnatural Mother" (1895), Gilman's short story of a young woman, Esther Greenwood, who risks the life of her child to protect her community; the town gossips call her an "unnatural mother." Gilman herself was also labeled an "unnatural mother" when she sent her daughter Katharine east to live with Walter

Stetson, following his remarriage to her close friend Grace Channing.

p. 200 Gilman may be alluding to a literary work here, but if so, the source remains unidentified.

p. 207 *Back door* is another word for *secret.* Hence, Jack is learning for the first time, along with the reader, that Ross was one of the "murderers."

p. 204 Nero Claudius Caesar (37–68 A.D.) was a Roman emperor who persecuted and murdered numerous people, including family members.

Afterword

In 1929, the year before her seventieth birthday, Charlotte Perkins Gilman (1860–1935) finished writing *Unpunished,* the last full-length fictional work of a long and highly productive career. Written during a time of waning sympathy for women's rights, *Unpunished* is a remarkable work. Gilman essentially follows the conventions of the popular detective novel of the 1920s but weaves in a thread of satire and a compelling message about the possible consequences of domestic abuse and sexual violence.[1] Both the dark humor that punctuates the pages of *Unpunished* and the theme of social injustices suffered by women were familiar territory to Gilman. The oppression of women was a common topic in her writing, and satire was often the vehicle Gilman chose to trumpet her cause.

Best remembered today for her short story "The Yellow Wall-Paper" (1892),[2] Gilman was heralded in her time as one of the leading intellectuals of the turn-of-the-century women's movement; her contemporaries often ranked her among the ten or twelve greatest women in the United States. Her body of work is impressive: she published novels, short stories, poetry, essays, an autobiography, and several full-length nonfiction books. She was an outspoken advocate for such radical reforms as social motherhood, kitchenless homes, and women's economic independence—issues she championed in her groundbreaking treatise *Women and Economics* (1898).

The great-niece of nineteenth-century American author Harriet Beecher Stowe, Gilman was no stranger to either adversity or controversy.[3] Her childhood in Rhode Island was not an easy one. Her father abandoned the family when she was a child, and her mother eked out a tenuous existence teaching school when work was available. The "repeated deprivations" throughout Gilman's childhood contributed to a "growing stoicism" that was "consciously acquired," Gilman recalled in her posthumously published autobiography *The Living of Charlotte Perkins Gilman* (44). She credited her mother's "profound religious tendency and implacable sense of duty" coupled with her father's "intellectual appetite" (44) as factors that influenced her unwavering "desire to help humanity" (70); by the age of sixteen she had decided to devote her life to public service. "Here was the world," she wrote, "visibly unhappy and as visibly unnecessarily so; surely it called for the best efforts of all who could in the least understand what was the matter, and had any rational improvements to propose" (70).

When, at the age of twenty-one, Gilman received a marriage proposal from Providence artist Charles Walter Stetson, she quickly declined. She reasoned that while "a woman should be able to have marriage and motherhood, and do her work in the world also," the course she preferred was one of "complete devotion to [her] work" (83). After a volatile two-year courtship, however, and despite grave reservations on her part, Charlotte Anna Perkins married Stetson (83). The birth of their only child Katharine ten months later triggered a serious depression that eventually led to her nervous breakdown at the age of twenty-six. It was her enforced "rest cure" which inspired her to write "The Yellow Wall-Paper" several years later. When she separated from her husband in 1888, her health improved, and she struggled to earn a living on her own, publishing stories (including "The Yellow Wall-Paper" in 1892) and collecting an edition of verse for publication in 1893. Gilman was granted a divorce in 1894; that same year she relinquished custody of Katharine to Stetson and began in earnest her public career, writing and lecturing throughout the United States and later in Europe. Her attacks on what she saw as a social and economic system which enslaved women were met with hostility by many, but they also won her numerous supporters. And with the publication, in 1898, of *Women and Economics* (which would eventually be translated into seven languages), Gilman became an international celebrity.

In 1900 she remarried, this time to her first cousin Houghton Gilman. Several influential books followed: *Concerning Children* (1900), *The Home: Its Work and Influence* (1903), *Human Work* (1904), *The Man-Made World: Or, Our Androcentric Culture* (1911), and *His Religion and Hers* (1923). From 1909 to 1916 Gilman wrote and published a monthly feminist magazine, *Forerunner*, which featured her stories, poems, articles, and several serialized books and novels. In 1915 she published *Herland*, a feminist utopian novel promoting collective child rearing and women's employment outside of the home. Written as a satire, *Herland* challenges social conventions based solely on gender.[4]

Because her ideas were considered radical, Gilman frequently had difficulty placing her work. She founded the *Forerunner* after American author and editor Theodore Dreiser suggested that if she wanted to sell her work, she should tailor her writing to more popular tastes. As she remarked in her autobiography, "[I]f one writes to express important truths, needed yet unpopular, the market is necessarily limited. As all my principal topics were in direct contravention of established views, beliefs and emotions, it is a wonder that so many editors took so much of my work for so long" (*Living* 304). Her desire to present a message "in direct contravention of established views" grew more urgent as she neared the end of her life. Despite Gilman's enormous popularity at the turn of the century, her fame diminished following the end of the First World War. Fearing that the fast-changing world would simply forget her contributions, she labored through the last years of her life to ensure that her legacy would continue. Several late projects, however, including *Unpunished*, remained unpublished at the time of her death.[5]

The writing of *Unpunished* in the late 1920s coincided with the decline in the women's movement. No longer able to secure a following, Gilman resented her fallen popularity. Moreover, she lamented the turn of events for women, who, in her opinion, had made little progress toward gaining equality, particularly compared to the widespread transformation she had envisioned for her society and advanced through her theoretical works.

Still eager to reach a wide audience in her later years, Gilman turned to the popular genre of detective fiction, completing *Unpunished* in 1929, during a post-feminist era not unlike our own. Ann J. Lane argues that the darkness and violence of the novel—its focus on domestic abuse, sexual violence, and the grisly murder of an evil patriarch—is the result of "frustration [Gilman] felt at having devoted a life to struggling for changes that did not occur. If she could not destroy patriarchy in reality, she could do it through literary fantasy" (*To Herland* 344). Indeed, *Unpunished* is laced with satire, the writing style with which she seemed to be most comfortable. The evil Wade Vaughn isn't just murdered; he is the victim of overkill, and we sense Gilman's delight in spinning out the dark tale of intrigue into a "whodunnit" with a satirical twist. Ultimately, however, her experiment with the detective genre was probably the result of a growing awareness of her economic vulnerabilities as she reached her later years.[6] Anxious to secure her financial future, Gilman likely saw the potential for marketability in detective fiction, which flourished between the two world wars—so much, in fact, that to accommodate the "increasing numbers of devoted readers, libraries and reviewers began categorizing mysteries separately from other forms of fiction."[7] Despite her attempts to place *Unpunished,* however, Gilman failed to find a publisher.

Like much of her fiction, *Unpunished* was hurriedly written and never edited for publication. It also reveals early-twentieth-century prejudices of Anglo-America evident in the works of other writers of Gilman's time; as much of her *Forerunner* fiction and journalism attests, Gilman was insensitive to the plight of racial minorities as well as working-class and immigrant women in her dream to build a new and better world.[8] But Gilman's inability to place the novel may have stemmed less from the quality of the manuscript than from her fusion of seemingly incongruous elements—the satirical twist on a popular genre with the darker themes of battered women's syndrome and sexual abuse. It is not unlikely that the editors who read the novel found the marriage of humor and pathos more than a little disconcerting. Still, her disappointment in their responses was obvious: "'I find your characters interesting,' said one 'reader.' 'That is not necessary in a detective story.' Evidently it is not, but I have often wished it was" (*Living* 332). In the final chapter of her autobiography, Gilman lamented that *Unpunished* remained "buried in manuscript heaps of some agent or publisher" (*Living* 332) and unavailable to the public she wanted desperately to reach.[9]

Three years after she completed the novel, Gilman was

diagnosed with breast cancer. As the disease advanced, she planned her suicide; on August 17, 1935, at the age of seventy-five, she inhaled chloroform and died peacefully at home. Less than two weeks later, daughter Katharine began exploring the possibility of publishing *Unpunished*.[10] She, too, was unsuccessful.

This publication makes available for the first time in its entirety Gilman's last significant work of feminist fiction.[11] Gilman's work was revived during the women's movement in the 1960s and 1970s. In 1966, a reprint edition of *Women and Economics* was edited and introduced by the prominent historian Carl Degler, who proclaimed Gilman "one of the leading intellectuals of the women's movement on both sides of the Atlantic" at the turn of the century (*Women and Economics* xix). Gilman's place in the contemporary literary canon was further established by The Feminist Press's 1973 republication of "The Yellow Wall-Paper," with an afterword by Elaine R. Hedges, who hailed it as "a small literary masterpiece" (37). Interest in Gilman's larger oeuvre continues to grow, as does the genre of feminist detective fiction. Thus, we believe the time is right to bring forward *Unpunished*, which has remained unpublished for nearly seventy years, virtually lost to the academic community and the reading public.

* * * * *

Gilman modestly acknowledges in her prefatory note to *Unpunished*: "Some of the tale is amusing"—and it is.[12] Perhaps because of the very seriousness of her message, she took pains to camouflage and offset it, making her work entertaining and thus more acceptable to the readership she desperately sought.[13]

Indeed, the pulpit-pounding didacticism that characterizes much of her poetry, fiction, and nonfiction is noticeably absent in *Unpunished*. Instead, the book has the elements of any lively detective novel. The opening scenes are characterized by playfulness and humor: a charming husband-and-wife detective team engage in spirited banter, paperboys "chant" about a murder, and we meet a corpse who has been "'killed four times over. Or four ways at once. Possibly five'" (16). Nevertheless, Gilman cleverly embeds a powerful message about the unequal role of women within a relatively conservative genre that was highly popular in the 1920s. Thus, *Unpunished* can be appreciated as a social reform novel disguised as detective fiction. As Lillian Robinson observes, "The idea, this time, was not so much to hurl feminism into the jaws of post-feminism as to pry open those jaws and slip in a sugar-coated pill" (277).

Undeniably, there is a pill beneath the sugar coating—a calculated message underlying each of Gilman's humorous plot devices. At the start, Gilman inflicts multiple wounds on her corpse to ensure that Vaughn's punishment by death fits his manifold crimes against women and society in general. Robinson remarks, "So we begin with the corpse, as is not uncommon in a murder mystery, but such a corpse has not been seen since the day some enterprising child pasted all the cards in the 'Clue' game together" (277).

Found dead in his study, Wade Vaughn has been shot, stabbed, choked, bludgeoned, and poisoned. Gilman comments in her prefatory note: "The mystery involved is not merely in the usual question of who did it, but in the unusual one of who did it first." As the plot unfolds, a number of "murderers" come forward, and Gilman, again playfully, ponders the order of the killings and wonders whether it is really a crime to murder a dead man, since "'A man can die but once!'" (44) Gilman saves the ultimate spoof for the end, when she reveals that Vaughn has actually died of natural causes.

The most corrupt patriarch in Gilman's fiction, Vaughn is a perverted villain, a marital rapist, an unscrupulous blackmailer, a sadist, and a misogynist.[14] Commenting on his constant cruelty and abuse of power, detective Bess Hunt deems him "'worse than Jack the Ripper'" (135). Gilman may have regarded Vaughn as the utmost manifestation of a dissolute patriarchy; she makes him an extreme case, and his death becomes an occasion for rejoicing. Moreover, as Lane points out, Gilman's *Unpunished*, like Agatha Christie's *Murder on the Orient Express* (1934), focuses more on justifying a homicide than unraveling the crime (xxxi).

In addition to her thoroughly despicable villain, Gilman's cast of characters and possible suspects includes the full range of stock characters found in any good melodrama: mysterious, disappearing servants with false identities (Norah and Nellie Brown and Joe White, all victims of Vaughn's blackmail); a fragile, innocent victim driven to suicide (Iris); a disabled and downtrodden but feisty heroine (Jacqueline "Jack" Warner); an honorable but maligned doctor (Ross Akers); a cheerful and righteous husband-and-wife detective team (Jim and Bess Hunt); and a corrupt and wormy rival detective (Gus Crasher). In Gilman's view, "the trouble with 'detective stories,' each and all, is that the Plot comes before the People" (*Forerunner*, September 1913, 252). For this reason, she considered Lily Dougall's *The Summit House Mystery* (1905) "the best detective novel I know" (*Forerunner*, September 1913, 252).[15] Gary

Scharnhorst suggests that Gilman "apparently designed her own detective novel . . . to redress the imbalance" (115). Many of the twists of the plot—overheard conversations, a secret hiding place, and the real surprise ending, a specialty of Gilman's[16]—can also be read as humorous exaggerations of the generic murder mystery. And as the mystery unfolds, we even learn that the butler really did "do it"—although he was not the first.

Gilman's notoriously dry sense of humor is also notable in her use of names.[17] Following Vaughn's death, shady detective Gus Crasher becomes a most unwelcome "gate-crasher" to the Vaughn household and admits that Iris "'gave me the gate'" (173). The play on "hunt" is even more obvious and sustained. The Hunts "hunt" for evidence: while "Bessikins" makes "'conscientious use of a dust cloth'" (66) and providentially finds Jack's revealing diary, Jim does "'some hunting in hospital records'" (133) to solve the mystery of Jack's father's second will. "Iris," the name of both Jack's sister and her niece, signifies a delicate flower and, in its Greek origin, "the senses." These sensitive women, particularly the elder Iris, become the express victims of patriarchy while Jack, with her decidedly masculine nickname, survives and succeeds.

Yet for all its lighthearted or stock elements, *Unpunished* remains more than just an "amusing" book. For Gilman, it was a literary vehicle; she worked within and subverted the genre in order to analyze and challenge the patriarchal construction of "woman." *Unpunished* makes a radical call for equal opportunity and power between the sexes.

Detective Bess Hunt, Gilman's mouthpiece, argues that the murder of someone as repugnant as Vaughn is indeed morally permissible. Throughout the novel, others echo her conviction.

We are encouraged to see Wade Vaughn's death as a justifiable homicide, not unlike the case of Minnie Wright's apparent murder of her abusive husband John in Susan Glaspell's one-act play *Trifles*, which was produced in 1916 and published in 1920. (The short story version of *Trifles* is entitled "A Jury of Her Peers" [1917].) Although there is no question that Minnie kills her husband, pithily described as a "hard man" (1357), Glaspell exonerates Minnie through her women neighbors, who discern Minnie's trying situation far more readily than their spouses do. Gilman similarly vindicates the heroine and prime suspect of *Unpunished*, Vaughn's sister-in-law Jack Warner. A wheelchair-bound invalid residing in Vaughn's house, Jack—who is scarred and disfigured—has her own motives for murdering Vaughn. His emotional and sexual abuse of his wife Iris (Jack's younger sister) drove her to suicide. Jack, too, is subjected to Vaughn's verbal and emotional abuse. He refuses to pay for Jack's reconstructive facial surgery: "[H]e said I was sufficiently useful to him as I was, and more likely to stay! Like the Chinese women" (71). Vaughn carries his crippled sister-in-law into his study, puts his arm about her, and insists that she give him "'a nice crooked kiss'" (82). Through their respective presentations of Jack Warner and Minnie Wright, Gilman and Glaspell were among the first women writers to explore a groundbreaking concept central to court cases today: women, at times, must take extreme measures to fight back against the males who enslave and abuse them. More graphic than *Trifles*, *Unpunished* illustrates and addresses both domestic violence and battered women's syndrome long before the phrases were introduced into our vocabulary.

Gilman uses the murder of the socially respected Vaughn to expose her patriarchal society without uprooting it, allowing corruption to persist as was the convention in Victorian and early-twentieth-century texts. Vaughn's murder occurs because he is a product of a sexist society that breeds and tolerates injustice to women. Although the act puts an end to his personal reign of terror over women, there is little hope that it will significantly reform the society which bred him. As Robinson notes, "the patriarch is done in, but patriarchy is not" (282).

While Gilman was writing for a "purpose" (*Living* 121), as she almost always did, *Unpunished* nevertheless adheres to—as well as subverts—some of the conventions of detective fiction. A prime example is Gilman's creation of a husband-and-wife detective team, a tradition in early detective fiction that has since largely died out. Critics Patricia Craig and Mary Cadogan, in their historical examination of the genre, point out that auxiliary women detectives were common in American and British detective fiction from 1913 to the 1970s. Had *Unpunished* been published, it could easily have been incorporated into Craig and Cadogan's chapter entitled "Spouses, Secretaries, and Sparring Partners" alongside Agatha Christie's and Dashiell Hammett's detective fiction featuring husband-and-wife detective teams (e.g. Christie's Prudence ["Tuppence"] and Tommy Beresford of *Partners in Crime* [1929] and Hammett's Nick and Nora Charles of *The Thin Man* [1932]).[18] Bess Hunt, an experienced journalist and stenographer, is detective Jim Hunt's wife and part-time secretary. Although Bess seems the bolder, more imaginative half of the team, she encourages Jim to take most of the credit. But we might best appreciate Bess's deference as another ploy Gilman implements to secure a late 1920s readership. Gilman makes Bess a conventional, contented wife and helpmate who eagerly engages in espionage in order to assist her husband. Her "honeymoonish greetings" (4) confirm that she is still deeply in love with Jim after four years of marriage. As an undercover maid, Bess cooks for the Vaughn household, and her capabilities as a housekeeper earn her more credit than her sleuthing. Jack commends Jim's "professional assistant" (139) for being "'super-efficient'" and making "'the best cocoa I ever tasted'" (141). Hal Warner laments the loss of Bess's morning muffins when her true identity is disclosed ("'Too good to be true! We never shall see those muffins again!'" [123]).

While Jim, Hal, and even Jack Warner view Bess as "too good to be true" and traditional enough to be unthreatening, perhaps this is precisely how Gilman hoped her contemporary readers would also view Bess and thus embrace her. Without the "ambitions to become detectives in their own right," some women auxiliaries, Cadogan and Craig observe, "were drawn into crime-solving by helping their professional-investigator husbands, lovers, brothers or fathers" (71). While it is Jim's case that undeniably "draws" Bess into investigative work, Gilman bolsters her character by showing that it is her own idea to go undercover. Neither merely a sexually attractive consort to a dashing detective nor a threatening femme fatale, Bess diverges from the sexist portrayal of women in the classical or hard-boiled detective formulas.[19] To readers today, Bess is undeniably a "partner in crime."

In addition, the Hunts have a true egalitarian partnership at home; Jim, in turn, assists in household chores. Through her development of Jim's domestic side and Bess's ingenuity, Gilman—who longed for an equal personal and professional relationship—finds another subtle way to make her 1920s detective novel decidedly more feminist: she challenges stereotypical gender roles, showing herself to be, once again, far ahead of her time. A partnership seems to have offered Gilman an acceptable vehicle to bring forward her female detective, who seems smarter than Jim, less quick to form a judgment, and far more intuitive (she suspects Jack before Jim does [32]). In these respects, Gilman's characterization of Bess Hunt—and of Jack Warner as well—anticipates the development of both professional (hard-boiled) female detectives (e.g. Sara Paretsky's V. I. Warshawski) and amateur (soft-boiled) female detectives (e.g. Amanda Cross's Kate Fansler), increasingly acceptable as characters in their own right following World War II.[20] We can only predict that Bess might have assumed an even more forceful role in future adventures had Gilman published a sequel about the escapades of Hunt and Hunt.

Pleased by his partnership with Bess, Jim Hunt humorously confesses: "'I'm mighty glad I've got you Bess, instead of a sheep like my dear Watson'" (6). As this reference reveals, Gilman enjoyed the Sherlock Holmes stories by Sir Arthur Conan Doyle—an affinity also documented by Scharnhorst (115). The allusion invites us to consider further the relationship between the Hunts of *Unpunished* and the male detective-assis-tant partnership of Conan Doyle's *Adventures of Sherlock Holmes*. It goes without saying that Jim's Bess is far cleverer than Holmes's "sheeplike" companion Watson. Rather, through her decision to go undercover as a servant in the Vaughn household, Bess plays the role of Sherlock Holmes himself, an association which bolsters the view of Bess as a forerunner of the indepen-dent female sleuth of contemporary detective fiction.

While Jim just thinks she looks "'funny'" in her blonde wig and makeup, Bess's ""transformation""" into a maid (63) is so convincing that her former reporter colleagues, who flock to the Vaughn household, do not recognize her. Bess's decision to assume a role of a lower station grants her the wisdom of the master of disguise, Sherlock Holmes. For example, in "A Scandal in Bohemia," Holmes adopts the guise of "a drunken-looking groom, ill-kempt and side-whiskered" (14) to gain quick information to solve his case. He admits his reasoning to Watson: "'Be one of them, and you will know all there is to know'" (14). In the case of *Unpunished*, it is Bess's handiwork that leads to the discovery of "all there is to know" about the Vaughn household: she finds the secret diary in which Jack Warner has carefully documented the cruelties of her brother-in-law. Reading Jack's journal, which Bess has smuggled home for the evening, Jim "'regret[s] that Mr. Vaughn is dead . . . so I cannot have the pleasure of killing him'" (113). Thus, Jim's view of the murder becomes aligned with the opinion of Bess, who earlier declares, "'If any people had a right to kill a man, they had'" (42).

Bess is not the only female character who helps solve the crimes in *Unpunished*. Mrs. Todd, an infirm but engaging and nosy neighbor from the opposite corner, admits she has "'nothing else to do'" but "'keep tabs on people'" (36, 37). Though Mrs. Todd might more accurately be called a useful snoop than an auxiliary sleuth, she recalls specific dates and curious activities of the Vaughn household and becomes indispensable to Jim Hunt.

Moreover, as a detective, Jack Warner herself—the one truly nongeneric character of *Unpunished*—upstages the Hunts. Jack's purpose in keeping a diary, she writes, is not only that it may prove "legally useful" (71), but, more importantly, that she finds it effective "as a 'release'" (71). Indeed, in chapters 7 through 10, Gilman invokes two of the devices she used so effectively in

"The Yellow Wall-Paper"—the first-person narrative account, presented in the form of a journal, and the idea of writing as therapy. In these undeniably therapeutic chapters that record information gleaned by her eavesdropping through an internal house phone, Jack assembles invaluable damning evidence in her "account of this man and what he has done to us" (70). She contributes insights into Vaughn's character and the real motivations for his multiple murder. In these chapters Jack adopts the persona of an undercover female sleuth, helping the Hunts to identify potential murderers and understand the legitimacy of Vaughn's murder. Readers can identify with "detective" Jack because of her direct narration, a feature of contemporary detective fiction. She provides the story-within-the-story. And it is Jack who draws an even more forceful comparison to Sherlock Holmes himself.

An actor, just as Holmes is, as well as an expert in disguise, Jack masquerades as her own dead sister and is so convincing that she literally frightens Vaughn to death. In the final chapter of *Unpunished*, Jacqueline Warner discloses this well-guarded secret. The surprise ending celebrates sisterhood; enraged further by Vaughn's marriage plans for young Iris, Jack succeeds in avenging her sister's death and saving her niece. As she explains to Akers and the Hunts, "'I made up my mind to—to—at least to make him *feel* for once! I made a fitted mask from the plaster one, and painted it. . . . [W]hen he saw me standing there he put up his hands before his face at first—then gave a choked cry, clutched at his heart'" (207).

The scene in which Jack describes appearing before Vaughn in her sister's death mask is particularly dramatic. To reach Vaughn's study, she crawls downstairs on her hands and knees.

The scene contains echoes of the conclusion to "The Yellow Wall-Paper": defeated and driven to madness by the rigid gender codes prescribed to women in her patriarchal world, that story's nameless narrator creeps in endless circles over her controlling physician/husband, who faints in disbelief as she declares "'you can't put me back!'" (36). But Gilman allows Jack to escape the fate of her earlier protagonist. In spite of her pain, Jack stands on her deformed feet; she rises from an infantile crawl, symbolically elevating herself above the seated Vaughn.[21] In doing so, Jack is both literally and figuratively taking a stand.

Jack has led a long battle against patriarchal control, which looms large in this novel. Her father, J. J. Smith, was himself a "strict, domineering" man "with antiquated notions about the education of girls, and particularly as to obedience" (71), who encouraged Wade Vaughn to marry his daughter while she was in a defenseless state. Vaughn, in turn, orders his delicate stepdaughter Iris to become Crasher's bride. Despite appearances to the contrary, Vaughn is, in fact, a professional blackmailer, but perhaps his most heinous actions are directed toward young Iris. Like her mother before her, Iris is subjected to the evils of a patriarchy in which marriages can be arranged, despite emphatic protests. However, in Gilman's fictional world, the reverberating cycle of coerced marriages is circumvented by women nearly every time. Jack and young Iris are ultimately granted the freedom to choose their own partners.[22]

Akers, Jack's chosen partner, is precisely the kind of Kevorkian-like physician for whom Gilman searched in vain as she planned her own suicide a few years later. Although Gilman might rightly be accused of playing God, she does not shy away from controversial issues that are still hotly debated today. Ross

Akers has performed euthanasia—an illegal but necessary "service," to Gilman's mind—and Jack Warner has used psychological warfare to terrorize her abusive brother-in-law. Jack is vindicated, however, because the murder is justified as retaliation for both the suicide of her sister and for the betterment of society at large. In Gilman's ideal world, then, mercy killings of suffering people and murders of evil people are forgiven.

This is but one example of how Gilman embedded her own inclinations into her detective novel.[23] The emphasis on physical culture is another obvious example. Gilman often fictionalized her belief in physical culture, which she not only practiced herself but also wrote about in numerous essays. Although confined to a wheelchair, Jack—whom Gilman likens to the wall-climbing Jean Valjean of Victor Hugo's *Les Misérables*—makes health a priority; she undertakes a regimen of fresh air, exercise, and a balanced diet as she cultivates a strong sense of self.[24] The desire to be independent is, of course, also a common theme in Gilman's fiction. Ever resourceful, Jack teaches herself and young Iris shorthand and typing so that when Hal enters college they can be economically self-sufficient.[25]

Jack's sister Iris, however, had been forced back into a dependent role after her marriage to Wade Vaughn. As her memory was restored, she was filled with "sharp anguish" and an "irresistible shrinking" (86) from Vaughn, whose control of his wife extended to her clothing, her behavior, and her sexual conduct. When Iris rebuffed his advances one evening, he threatened to have her institutionalized. "'If you care to remain at home with your sister and your child you must be calmer, more naturally affectionate, more obedient,'" Vaughn admonished her. "'If you make any noise or disturbance of any sort I am sure that an examining physician would quite agree with me that— restraint was necessary, and seclusion. . . . Come back to bed,'" he commanded (88).

In forcing his wife to share his bed, Vaughn has been guilty, in effect, of marital rape. In tormenting her with the prospect of medically ordered "restraint" and "seclusion," he recalls the role of John in "The Yellow Wall-Paper," who threatens to send his wife to Dr. S. Weir Mitchell if her health does not improve.[26] Gilman herself entered Mitchell's Philadelphia sanitarium in the spring of 1887 and agreed to undergo a one-month rest cure treatment for neurasthenia. When Gilman left his sanitarium, Mitchell provided this much-quoted advice: "'Live as domestic a life as possible. Have your child with you all the time. . . . Lie down an hour after each meal. Have but two hours' intellectual life a day. And never touch pen, brush or pencil as long as you live'" (*Living* 96). Following this regimen, Gilman found herself on the brink of a total breakdown. Rather than succumb to madness, as Gilman's nameless narrator does in "The Yellow Wall-Paper," Iris elects suicide and hangs herself with a black-and-white scarf.

The symbolism implicit in the scarf is striking. It is a scarf Iris "was very fond of" (87) but that Vaughn despised. The scarf signifies her choices, which were, indeed, black and white. She could continue to be subjected to the tyranny of a man she did not love, risking institutionalization, or she could quietly "escape from life" (89), as Jack characterizes the suicide. A fragile victim of patriarchy, Iris has been denied the fairy-tale ending Gilman grants Jack, who, like Jane Eyre, becomes the heiress to a fortune (Jack's inheritance is estimated at three million dollars) and agrees to marry her lover, but only after she can undergo extensive reconstructive surgery to repair her injuries.

It is in the final chapter of *Unpunished* that the title assumes significance. Gilman makes it clear that while Jack may have been physically disfigured, Wade Vaughn is morally deformed. The death-white mask that Jack wears to terrorize him is a reflection of his own dissipation. He, too, is guilty, after all, of wearing a figurative mask before the unsuspecting public, who saw "nothing but a rather genial man, benevolently taking care of his wife's relations" (91). Gilman leaves no question that Vaughn, ironically a criminal lawyer, deserved to die a criminal's death. After Jack's "confession" before her future husband and the Hunts, Ross Akers (who is also guilty of inflicting one of the post-mortem wounds) reaffirms that as far as he is concerned, the official explanation for Vaughn's death will remain that he "'just died of heart disease!'" (206) The Hunts concur: "'Verdict unanimous,'" they remark (206). The denouement of *Unpunished,* again, is not unlike that of Glaspell's *Trifles,* in which two women act as judge and jury by withholding from authorities crucial evidence that is needed to convict Minnie Wright. As Jack explains, "'You mustn't think me a heartless monster, my friends, condoning attempted murder and casual homicide. . . . But you know something of what I had to bear at the hands of that—unspeakable man!'" (199) Thus, Gilman renders Vaughn's death a case of justifiable homicide and Jack Warner a heroine.

Of the various characters who comment on the morality of Vaughn's murder, Bess Hunt most forcefully voices Gilman's philosophy: "'Here is this woman, widowed, crippled, disfigured, disinherited, and the only person on earth to look out for those two children. Even if she could have escaped with them, any sort of court would have given them back to him—what could she bring against him—that would hold? And being sane, and brave, and conscientious, she couldn't take her sister's way out—she couldn't leave the children'" (136). But Gilman never once allows her woman detective to upstage Jacqueline Warner. First and foremost, *Unpunished* is a story of a woman's survival. In spite of her physical disabilities, it is Jack Warner who possesses the courage and conviction to change the fate of nearly everyone who is terrorized by Vaughn. Jack emerges from the story both victorious and "unpunished."

In the final analysis, *Unpunished* aptly demonstrates Gilman's feelings about the possible consequences of domestic, emotional, and sexual abuse. Gilman, as an idealist and a champion of gender equality, fought against these injustices; her pen and her tongue were her weapons. Decades before battered women's syndrome became a defense argument in the courtroom, Gilman entertained, in fiction, the retaliation a brute might face if he continued to exploit and abuse others. Thus, the publication of Gilman's only detective novel—which regrettably had "No takers" (*Living* 332) in her lifetime—becomes a further tribute to her life and her legacy.

Whether a general readership in the late 1920s and early 1930s would have identified with Jack Warner or accepted Gilman's feminist message remains a mystery. But for readers today, Gilman's vision appears somewhat prophetic. She seemed to anticipate a time when "a man [who] thinks he has a right to manage his own wife" (87) had better think again, lest he be made to answer to a legal system that is finally holding men accountable for violence against women. Gilman would undoubtedly be gratified to know that, as we approach the twenty-first century, at least some women who are forced to defend themselves against the physical and emotional pain of chronic abuse are, indeed, going "unpunished."

Notes to Afterword

1. Gilman's only other fictional work featuring a woman detective is the short story "His Mother," originally published in the July 1914 issue of *Forerunner*, 169–73, and reprinted in *"The Yellow Wall-Paper" and Selected Stories of Charlotte Perkins Gilman*, 73–80. In "His Mother," detective Ellen Burrell Martin investigates her son, whom she discovers is involved in the white slave trade.

2. "The Yellow Wall-Paper" is a chilling and autobiographically inspired examination of a young wife and mother undergoing the "rest cure" for neurasthenia, or nervous prostration, a condition attributed to weakness of the nervous system. The rest cure, introduced as a treatment for nervous prostration in the nineteenth century and popularized by Dr. Silas Weir Mitchell of Philadelphia, required the patient to undergo extended bed rest, to be secluded from family and friends, and to eat a special, often high-fat, diet. The story was originally published in *New England Magazine* 5 (January 1892): 647–56 and became widely known after its republication in the early 1970s. See *The Yellow Wall-Paper*, with an afterword by Elaine R. Hedges. The story also appears in *"The Yellow Wall-Paper" and Selected Stories*, 39–53 and *The Charlotte Perkins Gilman Reader*, 3–19.

3. Readers wishing additional information on Gilman's life should consult biographies by Mary A. Hill or Ann J. Lane.

4. Significantly, *Herland* was out of print from 1915 until 1979. It was re-published shortly after renewed interest in Gilman's life and legacy arose.

5. Other late-in-life projects that Gilman was unable to place include an edition of poetry titled *Here Also*, a premise for a motion picture named "The Chosen Master," a nonfiction work titled *A Study in Ethics*, and a theatrical version of "The Yellow Wall-Paper."

6. Because Gilman was, in effect, self-employed, she had to contend with a precarious financial condition. The ventures in the last years of her life were often aimed at attaining financial security. Shortly after finishing the manuscript of *Unpunished*, she confided her inability to secure publishers to long-time friend Alice Stone Blackwell. She

wrote: "I'm not writing much now. Have failed to place my last three books. . . . These very young readers, editors, & critics have no use for writers over thirty." Letter to Alice Stone Blackwell dated 24 October 1930. Quoted in Scharnhorst 116.

7. See Klein 95.

8. Gilman's play with Italian names in chapter 12 surrounding the minor plot of Carlo's unknown murdered brother becomes increasingly irreverent, merciless, and racist by today's standards. Contemporary readers are no doubt disturbed that the Italian manservant becomes an unimportant casualty of the Vaughn murder and is "apparently not missed" (152). Unable to remember the exact name of Carlo's brother, Bess and Jim refer to him with a series of decidedly ethnic names all ending in *o* (128-32). Vaughn's chauffeur Joe White laments killing "'that little dago in the alley'" (199), who is earlier referred to as a "'Wop'" (29), but Jack concludes: "'that was no loss after all!'" (202). Racism is also evident when Bess arranges for "'little black Jenny to come as laundress'" (63) to the Vaughn household; and after leaving her undercover work as a household maid, Bess secures an "amiable colored helper" (167) to take her place.

Susan A. Lanser and Ann J. Lane have each also written about Gilman's racism. See Lanser; also see Lane, *To "Herland" and Beyond,* 251–54, 295–96.

9. Extant records show that Gilman sent her manuscript to Robert S. Tapley of the Macmillan Company in fall 1929. Tapley wrote to Gilman on 8 November 1929, that he had read *Unpunished* "with very great interest" and found it to be "exceptional" and "entertaining." He was obliged to send it on to other readers but promised to let Gilman know "as soon as there is anything definite to report." No readers' reports are extant, however, in the Gilman Papers at the Schlesinger Library, Radcliffe College. On 15 February 1930, Charlotte A. Barbour at G. P. Putnam, Inc. confirmed that she had "received two copies of *Unpunished*" and had sent one to Macmillan, per Gilman's request; the other was being considered for serialization. On 18 April 1930, Barbour informed Gilman by letter that there was "no luck yet with the book, but there are plenty of publishers still to try." Gilman Papers, folder 129. Quoted by permission.

10. Gilman's daughter, Katharine Beecher Stetson Chamberlin, wrote to literary agent Willis Kingsley Wing on 30 August 1935, asking him to try to locate the manuscript of *Unpunished* that was "in the hands of agents and publishers in New York" as "there might be an interest in [it]." Gilman Papers, folder 127. Quoted by permission.

11. Lane includes the dramatic chapter "The Record" in *The Charlotte Perkins Gilman Reader* (169–77), and discusses it in her introduction (xxx–xxxiv). The only full-length article to date is Lillian S. Robinson's. It is our hope that this publication will stimulate further scholarship on *Unpunished*.

12. Lane notes in her introduction to *Herland* that "Charlotte Perkins Gilman is not ordinarily thought of as a humorist, but her feminist utopia, *Herland*, is a very funny book" (v). Lane's comment can also be applied to Gilman's *Unpunished*.

13. Gilman uses a similar strategy in her feminist poetry in *In This Our World* (1893) when challenging women's subordinate place. For example, her poem "The Holy Stove" (158–60), which might be read as an argument for the kitchenless homes Gilman advocated, has a singsong quality to the rhyme scheme, offsetting her bitter message that women should not spend so much of their time in slavish house service.

14. A prototype for the evil Wade Vaughn of *Unpunished*, the misogynist playboy Terry Nicholson of *Herland* is one of three American males who stumble upon the utopian world of Herland—a highly civilized community of women who reproduce parthenogenically. While two of the males (Jeff Margrave and Vandyck Jennings) adapt to Herland to varying degrees, Terry tries to master his Herland wife Alima and is expelled from the peaceful utopian community for marital rape. While the laws, economics, and customs of Vaughn's society give him the power to carry out his wickedness, Herland, a utopian society, denies such transgressors any power and simply expels them.

15. These remarks occur in Gilman's comment and review of Ernest William Hurnung's *The Shadow of the Rope* (1902).

16. See, for example, the surprise endings in "Turned" (1911), "The Vintage" (1916), and "Making a Change" (1911). Likewise, the

denouement of Gilman's "The Yellow Wall-Paper" has a dramatic and theatrical ending; like *Jane Eyre*'s Bertha Mason, the nameless narrator circles around her room on all fours, creeping over her husband John who has fainted on the floor. Mary Jacobus further explores this connection. "Turned" is reprinted in *The Charlotte Perkins Gilman Reader*, 87–97. "The Vintage" is reprinted in *"The Yellow Wall-Paper" and Selected Stories*, 104–11.

17. Gilman plays with names in other works as well; for example, in her short story "Turned," which swells with water imagery, Marion Marroner feels herself drowning when she learns of her husband's betrayal.

18. Seemingly content with domesticity, Bess has a sympathetic, maternal nature. In this way she is like Nora Charles of *A Thin Man*. But Bess Hunt has a far less deferential role than Nora, who is not really her husband Nick's assistant. Much more like Christie's Tuppence Beresford, Bess eagerly engages in detective work and seems ripe for action.

19. See Cawelti, chapter 6, "The Hard-Boiled Detective Story" 139–61 (153–54 in particular). Jim's persona also departs from that of the archetypal private eye, such as Philip Marlowe or Sam Spade, who is tough, skeptical, and emotionally repressed.

20. Moreover, as Anne Cranny-Francis notes, in contemporary women-centered texts, the amateur woman sleuth may be married and still in charge of her own life, such as Amanda Cross's Kate Fansler. See Cranny-Francis 161.

21. The surprise ending is also reminiscent of "An Authentic Ghost Story," the famous scene in *Uncle Tom's Cabin*, by Gilman's great-aunt Harriet Beecher Stowe. Stowe creates a strong-willed female slave, Cassie, who dresses up as a ghost to frighten her evil master, Simon Legree. While Gilman's Vaughn dies from fright, Stowe's Legree collapses into a swoon (as does John in "The Yellow Wall-Paper"). The goal of both Jack Warner and Cassie is identical—each wants to escape the clutches of her oppressor and to exact vengeance at the same time. The parallels, in fact, between Simon Legree and Wade Vaughn are striking. Legree is a "short, broad" man with a "large, coarse mouth" and

"glaring" eyes (289, 293) while Vaughn is "stout" with "a thick red mouth and small hard eyes" (73). Even more significant is each man's insistence that those who are under his tyrannical rule be, in Vaughn's words, "'submissive and obedient'" (82). As Hal testifies at the inquest into Vaughn's murder, "'He was tyrannical—and enjoyed it. . . . we couldn't call our souls our own'" (164). Similarly, Simon Legree insists that he owns his slaves, both "body and soul" (309). And while *Unpunished* lacks the power of Stowe's popular antislavery novel, Gilman forcefully alludes to "slavery" several times, most notably in the "diary" chapters in which images of entrapment, enslavement, and disempowerment figure prominently.

22. Gilman also makes this point through her characterization of Esther Greenwood in her short story "An Unnatural Mother" (1895). Esther's father, a progressive doctor, raises his daughter unconventionally. He warns her of the dangers of venereal disease and encourages her to think carefully before "'choosing a father'" (62) for her own children. The story's title was changed to "The Unnatural Mother"; it is reprinted in *The Charlotte Perkins Gilman Reader*, 57–65.

23. There are also minor, but significant, biographical connections to her detective novel, most fittingly a family saga. After her death by suicide, Gilman's daughter had a death mask made of her mother. (That mask is now part of the Gilman collection at the Schlesinger Library, Radcliffe College.) Gilman's choice of a brother-in-law as the target of her fictional murder seems most pointed; during the period that she wrote *Unpunished*, Gilman felt enormous anger at her own brother-in-law, Francis Gilman, with whom she and second husband Houghton Gilman shared a house in Norwich Town, Connecticut, for twelve years. Although she discusses her life in Norwich Town in the penultimate chapter of her autobiography, Gilman omits any reference to the fact that her home was shared with her brother-in-law and his wife, Emily. During one particularly contentious exchange, Francis viciously remarked to Gilman: "I'll crack you between my fingers like a lobster!" (*Diaries* 2: 854) Hence, the fictional murder of Wade Vaughn can be seen as a revenge fantasy against a brother-in-law toward whom Gilman felt unbridled contempt.

Other biographical similarities between Gilman's heroine and her own experiences are evident. Jack Warner enjoys a brief career as a stage actress, a vocation that Gilman shared, in amateur theatre, in the early 1890s (*Living* 111–12). Moreover, just as Jack Warner constructs a fantasy world to help her son Hal deal with "the Cruel Enchanter" from whom they would escape "in time" (*Unpunished* 82-83), Gilman, as a child, also invoked a "dream world" to compensate for "the lack of happiness" in her own life (*Living* 23). Jack goes west to California for surgery, and Vaughn's household servants escape to California, where Gilman herself visited after the birth of her daughter Katharine and moved following her separation from Walter Stetson; the West emerges as a panacea in this and other fictions (e.g. *The Crux* [1911]) as it also served in Gilman's own life. Iris and Hal, first cousins in fiction, plan to marry, as Gilman herself married her first cousin. And Jack finds happiness as a middle-aged woman, as Gilman did in her second marriage to Houghton Gilman. The egalitarian marriages in Gilman's real life and in fiction, which also include that of Jim and Bess Hunt, serve as counter-testimonies to the abusive institution supported by patriarchy.

Another issue that Gilman confronted in *Unpunished* was her contempt for yellow journalists, which had its origins in the nasty and distorted press coverage of her divorce proceedings from her first husband, Walter Stetson, in 1894. Never one to miss an opportunity to advance a cause, Gilman castigates newspaper reporters throughout *Unpunished*. She sardonically characterizes "that great moral engine, the press" (48) for routinely engaging in "ample invention to support lack of knowledge" (154). Even courtroom sketch artists are implicated for drawing in "whatever expression they saw fit" (163). Only Bess Hunt, as a former journalist, is exempt from criticism, for she "had spent an instructive year in newspaper work, and was not impressed" (13) by the methods used to secure stories.

24. In her novellas, for example, Marjorie of *Mag-Marjorie* (1912) is accomplished in fencing, and Vivian Lane of *The Crux* thrives while running a summer camp in the West. In her short stories, Ellen Osgood of "Old Water" (1911) keeps in shape and excels at rowing, and Joan Marsden of "Joan's Defender" (1916) improves her self-esteem by climbing, swimming, and riding horseback. Both stories appear in *"The Yellow Wall-Paper" and Selected Stories* (122–29, 96–103).

25. Unhampered by her physical limitations, the self-reliant Jack stands in stark contrast to Ross's emotionally crippled, dependent stepsisters and stepmother. Gilman matter of factly explains that Ross must care for the "'Frail little things all of them, dead weights'" (6).

26. In her introduction to *The Charlotte Perkins Gilman Reader*, Lane suggests that *Unpunished* harkens back to "The Yellow Wall-Paper," but she does not develop the allusion (xxxii).

Works Cited and Consulted

Brontë, Charlotte. *Jane Eyre*. Ed. Richard J. Dunn. New York: W. W. Norton & Co., 1987.

Cawelti, John G. *Adventure, Mystery, and Romance: Formula Stories as Art and Popular Culture*. Chicago and London: Chicago University Press, 1976.

Christie, Agatha. *Murder on the Orient Express*. London: Collins, 1934.

———. *Partners in Crime*. New York: Dell, 1957.

Conan Doyle, Sir Arthur. *The Adventures of Sherlock Holmes*. New York: William Morrow & Co., 1992.

Craig, Patricia and Mary Cadogan. *The Lady Investigates: Women Detectives and Spies in Fiction*. New York: St. Martin's Press, 1981.

Cranny-Francis, Anne. *Feminist Fiction: Feminist Uses of Generic Fiction*. New York: St. Martin's Press, 1990.

DellaCava, Frances A. *Female Detectives in American Novels: A Bibliography and Analysis of Serialized Female Sleuths*. New York and London: Garland, 1993.

Gilman, Charlotte Perkins. *The Charlotte Perkins Gilman Reader*. Ed. with an introduction by Ann J. Lane. New York: Pantheon Books, 1980.

———. *The Crux*. Serialized in *Forerunner* 2 (1911). Reprint. New York: Charlton, 1911.

———. *The Diaries of Charlotte Perkins Gilman*. 2 vols. Ed. with an introduction by Denise D. Knight. Charlottesville, Va.: University Press of Virginia, 1994.

———. *Forerunner* 1–7 (1909–16). Reprint, with an introduction by Madeliene B. Stern. New York: Greenwood, 1968.

———. Gilman Papers, Schlesinger Library, Radcliffe College, Cambridge, Mass.

———. *Herland*. Serialized in *Forerunner* 6 (1915). Reprint, with an introduction by Ann J. Lane. New York: Pantheon Books, 1979.

———. *The Home: Its Work and Influence*. New York: McClure, Phillips & Co., 1903.

———. *In This Our World*. Oakland: McCombs & Vaughn, 1893. 3d ed. Boston: Small, Maynard & Co., 1898. Reprint. New York: Arno, 1974.

———. "Joan's Defender." *"The Yellow Wall-Paper" and Selected Stories of Charlotte Perkins Gilman*. Ed. Denise D. Knight. Newark, Del.: University of Delaware Press, 1994. 96–103.

———. *The Living of Charlotte Perkins Gilman: An Autobiography*. Foreword by Zona Gale. New York: Appleton-Century, 1935. Reprint, with an introduction by Ann J. Lane. Madison, WI: University of Wisconsin Press, 1990.

———. *Mag-Marjorie*. Serialized in *Forerunner* 3 (1912).

———. "Making a Change." *The Charlotte Perkins Gilman Reader*. Ed. Ann J. Lane. New York: Pantheon Books, 1980. 66–74.

———. "Old Water." *"The Yellow Wall-Paper" and Selected Stories of Charlotte Perkins Gilman*. Ed. Denise D. Knight. Newark, Del.: University of Delaware Press, 1994. 122–29.

———. "Turned." *The Charlotte Perkins Gilman Reader*. Ed. Ann J. Lane. New York: Pantheon Books, 1980. 87–97.

———. "The Unnatural Mother." *The Charlotte Perkins Gilman Reader*. Ed. Ann J. Lane. New York: Pantheon Books, 1980. 57–65.

———. "The Vintage." *"The Yellow Wall-Paper" and Selected Stories of Charlotte Perkins Gilman*. Ed. Denise D. Knight. Newark, Del.: University of Delaware Press, 1994. 104–11.

———. *Women and Economics: A Study of the Economic Relation Between Men and Women as a Factor in Social Evolution*. Boston: Small, Maynard & Co., 1898. Reprint, with an introduction by Carl Degler. New York: Harper & Row, 1966.

———. "The Yellow Wall-Paper." *New England Magazine* 5 (January 1892): 647–56. Reprint, with an afterword by Elaine R. Hedges. New York: Feminist Press, 1973. Revised ed. 1996.

———. *"The Yellow Wall-Paper" and Selected Stories of Charlotte Perkins*

Gilman. Ed. Denise D. Knight. Newark, Del.: University of Delaware Press, 1994.

Glaspell, Susan. *Trifles. The Norton Anthology of Literature by Women: The Traditions in English.* 2nd. ed. Eds. Sandra M. Gilbert and Susan Gubar. New York: W. W. Norton & Co., 1996.

Golden, Catherine, ed. *The Captive Imagination: A Casebook on "The Yellow Wallpaper."* New York: Feminist Press, 1992.

Hammett, Dashiell. *The Novels of Dashiell Hammett.* New York: Alfred A. Knopf, 1965.

Hill, Mary A. *Charlotte Perkins Gilman: The Making of a Radical Feminist, 1860–1896.* Philadelphia: Temple University Press, 1980.

Irons, Glenwood, ed. *Feminism in Women's Detective Fiction.* Toronto, Buffalo, and London: University of Toronto Press, 1995.

Jacobus, Mary. "An Unnecessary Maze of Sign-Reading." In *The Captive Imagination: A Casebook on "The Yellow Wallpaper."* Ed. Catherine Golden. New York: Feminist Press, 1992. 277–95. Reprinted from Jacobus, Mary. *Reading Women: Essays in Feminist Criticism.* New York: Columbia University Press, 1986. 229–48.

Klein, Kathleen Gregory. *The Woman Detective: Gender and Genre.* 2nd ed. Urbana, Ill: University of Illinois Press, 1995.

Lane, Ann J. *To "Herland" and Beyond: The Life and Work of Charlotte Perkins Gilman.* New York: Pantheon Books, 1990.

Lanser, Susan A. "Feminist Criticism, 'The Yellow Wallpaper,' and the Politics of Color in America." *Feminist Studies* 15.3 (1989): 415–41.

Reddy, Maureen T. *Sisters in Crime: Feminism and the Crime Novel.* New York: Continuum Publishing Company, 1988.

Robinson, Lillian S. "Killing Patriarchy: Charlotte Perkins Gilman, the Murder Mystery, and Post-Feminist Propaganda." *Tulsa Studies in Women's Literature* 10.2 (Fall 1991): 273–85.

Scharnhorst, Gary. *Charlotte Perkins Gilman.* Boston: Twayne Publishers, 1985.

Stowe, Harriet Beecher. *Uncle Tom's Cabin.* Ed. Elizabeth Ammons. New York: W. W. Norton & Co., 1994.

REDISCOVERED CLASSICS
OF AMERICAN WOMEN'S FICTION

from the Feminist Press at the City University of New York

Brown Girl, Brownstones (1959) by Paule Marshall. $10.95 paper.

Call Home the Heart (1932) by Fielding Burke. $9.95 paper.

Daughter of Earth (1929) by Agnes Smedley. $11.95 paper.

Doctor Zay (1882) by Elizabeth Stuart Phelps. $8.95 paper.

Fettered for Life (1874) by Lillie Devereux Blake. $18.95 paper, $45.00 cloth.

Guardian Angel and Other Stories (1932) by Margery Latimer. $8.95 paper.

I Love Myself When I Am Laughing . . . And Then Again When I Am Looking Mean and Impressive: A Zora Neale Hurston Reader, edited by Alice Walker. $14.95 paper.

Life in the Iron Mills and Other Stories (1861), by Rebecca Harding Davis. $10.95 paper.

The Living is Easy (1948) by Dorothy West. $14.95 paper.

Not So Quiet . . . Stepdaughters of War (1930), by Helen Zinna Smith. $11.95 paper, $35.00 cloth.

Now in November (1934) by Josephine W. Johnson. $10.95 paper, $29.95 cloth.

Quest (1922), by Helen R. Hull. $11.95 paper.

Weeds (1923), by Edith Summers Kelley. $15.95 paper.

The Wide, Wide World (1850) by Susan Warner. $19.95 paper, $35.00 cloth.

The Yellow Wall-Paper (1892) by Charlotte Perkins Gilman, $5.95 paper.

To receive a free catalog of The Feminist Press's 150 titles, call or write The Feminist Press at The City University of New York, 311 East 94th Street, New York, NY 10128-5684; phone: (212) 360-5790; fax: (212) 348-1241. Feminist Press books are available at bookstores, or can be ordered directly from the publisher. Send check or money order (in U.S. dollars drawn on a U.S. bank) payable to The Feminist Press. Please add $4.00 shipping and handling for the first book and $1.00 for each additional book. VISA, Mastercard, and American Express are accepted for telephone orders. Prices are subject to change.